"[A] POWERFUL NEW NOVEL."
—*San Francisco Examiner & Chronicle*

"With unerring skill and deep compassion, Golden gives us a whole suffering family caught up in the throes of love, violence, ambition, grief—and finally, redemption. Each believable character is deeply imagined and fully developed; each chapter pulls the reader straight into the next. I couldn't put *The Edge of Heaven* down until I had reached its wrenching and satisfying end."

—Lee Smith
Author of *News of the Spirit*

"Marita Golden's new novel brings us—with sensitivity and deft artistry—the precious stories of three generations of women in the aftermath of a tragedy that has torn each from herself and each from the others. Golden's women are altogether knowable and most unforgettable: their struggle to find their way back to some tiny form of normalcy will make a place in a reader's memory and heart."

—Edward Jones
Author of *Lost in the City*

"Fresh, original . . . Golden goes for the emotional jugular with such skill and intelligence that it's likely even the most jaded reader will be won over."

—*Time Out New York*

"Compassionately peels away the layers of a family's grief to reveal one woman's passage from repentance to renewal . . . These vividly rendered characters come to life, leaving the reader to cheer their strength and humanity. Highly recommended."

—*Library Journal* (starred review)

"An acclaimed chronicler of black women's lives . . . Golden, in her fourth novel, is writing in top form."

—*Kirkus Reviews*

"Golden has vividly captured aspects of the experience of race in the U.S. in the late twentieth century."

—*Booklist*

THE EDGE
OF
HEAVEN

Marita Golden

One World
The Ballantine Publishing Group
New York

A One World Book
Published by The Ballantine Publishing Group

Copyright © 1998 by Marita Golden
Reader's Guide copyright © 1999 by Marita Golden and The Ballantine Publishing Group, a division of Random House, Inc.

www.randomhouse.com/BB/

Library of Congress Catalog Card Number: 99-90084

ISBN 0-345-43172-3

Cover design by Kristine V. Mills-Noble
Cover art: *Get me another heart, this one's been broken many times,* by Valarie Maynard

Manufactured in the United States of America

First One World Edition: August 1999
10 9 8 7 6 5 4 3 2 1

ACKNOWLEDGMENTS

I want to gratefully acknowledge and thank Mary Treadwell, Brenda Smith, Lisa Greenman, and Tracey Payne for sharing their experiences and insights through numerous interviews and conversations, which turned research into a wonderful journey. My editor Casey Fuetsch once again helped me find my way through unfamiliar waters. She waited with patience and a sense of humor for me to finally hear what SHE was saying, and to stop resisting my narrator's voice. My husband Joe Murray drove me to West Virginia to a woman's prison, answered countless hypothetical questions that my characters had to wrestle with, and just kept loving me every day, which was the most important of all the things he did while I wrote this book. Kathleen Halley read the manuscript in the beginning and in the end and her com-

ments were invaluable and compassionate and wise. My agent Carol Mann was understanding as I set this book aside to write another one. She never pushed. She just waited and turned that into a generous act of faith.

THE EDGE

OF

HEAVEN

My mother returned that summer from an exile both imposed and earned. Nothing had prepared me for her departure. I was unsure how to claim her homecoming. But I share her talent for perseverance, for we are joined by more than I can bear. My mother came back to recognition and reckoning. I thought she came home to me.

At ten minutes after seven the morning of her return, it was already eighty-five degrees according to the deejay on the all-news radio station that woke me up.

All news, all the time, the station promised and delivered, and so even as I lay, partially asleep, poised to wake, I learned that the pollution and humidity made it a bad day for breathing and that the body of a young pregnant Black woman had been found in a park in Northeast Washington the night before. She had been stabbed and bludgeoned.

My cynicism was ornate and entirely deserved so I knew that only someone who thought they loved her could have unleashed such a torrent of rage. What had happened to us, my mother, my father, my grandmother, and me, had not dampened my curiosity about death, but perversely seemed to stoke it. If I saw a traffic accident in which the cars had been reduced to metallic rubble, I'd linger long after others had departed. The yellow police tape enclosing the scene was not a border, but simply a line to be crossed in my imagination. Standing before the carnage, I could never decide who was luckier, the covered, lifeless bodies on stretchers (the white sheets draped but never covering everything so that a foot or a shoe or the top of a head cheated anonymity), or those suffering pain, bruises, injury, but still alive.

Did she and her assailant argue in the park? I wondered of the dead woman as I rolled over and reached behind me to turn the volume down and switch to the soulful early morning gossip, music, and banter of WHUR, or was she murdered someplace else and her body dumped near the picnic tables? Lying on my back, I felt my hands roaming the terrain of my body, as though propelled by thoughts of their own. Once my palms and fingers confirmed limbs, skin, the tautness of my stomach, the veins in my neck, a sigh of relief fled my heart. A storm had awakened me in the middle of the night. The thunder clamored and menaced. But as an aggressive sunlight filtered into my room that morning, I wanted to know if the young woman was already dead when the rain began. Did the storm revive even a moment of her life? Did she open her mouth to whisper for help, only to have raindrops clog her throat?

My lavender sheets were humid and musty and my body grew numb each time I thought of my feet hitting the floor. My mother was coming home. And though I was terrified by the thought, the night before, within the boundaries of slumber, my mother's face spilled forth like a comforting hallucination, one induced by the potent alchemy of desire.

I lay in bed until seven-thirty, the numbers on the illuminated digital clock radio a neon countdown. When I finally got up, it was because I realized that my mother might arrive earlier than she had told us. Delay on my part would give her an advantage. I did not want to be caught, unawares, in the glare of my mother's love. Premeditated affection is what she would offer. I wanted a chance to choreograph my response too.

Drying off in front of the bathroom mirror, I confronted my face. It was then, as it is now, my mother's face. Undeniably hers. We share a curvature around the jawline that defines our visage, in the estimation of others as unremitting, even stern. But for us both, I knew, there was mostly reticence trembling beneath those bones. It was an unremarkable face, the only striking feature being the thick brows we shared, their natural arc softening what the jawline seemed to imply.

I applied more makeup than usual, my hands trembling and unsure as I lined my eyes and brushed on a thick coat of mascara, hoping to erase any hint of my mother's imprint. I had hoped to create a mask. My inept artistry had merely sharpened and clarified just how much I was her child. After I dressed I walked down the hall and knocked on my grandmother's bedroom door.

"Come in," she called softly. A proliferation of plants and flowers, philodendrons and wandering Jew, African violets, even a miniature cactus, made entering Ma Adele's room comparable to stepping into a rain forest. Some days I had heard her behind her door conversing with the plants. She had named the cactus Butch and the azaleas that hung from the ceiling Aretha.

"I just got through talking to your mother a few minutes ago. Didn't you hear me calling you?" My grandmother sat enthroned in the king-sized bed among half a dozen pillows, her white hair uncombed, her purple and green floral robe open, exposing the wrinkled crevice between her breasts.

"I was in the shower," I told her as I sat on the foot of her bed, the gently perfumed scent of the pink hyacinths in bloom on her nightstand, the eucalyptus stationed in the window, making me slightly dizzy. "I didn't hear you."

"Well, it would've been nice if you could've spoken to her," she said, dismissing my defense with a skeptical glance over the tops of her bifocals as she thumbed through *The Daily Word.* "You come straight home from work this evening, you hear?"

"Yes ma'am."

"Straight home."

The TV remote control, a paperback mystery, an aged, tattered leather phone book, knitting needles, a ball of yarn, and a stack of bills littered my grandmother's bed. I saw as well a pile of letters from my mother. The sight of my mother's handwriting—small, precise, and legible, so unlike my own, ignited a keen spark of longing I could almost taste. The letters lay spread like a fan. The envelopes had been slit open neatly and remained white and crisp. Where had my grandmother stored them?

The letters my mother had written me had ragged envelope tops, for I had impatiently, even brutally, pried them open with my thumb the days I came home from school to find them on my bed. The pages were grimy, laden with fingerprints, and crinkled, as though they had lived a lifetime in my hands. I stored them in my desk drawer with my diary, pens, school assignments, phone numbers, spare change, loose earrings, photos of friends, verses from poems I had written, and a broken Timex watch. There the letters mingled with the other secrets I wished I could tell.

"How do you feel? Now that she's coming home?"

"I'm just glad it's over," my grandmother said, her voice thick with weariness. Yet I heard beneath that familiar sound the simmering, satisfied whisper of anticipation.

"Do you really think it is?"

Each time I looked at my grandmother's face I saw the shadow and the promise of my mother and myself. My grandmother had aged with staunch dignity. Each year her high cheekbones, Cherokee nose, and burnished dark skin grew persistent, more right. I took refuge in that face as I awaited her response, which came convicted and sure.

"Of course it's over." She chided me with a relieved laugh, look-ing at me in annoyance and returning to the inspirational *Daily Word* paragraph for that morning. My doubt inspired her to suddenly read quite loudly and with dire oratorical belief "The power of God pro-tects me, the presence of God watches over me," looking up from the page in triumph when she had finished.

In self-defense I thought of but did not dare give voice to the quote from Faulkner I'd read once when I was writing a paper for an American literature class: "The past is never dead. It's not even past." Didn't my grandmother know that? Would I be the only one who knew this, even when my mother took up residence in a room across the hall from mine?

"Teresa, it's time to move on."

"Just like that?"

"Your mother's coming home expecting to find a daughter here. Don't disappoint her."

"And what do I get?" A ripple of nausea crossed the plain of my stomach.

"You get your mother back. You're not the only one who suffered, Teresa, she suffered worst of all."

"Do you really think *she* suffered worst of all, do you really believe that?"

"She lost everything."

"I did too. What do I do with everything I feel?" Clumps of sickness congealed in the pit of my stomach as I bit my tongue and bunched it at the back of my throat to keep from throwing up.

"You let it go. She'll need you to love her, love her to the bone."

"I need the same thing."

"Don't turn this into a contest, to see who needs more. You ought to be glad you still have a mother."

"I haven't had a mother since she left. I won't automatically have one when she comes back."

"Don't bring that attitude into this house tonight, you hear?" she warned me, her hands suddenly implacable, serious, stationed on her hips, a sign I had slipped into deep waters.

"What if it's all I've got?" I whimpered.

"I don't believe that. Neither do you."

My grandmother's understanding edged toward me like a malevolent impulse I dared not trust. Bolting from her bed, I ran from the room, ignoring her pleas for me to come back. Before her there was nothing I could hide. Even in my flight there was nowhere really to run.

On the front porch I closed the door behind me and slumped against it for several minutes. Finally I braved a step off the porch. The grasp of the sun was punishing as I walked down the hill toward Fourteenth Street to catch the bus, wondering not when but if this day would end.

On the bus I stood pressed against a young Black woman wearing blond cornrows, whose hands, clutching the back of a nearby seat, were large and thick, the nails of her fingers bitten so low, I winced at the sight of them. In the back of the bus the clipped, jocular Spanish of a group of Salvadoran men competed with the incantations of a boom box planted on the shoulder of a slick-haired, tawny-skinned boy dressed in black leather. He belligerently claimed the empty back row of seats. The air-conditioning didn't work. Halfway downtown I got a seat, and behind me one of the windows, loosened from its frame, slammed against the side of the bus each time the tires rolled over a pothole. Teenage girls with finger waves, and gold earrings the size of cereal bowls, burst onto the bus like unexpected turbulent weather. Instinctively they headed for the back.

When I got off the bus downtown, I missed the last step and tripped and fell. Briefly, I thought of remaining on the sidewalk, wounded and immobile forever. But hands, attached to faces that in my confusion and embarrassment I could not see, reached out to help me stand up. My knees and the palms of my hands were raw. Pinpricks of blood bubbled beneath my broken skin. Warm and merciless tears streamed down my face as I struggled to regain my composure and hurried past the curious gaze of the people waiting to board. The tears ceased as suddenly as they began, and when they released me, I stopped before the window of Ann Taylor, my reflection a humbling sight. I wiped my knees and the palms of my hands with a tissue someone I didn't know had thrust at me moments before.

Wobbly, and experiencing my body as untested and new, I walked the three blocks over to Seventeenth Street. Hollingsworth, Jacobs, and Lee was housed in a twelve-story glass and chrome tower on the corner of K Street. The entire east, west, and south wings of the building were occupied by the firm. Opening the heavy glass doors, I found myself in a gray, pale pink, and white sea of marble floors, walls, and ceilings. The foyer was an open, unbroken space, one so oppressive that it dwarfed the uniformed receptionist who was really a security guard, stationed in an elevated teak, oval desk below a chandelier that hung fifty-four feet overhead. The sheer width, depth, and length of the space had clearly been designed to intimidate. This was an edifice built for lawyers. I felt most days that if I could just get through that foyer, there was nothing in this life or the next that I couldn't do.

Hollingsworth, Jacobs, and Lee's clients were banks, corporations, television stations, and major newspapers. In my few weeks with the firm I had seen two congressmen and a senator stride down the plushly carpeted halls toward a meeting room to sit with a dozen others around a cherry wood table as large as a small Central American country. The pink-faced, middle-aged-to-elderly, tastefully prosperous clients, nearly always male, possessed information, influence, power, and wealth that the firm's lawyers were hired to consolidate, enhance, or protect. These were people whose sense of their own importance sculpted the unhurried, assumptive timbre of their voices and drenched their eyes with impatience when forced to gaze at anyone who could not be of service.

I was working at the firm as part of a program sponsored by George Washington University, where I was a junior. I interned through one of those liberal uplift programs that gave Black kids a taste of their chosen profession. I was a gofer and fill-in word processor because I could type pretty fast. Sometimes Bradley Hampton, the only Black partner, and the lawyer who had come to G.W. to speak about the program let me look at paperwork on his more innocuous cases and take notes in meetings for the pro-bono ones. I'd fill in for the receptionist if she was out or at lunch. Mostly, I was just breathing in the atmosphere of a law office, not much more. But the summer my mother came home I was drawn to the law as much as an idea as a profession. I was more puzzled than ever about the meaning of justice. The law seemed both arbitrary and fluid. Bradley had told me that the law didn't necessarily have anything to do with justice. I had come to that conclusion on my own. Truth and facts were relative. But the facade of absoluteness that the profession and its practitioners effused was irresistible to me then. I wanted to claim all that as mine too.

As soon as I got off the elevator on the twelfth floor, I headed for the bathroom. I washed my knees and my hands with cool water and then I threw up. This sickness was my friend, becoming, in my mother's absence, my alter ego. It hounded and relieved me and joined me in my mind to my mother, conquered the miles, the present and past time that so dauntingly separated us. When she first went away, I'd get sick to avoid going to school. Lying in bed, feverish with no appetite, I'd watch soap operas, reruns of *The Andy Griffith Show,* cartoons, and the daytime talk shows that turned genuine misery into something despicable and hilarious. Sometimes I got sick in the presence of my girlfriends' mothers, grew queasy with covetousness. On my mother's birthday, or the anniversary of the day she went away, my sister's birthday, or a day when my father promised to see me but failed to come, illness invaded me.

Nadine, Mr. Jacobs's secretary, found me in the ladies' room and from behind the locked door I assured her that I wasn't pregnant. By the time I came out of the stall I was headachy and exhausted. My skin was clammy, a thick film of perspiration clung to my face and arms. Murderously hot, inexplicably cold, I wanted to go home. But I couldn't remember the exact time my mother was going to arrive, and I had decided that I didn't want to be there when she walked through the door.

I stood before the bathroom mirror, assessing my face for the second time that morning. I've never been able to hide anything I feel. The makeup that seemed expertly applied an hour before was melting into jagged lines around my eyes. My face was puffy, my skin raw. My gaze was depleted, fully in retreat.

Nadine watched me skeptically in the bathroom mirror as she dried her hands.

"Are you all right?" she asked, the question so hesitant, so skittish it was clear she was afraid of my answer.

"I'm okay. It's nothing."

"Come on, Teresa. Are you sick?"

"No, I'm fine." I leaned over the sink, opening the tap, burying my face in the cool water filling my palms. I was not sure whether I wanted to disappear or just wanted Nadine to leave.

Nadine handed me a paper towel as I turned the water off, and she stood unflappable, forthright beside me. I smelled the faint odor of a delicate musk that I'd seen her apply to her wrists some evenings before heading for home. The hem of her pale yellow skirt lay against the exact middle of her knees. A sliver of black silk blouse was discreetly exposed by the open top button of her jacket. Her permed shoulder-length hair framed a bronze face.

As the secretary of the senior partner, Nadine was rumored to know everything about everybody in the firm. Who was going to get a raise, a promotion, get fired, who'd reached a glass ceiling, why Hollingsworth and Lee weren't speaking anymore. But Nadine, like everyone else in the office, knew nothing at all of substance or value about me.

"Is it something at home? Do you need the day off?" she insisted.

Crumpling the towel in my hands, I smiled at her, squelching the perverse desire to laugh, saying only "No, Nadine, I don't want to go home."

"Well, what is it?"

I opened my mouth but had no idea what to say. The sight of my attempt to speak widened Nadine's eyes, set them sparkling with hunger. Her naked curiosity pushed me back into the realm of the silence and caution I'd cultivated. The secretaries knew all about my boyfriend, Simon, my classes at G.W. I'd even mentioned Ma Adele. When they asked more, I gave them an answer that told them nothing but sounded like a revelation. I'd then gently interrogate them, listening so enthusiastically, they'd soon forget they knew nothing much about me at all.

"You can trust me," Nadine said.

I knew I could not. "I'll be okay."

"Are you sure?"

I finally found the strength to look at myself in the mirror, this time briefly, not comforted by what I saw. I smiled furtively at Nadine and hurried past her, saying, "Not just sure, I'm positive."

I got through the rest of the day, but I am not really sure how, for I was full near to bursting with emotions I was ashamed to own, much less express, the same as I'd been since my mother went away. During her absence I never told anyone how I felt. How could I?

Once, behind the locked bathroom door in my grandmother's house, I carved my sister's name onto the tender, yielding flesh of my inner forearm, where you could see, if you looked closely, the long blue tributary of vein linking your innards, holding you together. It didn't hurt. Because the knife was dull. But mostly because, like some primordial species, by then I had evolved beyond feeling anything.

After the blade, dull but plunged all the deeper because of that, drew its first blood I *did* feel a tiny, almost playful nick—I imagined myself some tribal female decorating herself for marriage or a fertility dance or merely the rest of her life. I was patient, dedicated to my task as I cut through my skin. The years have softened but not eradicated the wound. The slender, two-inch-long ropelike twisting of my flesh into the letters K and E, is a delicate yet horrible brand the doctor my grandmother took me to said would probably remain.

And I had kept a diary for a while, but one day when I recorded five anguished, confessional pages with an accuracy that appalled and frightened me, I never wrote in it again. I had translated feelings into words that I thought lay as immutable as bricks or stones. But when I read them and saw that they didn't rest easily on the page, pristine and polite but that the words hurled themselves in fury, tripped me up, breathed heavily in my face, I was afraid my grandmother would find what I had written, read it, and never forgive me.

In those days I lived an expansive, opulent fantasy life, reclaiming the years before my mother left us, and coloring that life in tones so vivid that some part of me was always living in that place I had invented even as I sat in my classes, watched television, or talked on the phone to friends.

In my dreams I was always back in our house on Sycamore Street, a large, sprawling house that in remembrance was perfect. I remembered small, mundane things, like the sheen of the hardwood floors and the smell of the attic where my father worked, and the sight of the house when I'd come home to it after school, just there waiting, it seemed, only for me. And when I thought of how we'd lived in that house, the only voices I resurrected were the murmuring, surprised, sometimes pained sound of my parents making love, a sound that crept like some enticing yet garbled foreign language into the hallway sometimes at night even when they locked the door.

I remembered the hamster my father gave me for my seventh

birthday and how I named him Alexander and fell asleep to the squeaking, fevered sound of him running, running into the night on his tread wheel. The faces of Black angels made of cardboard and cloth and yarn and cotton that we'd decorate the Christmas tree with each year, those faces filled my dreams day and night. There was my mother filling up the house, reigning over it. And my sister, my sister, she was always there.

When my mother was away I could not feel the way other girls my age did. While I was brimming with unexpressed anguish, I felt hollow as well. It was a strange feeling of being both empty and full, and because of that, feeling off center. Walking down the street, I sometimes felt wind-whipped and unsteady, as though reeling in the midst of a private hurricane. In bed at night I imagined my mattress a rickety lifeboat, the sheets monstrous, violent waves. More than once I knew, absolutely, I had capsized and woke up wet and shivering. On the occasions when I did express what I felt I always overdid it. Ma Adele gave a party for me for my sixteenth birthday. All my girl-friends were there, and there were boys, and this one special boy, Elton Hughes, whom I liked a lot. Everyone was huddled around the dinner table, adults snapping pictures, my friends singing "Happy Birthday," haltingly, because we were really too old for the song yet we could not escape the requirement to sing it. And when I cut the cake I began to giggle. It was a chuckle at first, a little pop going off in my stomach. Then it burst into laughter that quickly became too loud, too much, frosted with a bitter edge. I couldn't even hold the knife I was cutting the cake with, the laughter set my fingers to trembling so. The room began to swirl feverishly around me. The faces I had seen clearly moments before dissolved into a lurid color-stained blur. I was laughing, I thought because I was so happy. Then tears filled my eyes and there were these two feelings erupting, competing, inside me. The twirling sensation stopped as abruptly as it had come upon me. Everyone's face was suddenly in focus. Through this haze of impossible emotions I saw everyone looking at me. We were all ashamed, uncomfortable. Ma Adele came up beside me, mouthing a stream of apologies and explanations that she spread over the moment like a balm and whisked me away to my room, where she made me lay down.

I remember this laughing/crying going on for some time as I lay on my bed in the dark. When it was finally over and I was spent, lying on my bed, as still as a corpse, I heard Ma Adele and her friends washing dishes, cleaning up on the first floor. Then I felt nothing at all.

When I left work at five o'clock, I knew that my mother had probably arrived home. I found myself getting on the Red Line to Dupont Circle instead of taking the bus home. I bought a ticket at the first theater I passed. Looking back, I don't remember what I saw, have no idea who was in it or what it was about. A movie would use up at least two hours. And I wanted to be in the dark, in a room with people I didn't know. I wanted to be anonymous, for my life to matter much less than the lives unfolding before me on the screen.

When I came out of the theater, it was still light, but dusk had begun to gently claim the sky. Darkness seemed an option, not an inevitability. Standing at the bus stop, I felt sick once again, but willed a cessation to the upheaval in my stomach. The bus arrived and I got on, finding a seat three rows from the front. Staring out the window, I knew that before I told her anything I wanted to hurt her, to make *her* cry. Before the day was over I would wound her. I could defeat her by denying her an embrace. I could damn her forever. But fate already had.

The cabdriver was from Afghanistan. His broken English sputtered like an enticing but dense and nearly indecipherable song as he explained to Lena that he had been in America two weeks, and driving a taxi for three days. Not long after she settled in the backseat, Lena discovered that Mohammed Amin—she saw his name beside his picture on the sun visor above the front passenger seat—could not have found his way to the White House if it were three blocks away. Panic clouded the cabdriver's dark, bearded face as he repeatedly asked Lena for directions to her mother's Ingraham Street address. With a broad sweep of his hands, the cabdriver generously urged, "You show me way. You show me way."

Lena told him the most direct route and then huddled in the backseat, surveying the streets of a strangely unfamiliar downtown. Sleek new office buildings were rooted on nearly every corner. The buildings' colorful facades, tinted windows, and offbeat symmetry was playful yet resolute. The architecture deconstructed the awesome self-consciousness, the longing for grandeur and empire that studded the columns of the federal buildings that had always invested the city with a slightly grim demeanor. These new buildings were quirky, yet they too spoke of commerce and contracts. What else had changed,

Lena wondered even as she remembered that Teresa worked in a building like the ones they passed. It was three o'clock. Inside some her-
metically sealed office was Teresa swamped with work or in the middle of an afternoon break. Was she eager to come home that evening,
or plotting, even in the midst of her job, some insurrection to greet
her return.

During the bus ride through the craggy hauntingly eloquent
mountains of West Virginia, Lena had slept. The thought of what
awaited her frightened Lena so that she slept hard and deep most of
the ride down as a defense against the encroachment of thoughts of
what she longed for and feared most—home. What was there to
sleeping? You closed your eyes, but then your subconscious woke up,
went on foot patrol across your mind. It was nearly a year after
Kenya's death before something like slumber returned, rest without
pills, without the fear that despite the pills she would not sleep, fear
pumping her so full of anxiety that she lay awake, energized and
anxious until dawn. Retrieving that skill, that blessed ability, she had
spent long hours in her room prone, feigning a kind of temporary
death, sleeping just because she could. Now she was groggy, headachy, betrayed by sleep that had offered escape but not rest.

Above Colorado Avenue the taxi entered Petworth, and the houses
became large, even grandiose, surrounded by huge yards, and eerily
quiet streets. At Ingraham, Lena told the driver, "Make a left." When
he stopped before the wrong house, Lena thrust a ten-dollar bill
toward him, waved away the change, and, grabbing her suitcase, fled
the interior of the taxi. Standing at the curb, Lena wished she could
beam herself behind her mother's door.

Across the street on the porch of a dark green Cape Cod, she saw
Odelle Anthony and Edith Ferguson, both widowed and retired, rocking in the shady recesses of the screened-in porch. The two women sat
aged but not withered, well tended, highly prized flowers. Lena knew
that Mrs. Anthony earlier in the day had pruned the rosebushes, red

and luxuriant in the afternoon sun, and watered the plants curling in gay, ribbonlike profusion around the porch. Someone next door to Mrs. Anthony had watered their lawn, and rivulets of water veined the newly laid cement of the street, flowing quietly off the curb. The block smelled tropical, fertile. Lawns had been mowed, backyard gardens dug.

They all knew her. Had watched her grow up. Had seen her fall. Lena stood at the curb, her suitcase beside her, the sun unbearable against her neck and shoulders, certain that the walk to her mother's door would take longer than the bus ride. She reached to pick up her suitcase and felt someone beside her, then she looked up into a face that quickened her pulse with memory. "Your mother told me you were coming home today. Welcome back."

Ellington James stood before her, his bearded face, the light brown eyes, eradicating the cowardice that rooted her to the curb. He was standing close to her, like always. In high school at McKinley Tech, Lena watched Ellington pass her as he walked down the halls, his step assured, springy, and she'd call out to him, "Hi, Ellington James," always saying his whole name because it sounded to her like the beginning of a vow, a prayer or some promise she could not live without. He'd tease Lena, stopping in mid-stride to turn brusquely and look at her in feigned irritation and ask, "What you want, girl?" Listening with his whole body, Ellington never let his eyes leave your face once you started talking. Lena remembered feeling as though he'd kissed her just because he stood so close. When she was in high school and he'd come home in the summer from Temple University, they sat on the front porch at night. Sometimes before he went out with some girl prettier and older than her, Ellington would tell her what college was like. She felt as if they'd made love.

"What're you doing here? Visiting your father?" Lena asked, allowing Ellington to reach for her suitcase, and finally initiating a slow shuffle toward her mother's house.

"I live here now. My sister and I take care of my old man. He's got Alzheimer's."

"My mother told me. I'm sorry."

"Let me put this on the porch for you," he offered. Lena followed him up the steps.

"Looks like we just can't leave this street," she said, the words piercing her throat, then plunging into her stomach, where they bled like a sudden hemorrhage. "I thought when I left, I'd never call this house home again."

"That's the difference between you and me, Lena, I left the street but I didn't leave home." Looking at his face, Lena saw everything that had happened to him since high school—two divorces, a child he was a stranger to, a job he paid for with his life, his halting, blind stumble toward happiness and grace. She saw that and still could not turn away from the eyes amazingly flecked with sunlight, patiently awaiting surprise. Lena turned away only when she wondered what he saw when he looked at her.

And in the moment she turned from him, Ellington touched her cheek, his large hand resting there for a moment, and he said, "Take it one day at a time. I'll see you around. And don't be a stranger." He hadn't said a word about why she went away. He knew, of course. Everyone did.

Just as she raised her hand to knock, Adele's brisk, purposeful footsteps filled the hallway. As Lena heard the noisy, metallic, foreboding sound of the two locks being turned, she envisioned her mother dismantling the safety net that Adele Ramsey, like everyone, hoped would keep disaster at bay or drive it to someone else's door.

"Well, it's about time, I was getting worried," Adele said, hugging Lena, engulfing her in the overwhelming scent of a thick cologne.

"I had a cabdriver from Afghanistan. He didn't know how to get here." Now that she was inside the house, Lena longed to be outside once again.

"Afghanistan?" Adele asked as she placed Lena's suitcase beside the coffee table.

"It's in Asia, Mama, near Pakistan."

"Last year, when Loretta and I came back from the Bahamas, we arrived at Dulles and had a cabdriver from Iran," Adele said with a dismayed shake of her head. She settled on the sofa, watching Lena stand for several seconds beside a chair, her eyes scanning the room as if searching for clues to where she was. An expectant, tense moment blossomed between the two women. Finally Lena sat down, tossing her purse onto the floor next to her chair.

"How was the ride down?"

"Exhausting."

"You look good."

"You sound surprised."

"I didn't know what to expect. It's been a while since we visited you last."

"I went on a diet a few weeks ago, started running in the morning. It was important for me to come back looking better than people would expect."

"Don't mind people."

"Are you saying you never do?"

"I'm saying you don't owe anybody any excuses or anything you don't want to tell."

"What's left to tell? What's left that anybody doesn't know?" Lena shrugged.

"More than you think," Adele said gently.

"What time will Teresa be home?"

"Around six."

"I'm almost afraid to see her."

"I'm just glad you're finally back."

The kitchen telephone rang and Adele rose to answer it. Lena sat alone in a room of lace curtains and a Waterford vase stationed on a starched doily atop an ancient but sturdy, gleaming black upright piano. Baby yellow roses picked from Adele's quarter-acre backyard garden filled the vase. The walls held dozens of framed photographs of relatives. In the sepia-tinted pictures the expressions were solemn, whether posed on a beach or before some tacky fake background at a carnival or circus. Lena sat surrounded by everything she once knew and that she now felt she had lost.

Adele had worked three jobs to purchase the brick, two-story house, supplementing her teacher's salary by giving Saturday afternoon piano lessons and helping one of her friends cater weekend parties. For much of Lena's childhood, they shared the house with Thelma Louise Jenkins, who rented the room next to Adele's. In "Miss Thelma's" room Lena was given small, surreptitious sips of Manischewitz wine and told stories about all the men Miss Thelma swore wanted her but who just weren't good enough. A milliner for Woodward and Lothrop's, Thelma Jenkins lived in a region where the fanciful seemed necessary and beauty was the answer to everything. Words like *magenta, rose, turquoise* dripped from Miss Thelma's lips like the sound of poetry carved from teardrops or some savage timeless chant that would speak to everyone forever. Sequins, beads, strips of velvet, a swath of crinoline, were instruments of magic in Miss Thelma's wiry, gifted hands. Her room was eternally littered with bolts of cloth lined against the walls, swatches of lace and silk draping the night table and the chest, as if for dramatic effect. There were knee-high stacks of *Vogue, Harper's Bazaar,* their pages slick, shiny, hypnotic. Small rivers of material clung to Lena's ankles as she entered the room, grazing her skin, introducing her pores to sensations she could not describe but that she suspected lay in wait for her. A large canopied bed, whose sheets and blankets held and hid clothing, patterns, and cloth inside their folds, presided over the room's gorgeous disarray. Color and texture crowded the room with emotion and possibility.

While Adele worked her evening catering jobs, Thelma Jenkins designed hats for rich white ladies who drove onto Ingraham Street at night in long, sleek dark cars—Chrysler Imperials, Buicks and Lincoln Continentals—to pick up a hat for a luncheon or tea or some occasion that seemed peculiar to white people's lives. Some evenings, Lena watched the swift yet perpetually nervous hands of her mother's friend create hats as startling as some forbidden, finally revealed desire. Inside the room that Adele called sloppy but that was a universe to Lena, Thelma Jenkins showed Lena a picture one evening of the keen-featured daughter she had left behind with family in 1946 so she could come to Washington. A girl whose daddy, she proudly told Lena, was the richest Negro undertaker in North Carolina, but who was married to someone else.

The white ladies gushed over Miss Thelma's hats as Thelma stood beside them before the mantelpiece mirror in the living room, ostentatiously fussing over or pretending dissatisfaction with the clearly splendid creation.

Adele found Thelma Jenkins dead one Sunday morning in her room, slumped over the black Singer sewing machine, her foot still on the pedal, clutching a small black-felt triangular hat with a pink silk rose on the side, her face gnarled in an expression of surprise that death had arrived with so little fanfare. And although Miss Thelma herself had rarely worn hats, Adele decided that she would be buried in the hat she had held when the heart attack struck.

Lena would stay in Miss Thelma's room while she lived in her mother's house. Whenever she entered the room, she thought not of her mother finding Thelma dead, but of what she had felt and learned sitting on the floor, watching Miss Thelma sew, listening to her talk.

"That was Odelle Anthony calling from across the street. Naturally her feelings were hurt that you didn't stop and chat, as though that's the first thing you'd do," Adele said, entering the room.

"I'll go over. Maybe tomorrow."

"Please do. If you don't, I'll never hear the end of it." Adele settled on the sofa.

"I ran into Ellington James as I was getting out of the cab."

"It's a shame about his father. A college professor and now he can't even remember his own name," Adele said wistfully. "And Daniel Jackson, who lived at the end of the block, he died last year of a stroke."

"You told me, Mama."

The upwardly mobile strivers who had purchased the houses thirty, sometimes forty, years ago were passing into illness and death, swept there by a force that would claim her one day too, Lena thought. She did not want to know the names of anyone else who had died while she was away or been crippled by some awesome, incurable disease. She knew she would have to visit Ellington's father. But what could she possibly say that he would hear or understand? How could she look at him and not wonder if she was looking at who she might one day be?

"What has it meant, Mama, all these years to have this house?" She asked the question, moving from her chair to sit beside Adele on the plush navy blue velveteen sofa, longing to sit so close to her mother she might hear her heart beat, feel the warmth of her breath.

But before Adele could answer, Lena spoke the words she had tried to exorcise since she woke that morning. "What do I do now? Mama, I've got nothing left of my life." Finally she had said the words, but felt only terror, felt them gagging her, twisting her arms behind her back. The question languished in the air as both verdict and destiny.

"Lena, you know I never had a lot of time for pity parties. You've got your health, Teresa, and you've got no time to waste on feeling sorry. If you want pity, then maybe you should stay someplace else," Adele told her with a steely calm.

Then she stood up and began walking around the room, straightening the objects on the mantel, the magazines atop the television, clearly liberated by the distance she had placed between her daughter and herself.

"Do you think it was easy for me?" she asked, continuing to pace. "I'm seventy years old. To raise a teenager, at my age? I wouldn't have had it any other way. Ryland could hardly get through the day after you left, much less be responsible for Teresa. But I had already raised you. I didn't plan on raising any children again."

Standing before the picture window, Adele's hands smoothed the bodice of her crisp salmon-colored sleeveless dress, the movements offering the comfort that, Lena could now see clearly, her mother never got any other way.

"And I lost my granddaughter, lost her in some way none of us can explain. It's terrible to lose your grandbaby, Lena." Adele's soliloquy gained fervor in the room's appalling quiet. She might have been addressing a gathering of ghosts lined up on the other side of the window. "That's what Kenya was. She was my baby too because she came out of you and you came out of me. You didn't grieve alone. And you weren't in prison by yourself."

Adele turned around but did not look at her daughter, avoided Lena's eyes as she continued her reconnaissance of the room, tinkering, puttering with the scores of ceramic objects and photos on the tables.

"And losing you." She shook her head. "Those visits to Farmingham just made it worse. I was afraid every day something would happen to you there. Something more awful than what already had. The calls, the visits, the letters—they never put my fears to rest."

Having circumnavigated the room, she found herself once again sitting beside Lena. "What happened was terrible. And now we all have to go on."

"I'm sorry," Lena said, wiping her eyes, recomposing herself.

"Maybe what you need is understanding." Adele relented slightly, her eyes resting on Lena, narrowed in bold assessment.

"I'll try to understand. But I want you more than anything to have faith, Lena. In yourself. You had a good life before this happened. Doubt didn't take you there, belief did."

One night over dinner Adele had called Thelma Jenkins weak and infantile. She told Lena this as Thelma prepared to go out in the middle of the week to the Birdland or the Bohemian Caverns and the sound of Nat King Cole singing "Unforgettable" oozed down the stairs from beneath the door of her room.

Her escort was a man who waited impatiently for her in the living room and who, with his gleaming, slicked-back "conked" hair and gold tooth, looked to Lena's eyes like the personification of the words "good time."

"What's infantile mean?" Lena asked, the word threatening upheaval of all she knew and cherished about Miss Thelma.

"It means weak," Adele snapped, her judgment falling prickly and dangerous through her lips, hurled like some form of damnation. "She could've had her own hat shop by now. But lets these men sweet-talk her out of her money. Ever since we were children in Wilson, it's been me bailing Thelma out. She's a genius with those hats. But she lives just for today and can't see farther than the hat she's got in her hand."

Watching her mother's lips tighten in dismissal that evening, Lena wondered if the word *infantile* had anything to do with the way Miss Thelma's hands so easily touched her on the shoulder or squeezed her arm when she was telling her a story. Sometimes those hands just hugged her too, for no reason at all, touched her and turned the pages of a narrative her mother refused to tell.

"You'll have to go on from here, from this awful place, even if you don't know the way," Adele said, standing upright and gazing at her daughter, remembering how she had "gone on" from a similar dreadful starting line after the sudden death of her husband. She had endured widowhood, raising Lena alone, working ceaselessly and with a kind of valor to buy this house, claiming a trenchant resurrection of spirit at forty-eight after she survived breast cancer, wedding herself firmly, blatantly, to God, teaching thirty years in a school system that she had watched turn chaotic by the time she retired. She had "gone through" Lena's triumphs in college and career, boasting each time her bridge club met about Lena's job as an accountant with a Big Eight firm though Adele didn't know what the term meant except that it sounded important, and then witnessing Lena's marriage, not to the kind of man she had envisioned for her, but to a man who loved her, and loved her granddaughters with an exquisite, nearly frightening abandon. Adele had seen her daughter's life unfold like a charming, delicious antidote to her own. Then it was over, and Adele struggled to get through what came next.

"You're right, Mama," Lena said, rising to go upstairs.

"I fixed the guest room up for you," Adele said with a hastily marshalled brightness, watching Lena head up to the second floor.

"I'll just take a nap, get some rest before Teresa gets home."

"That's a good idea," Adele said, her relieved gaze nudging her daughter up the stairs.

Once in the second floor hallway, Lena immediately ventured into Teresa's room, hoping to stumble upon full disclosure of her daughter. She sat on the unmade bed, the rumpled sheets warm with sweat. Lena tried to imagine Teresa asleep, and she stretched out and closed her eyes, inhaling the thought of Teresa like a scent. Lena thought to rummage through her daughter's drawers, look in her closets, go through the papers stacked on her desk. All too brief letters, infrequent visits, had fractured the possibility of revelation. Even if Teresa were to tell her everything she did not know, how would she use it? Her first child, the one everyone said she "spat out," they looked so much alike. There was always, even when Teresa was a baby, the charisma that surprised and enraptured. She was a tomboy, athletic and precocious. Lena remembered now, lying on her daughter's bed, Teresa racing the boys in the neighborhood to the corner, and each time beating them all; Teresa falling from a limb of the oak tree in the backyard; Teresa reading the encyclopedia with a flashlight at night under the sheets in her bed; Teresa growing into Ryland's tight, angular build. Teresa was the one she had always wanted.

But Teresa grew up and Lena lost her over and over, again and again. She had missed Teresa's high school prom, her graduation, had never met her boyfriend. Her daughter's teenage years were as elusive yet seductive as a legend that could not be verified but that to believers had surely happened. It had happened, Lena banished to the ever-shifting and out-of-reach borders of her daughter's life.

The first year or two of her imprisonment, Teresa had written her weekly. Lena answered those letters nearly always the very next day. And each letter lay in a cherry wood box one of the women at Farmingham had given Lena as a birthday gift. After Teresa entered college, her letters came once a month if Lena was lucky. The visits deteriorated into small, destructive melodramas in which Teresa held all the power. There was no admonition, no punishment, no anything Lena could propose and implement. Her daughter now wore a size 36D bra, makeup, and often didn't even pretend to listen to what she said.

In the spring of her freshman year, Teresa failed an anthropology course.

"What happened?" Lena demanded.

"I flunked the course." Teresa shrugged with the insolence that had become a nervous tic. The sight of her daughter—eighteen, smug, and unrecognizable—made Lena tremble so that she held on to the sides of her chair to steady herself.

"I *know* that. I can *see* that," Lena said, pointing to the Xerox copy of Teresa's grades that Adele had sent. It lay on a Formica table between them in the visitors' lounge.

"But why? You don't flunk courses."

"I had a problem with the teacher."

"What kind of problem?"

Teresa said nothing.

"What kind of problem?"

"What you all call these days sexual harassment," Adele said quietly.

"What?" Lena shouted.

"I was having a conference with the professor in his office and he touched me."

Lena sprang from her chair in anger.

"Lena, sit down," Adele admonished her, looking around the nearly deserted lounge. It was a beautiful spring day, and almost everyone else was outside.

"What happened?" Lena asked, sinking back into her chair.

"We were having a conference and I was sitting next to him and he touched me in a place and in a way he had no right to. I was so upset, I never went back to his class."

"Why didn't you tell me?" Lena looked at Adele.

"I didn't want to upset you. And I've already got a lawyer talking with the university now. That F won't stay on her record and it isn't the first time this professor has been reported. Something will be done. But I'm doing all this quietly for Teresa's sake."

Her irrelevance bloomed as a sensation so intense, Lena felt nearly faint.

"Why didn't *you* tell me at least, Teresa, I deserved to know."

"What could you have done from here? Written a letter? A lot that would've done. How much weight do you think a letter from someone with a number instead of a name would carry?"

Remembrance mingled with grief and throbbed alive inside

Lena's skin. She had prayed to forget. But how could she? Sometimes if she shoved memory into a place so distant that everything and everyone seemed harmless, Lena could live and breathe inside her mind. And so, lying on her daughter's bed, she closed her eyes against the bookshelf lined with college texts, and paperbacks, the posters of Winnie Mandela and Tina Turner, their faces taut and intrusive on the walls of the room. Lena shut out the sight of the framed photos on Teresa's chest of Kenya and Ryland, the hot pink bathing suit drying on a hanger on the closet doorknob, the large box of tampons on the floor beside her desk, the high-heeled leather sandals lying casual and seductive on the floor beside the bed, the white cotton nightgown thrown onto a chair near the window.

She saw, instead, herself reading to Teresa as she lay in her womb, certain that she could hear her. Lena succumbed to the memory of evenings when, on her return home from work, she felt the stress of her job accumulated, festering in her bones as she soaked in the bathtub, trying to relax. Teresa and Kenya entered the bathroom giggling and speechless at the sight of their mother, nearly hidden beneath a mountain of bubbles. They stood excited yet unashamed in the presence of Lena's nakedness, the steam, the closeness of the room, the bubbles Kenya joyfully shaped into small hills, enclosing them in an alternate space, a world where they ruled, female and unpossessed.

Teresa sat on the side of the tub, reading to Lena some story she'd made up, some tale that always had a happy ending, while Kenya, tired of the bubbles, sat on the floor, combing the lint-filled hair of her brown baby doll. The last image Lena saw before she fell asleep in Teresa's bed was of Kenya on the floor, beside the tub. She was listening to the story too.

S treetlights flickered on just as the bus pulled up to the corner of the old Tivoli Theater, where my mom had told me she used to go to the movies on Saturday afternoons when she was a kid. Back then, there was a crystal chandelier, marble staircases and floors, and elegant murals in the foyer and lobby. A balcony stretched the width of the hall, and the whole theater seated over two thousand people.

But the Tivoli had been reduced to a boarded-up, brooding disaster. It claimed the corner of Fourteenth and Park Road like some beaten but still possibly dangerous animal. A poster advertising a concert by "King Sunny Ade" was pasted on the side of the theater. The bus loaded up and pulled off sluggishly into a neighborhood that was an energetic jumble of immigrants and old-timers, those barely staying alive and the entrenched middle class. This part of Fourteenth Street was crowded with rib joints, funeral parlors, liquor stores, hairdressers, and bodegas.

At Newton Street the bus stopped again, this time before a tiny Spanish church whose congregants overflowed onto the sidewalk. My father used to tell me that if America stayed out of those people's wars they'd probably never leave countries so beautiful he called them "God's Valium."

When the bus entered my grandmother's zone, the commercial upheaval just past was nowhere to be found; it felt as though years rather than hours had passed since I left that morning. The street lamps frosted the surface of the newly arrived darkness with a tenuous light. Was I coming home or entering another world? Too tired now to be anxious or afraid, I simply put my key in the door and turned the lock. Entering the living room, I saw that Ma Adele was knitting. My mother was curled up like a very small child, shoes off, her legs and feet tucked beneath her, staring at the TV screen.

"I'm sorry I'm late, but I couldn't help it, Nadine needed my help preparing some briefs for an important case," I said. I had chanted this lie to myself like a mantra all the way home.

"You've never been this late before," Ma Adele said, tossing the yarn she was knitting into her lap, her eyes gleaming with a righteous knowledge of what I had really done. I turned quickly to face my mother and pleaded, "I'm sorry, I really am."

My mother possessed the spartan, functional look I had seen evolving over the past four years. With her short hair brushed back, her face was a declaration. In jeans and a sleeveless blouse, she was trim and almost muscular. Her clear, eager gaze seized me.

She stood, a bit awkwardly, unsure of the etiquette of this reunion. We had argued the last time we'd visited, yet at that moment I couldn't even remember why. She walked toward me, her arms opening a world I was expected to enter. My mother pulled me so close, my arms ached. Then she launched an intricate physical rediscovery of me, hugging me, and then pushing me gently away from her a bit to inspect me closely. Her touch felt unfamiliar and new. I looked back unflinching, with a vision honed to salvage anything I could find. She held me against her breast. Her fingers played in my hair, outlined my ears, caressed my neck.

"Welcome home, Mom," I whispered, astonished that the words had thrust themselves into speech. My grandmother sat watching our display as though a long-overdue vindication had finally arrived.

Pleased by what she saw, Ma Adele left to clear the dishes off the dining room table, where I could see they had already eaten. My mother and I untangled our arms and sat on the sofa.

I was really seeing her now, almost as if cataracts had been removed from my eyes. Home to stay, my mother was clarified and focused, reminding me how counterfeit the visits in prison always were. Maybe I hadn't really looked at her closely then, terrified of what I might actually see. How had she masked the warm, total presence that sat next to me now? Although the visits were always unnatural and unreal, still I'd bring a list of things to tell her written on a spiral notepad.

Nearly every time, during the ride back home, I'd remember a joke that would have made her laugh, a question only she could answer, a story I had practiced in anticipation of a response I could predict and that was all the more precious because I could. My absent-mindedness made me ache with a sense of betrayal, for it always felt like the chance to tell my mother that specific thing had been swallowed by time. Time I would never get back.

Her gaze fell upon me ravenous, loving, amazed. If I was really seeing her, then she too must have been sated by the sight of me. A family of prickly gray hairs had claimed the hairline around her temples. I had not seen them before. A profusion of tiny moles mapped the space around her left eye. No, I had not really looked at my mother in four years. Suddenly I wished I had.

We sat quietly before one another. She looked at me as though I were a miraculous, rare discovery. I found the silence a comfort. I didn't know what to say. I hoped in my heart she'd say nothing too. But she wouldn't leave well enough alone.

"I'd like to call Bradley Hampton, thank him for what he's done."

She sat, lighting a cigarette, a habit she had picked up in prison. I sensed that she needed something to do with her hands. But once she took a drag, not inhaling, she began to relax. Clearly she thought this was going to be easy.

"That's not necessary, really, Mom, it isn't."

"I'm sure he'd be glad to hear from the parent of an intern."

"I just think it'd be better if you didn't call."

"Why?"

The question was rimmed by only a mild coating of surprise. I pressed my luck, however, engaged already in a game I had not consciously known I needed to play.

"Why?" she asked again.

I don't know how long I sat there saying nothing, obstinate beneath her confused stare. I flirted with the possibility of not answering. But the stiff-edged demand of the second request reminded me that this was not a visit. My mother was home to stay.

"No one there knows what happened," I said meekly.

"What do you think, I'll contaminate him over the phone?"

I didn't answer.

"Why don't you want me to call him?"

"I've worked hard to be like everyone else."

"They'll know you have a mother, that's all."

"No, that's not all. Can't I have something, some place that's mine that you can't spoil?"

"Is that what my coming back does, spoil your life?"

"I didn't mean that."

"It's what you said," she bitterly reminded me.

"Please, Mom, just leave things like they are."

"And how are they?" she shouted. "Maybe if I went upstairs, packed my bags, and went back to Farmingham, you could have your precious little life back."

"You don't understand," I said, standing up, feeling myself gaining some advantage over her just by this move. "It didn't happen only to you. That's what you think. That's what you've always thought. It happened to me too."

I had hoarded this blast, carved each word in my sleep, polished them in daydream until they glistened. I had imagined them marching like soldiers. Instead, they scattered in all directions and lay sprawled, whining and bothersome, between my mother and me.

Just then Ma Adele called to me from the kitchen, "Do you want me to fix you a plate, Teresa?"

"Yes, ma'am," I told her, grateful for an excuse to look away from my mother. When I looked back at her, only because I had to, she asked, "Are you going to fight me all the way?"

"I wasn't the one who left."

I saw Ma Adele set my plate on the dining room table and I stood up, eager to flee. As I walked past my mother, she grabbed my wrist and asked me again, "Have I lost you?"

I didn't know what to say.

My mother left me alone while I ate. She and Ma Adele settled before the thirty-six-inch Sony as though they were assigned to watch it. They sat wedded to the screen yet clearly unsatisfied by what they saw. The television provided a kind of visual Muzak my grandmother found comforting as she sat intent on her knitting. The click of the needles, a sound I had grown used to, was the one aspect of the picture my mother and grandmother presented that I welcomed because it was innocuous, requiring nothing of me, not even that I listen.

I used to watch a lot of shows on cable, black and white movies from the forties, and nature and educational programs. I loved the nature programs. The predatory, relentless lives that tigers and elephants and snakes and wolves lived was much more bearable than the culture of humans. Geese didn't have a conscience, rabbits couldn't feel guilt. There were no serial killers in the forest, no terrorists in the

wild. It was nothing personal when a lion devoured a family of ante-
lope. It was just the need to survive, and I began to see an unexpected
beauty in that.

Sometimes when I wanted to feel close to Ma Adele I'd crawl in
her bed and watch television with her, let the energy, colors, and
sounds emanating from the screen join us. I don't know what we were
doing in those moments, what was being done to us in the dark, lying
in my grandmother's king-sized bed. But I know I didn't feel lonely,
or afraid.

My mother's boredom was flagrant. She sat on the sofa, enduring
a rerun of *The Fresh Prince of Bel-Air.* A battered Samsonite sat beside
the sofa. Was she back for good? Or was the suitcase a reminder that
she had other options more attractive and certainly easier than the
decision she had made to return to me?

I finished my dinner and went to my room. My mother came
upstairs a few minutes later and entered her old bedroom across the
hall as cautiously as a guest in a stranger's house. She left her door
open. Ma Adele had bought a new blue and gold spread with matching curtains and had put a vase of daisies on the chest of drawers. The
room was oddly uninviting despite the purposeful sense of cheer Ma
Adele had tried to instill.

I heard my grandmother heavily climb the stairs, the banister
creaking morbidly as she pulled herself up each step. She entered my
mother's room and I heard their voices. I could see my mother hugging my grandmother and then longingly watch her walk slowly
down the hall.

I knew my mother saw me stretched out on my bed in my nightgown, pretending to read. She said nothing and began to put away the
things she had brought back with her—clothes, toiletries, books—
placing them neatly in the chest of drawers. She turned on the radio
next to her bed very low, and I could hear Smokey Robinson's exqui-

site purring falsetto fill the room with the opening lyrics of "Quiet Storm."

When she had put her clothes away, she sat in the middle of the bed, very still, her hands folded, as if in her mind she were trying the room on for size. Then she closed her eyes and she hugged herself the way I had refused to do. She fell back on the bed and lay there for a long time. Then she turned out the light. I heard Ma Adele in her bathroom brushing her teeth, showering. I could tell when she got into bed and turned off her light.

Of course I did not sleep, and several hours later I heard my mother. I heard her leave her room and go downstairs, pacing the first floor, walking back and forth between the living room and the kitchen. I lay in my bed and counted how many times she traveled that route. After a while I lost count. Was her first night in prison like this too, a time of searching for limits, boundaries, trying to conquer the dark. Then I heard the hum of the television. I could tell that she was changing channels mindlessly. For nearly an hour I did not hear her footsteps. Then I heard the front door open. I got out of bed and looked out my window to see my mother in her nightgown and robe, sitting on the steps, smoking and staring into the night. I felt her every move, heard each breath. I could not rest until she was still. I could not sleep until she closed her eyes. When she came upstairs some time later and entered her room finally, the house was quiet. But still I did not sleep.

I listened to the crickets outside my window, the blasting backfiring of a motorcycle a block away, and the confident repose, even on this night, of my grandmother's house. I lay listening to all that I heard and could not hear, lay listening for some sound from my mother's room. When the silence achieved a voice of its own, I walked across the hall. My mother had shifted in her sleep, was curled tight, coiled almost. The light from the hallway filtered over my shoulder but did not wake her. I watched her sleep, then I kneeled beside the bed and felt her breathing, a muted rumble filled with a sorrow I knew too well. Her fists were balled beneath her head. And I touched her face, brushing my fingers against her skin so quickly, so hesitantly, she might not even have felt it. I was afraid she would wake, and I wanted her to. I sat in my mother's darkened room, staring at her face, hating it even as I was anointed anew by love for her. I sat there, I don't know how long, watching her sleep. At five-thirty the next morning I woke up on the floor next to my mother's bed and went to my room. Sometime later I felt her watchful, expectant presence stationed in my doorway. I lay still, feigning sleep, as I imagined she had the night before, just so I would not leave her side.

My mother's first Sunday back, I woke to the mournful strains of Lionel Ritchie's gospel anthem, "Jesus Is Love." As on nearly every Sunday morning, the song flowed throughout my grandmother's house, rallying and bolstering sagging faith, mostly mine. As the song filtered into the bathroom where I showered, or trailed me as I decided what to wear to church, I listened for sounds of my mother stirring in her room. I heard none.

My mother had been baptized at Metropolitan Baptist Church, but she stopped attending when she became an atheist in college. Even after I was born and she started believing in God again, she still did not resurrect the rituals of the Sabbath. She and my dad hadn't even gotten married in church, choosing to have the ceremony performed by a judge at the Superior Court downtown, where her maid of honor read Gwendolyn Brooks's poem, "A Black Wedding Song." "This love is a rich cry over the deviltries and the death. A weapon song. Keep it strong."

And in our home, my real home, the one my parents made for me, my mother spent Sunday mornings reading *The Washington Post* and *The New York Times* and my father worked in his studio in the attic.

Once a month Ma Adele called my mother on Saturday evening

and ordered her to have Kenya and me ready for church the next day.
She'd warn my mother that we'd grow up pagans if she wasn't careful.
My mother just laughed. But watching Kenya and I descend the stairs
those Sunday mornings wearing dresses of velvet or frills and lace, our
feet uncomfortable in the patent leather shoes we rarely wore, ribbons
sprouting among Kenya's braids, my hair still smoky from the curling
iron she had used to transform it into a neat bouffant only an hour
earlier, my mother was clearly proud of something I could not
fathom.

After I went to live with my grandmother, when we attended the
eleven o'clock service the sheer size of the congregation meant that we
could maintain a kind of solitudinous dignity. My grandmother was
not the only member of Metropolitan who had a child in prison. But
the nature of my mother's crime so stunned the congregation that
many members were inarticulate in the face of our grief or could only
offer platitudes that were more offensive than silence. I was not at all
sure about God the summer my mother came back to us. I went to
church with my grandmother out of respect for her. And each Sunday
I relived Kenya's funeral, her small aluminum casket stationed at the
front of the church, my parents sitting side by side, my mother doped
up on tranquilizers, my father's face frozen in a harsh, masklike expression of resignation, my grandmother's weeping. I'd often recall
the image of Ma Adele's white handkerchief dabbing at her eyes each
time I had turned to look at her, the cloth offered up like a sign of
capitulation to an agony she could not have foreseen but expected,
because her mere existence made it possible.

Kenya did not appear to be asleep, as I'd heard dead people
looked. Despite the casual way her palm rested on her chest, the
beauty of the light green taffeta dress she wore, and the tiny pearl
studs in her ears, my sister was dead. I knew that. Her ten-year-old
face betrayed only anguish, rooted in the downward curve of her lips
and in her eyes, closed, and dusted with a thick coating of that awful

powder, eyes that I was convinced might open any moment and indict us all.

Each time I entered Metropolitan I embraced my sister again. Surely, I thought that Sunday morning, fear was what had my mother holed up inside her room. When I came downstairs and entered the kitchen, Ma Adele turned from the stove and asked me, "Is your mother up?"

"I don't think so." I shrugged, sitting down before a plate of waffles and bacon.

"Why didn't you wake her up? You knew she was going with us."

"She did too," I protested, reaching for the orange juice.

"Watch yourself, young lady," she ordered, untying her apron and casting a disgruntled glance behind me into the hallway, where she should have seen my mother standing, on her way into the kitchen.

Ma Adele marched resolutely out of the kitchen and up the stairs. I heard her knock gently on my mother's door and then enter the room. A few minutes later, when she returned to the kitchen, she placed two waffles onto her own plate and informed me, "She'll be ready in twenty minutes."

"What was wrong?"

"She didn't want to go, she said she was afraid. I told her we went every Sunday. If she didn't believe in God, she could at least believe in us."

Metropolitan Baptist Church occupied a block of Thirteenth and R streets in the midst of a zone of Black religious faith that had flourished in the area for over a hundred years. Vermont Avenue Baptist Church sprawled over an entire block around the corner from Metropolitan. Sometimes when we'd drive past that church, I'd turn my head to see the wall-high, pink-skinned Caucasian-featured Jesus, arms extended, surrounded by an angelic glow, staring out through the glass doors of the church entrance. It was an unsettling sight. Jesus always struck me as an interloper, not a savior on this block, pockmarked by boarded-up houses, abandoned cars—the vision that met this savior as he stared out onto Vermont Avenue—graffiti-scarred buildings, small glass- and rubble-filled alleys that seemed to lead nowhere.

Metropolitan was marked by the huge crosses hung on the front of the nearly nondescript, almost utilitarian redbrick building. Even the stained glass windows, opulent and rich with story at other churches, were muted at Metropolitan, composed of jagged, triangular colored glass fashioned into a modern motif. The real beauty of the church was inside the huge sanctuary. Its sense of omnipotence was breathtaking. As large as the sanctuary was, with its balcony stretching the width of the church with tiers of pews overlooking a huge lower level, there was often an overflow crowd and folding chairs had to be set up in the aisles by the white-gloved ushers who were as precise and disciplined as well-trained soldiers as they led the late-comers into the service.

Small clusters of women waved or nodded to Ma Adele and me and then paused in openmouthed curiosity at the sight of my mother as we entered. The women who normally chatted with my grand-mother in the minutes before the service began clung to the people they were with, as if for protection against what my mother intro-duced into their midst.

When the service started, my mother stealthily reached for my hand. It cost me nothing to submit to her touch. Sometimes I was convinced I'd seen Kenya, a phantasm and blessedly real, hovering over the minister's shoulder as he read the weekly announcements. There were times in those pews I fought the urge to will my own death even while the choir sang. My mother's fear passed like an awful adrenaline into me as she gripped my palm.

At the end of the service, when the assistant pastor called all those forward who wanted to join the church, I wondered what my mother was trying to prove. Watching her walk down the aisle, I wondered if she really thought forgiveness was so easy. When my mother finally made it to the aisle, brushing clumsily past Ma Adele and me, she just stood there as if she didn't know what to do. She looked back at us, searching our faces for something I wasn't sure we could give but she clearly thought we owned. Whatever my mother sought in that backward glance, she must have found, for she surged toward the front. I sat counting her every step. The farther away from me she moved, the more I yearned to run into the aisle too. For it seemed that all the roads my mother chose or was forced to take led away from me.

I no longer sang, my voice aching, instead, for words I could both summon and express. Beside me, Ma Adele stood holding her breath as though watching my mother embark on her first steps ever.

That languid and sultry afternoon, Ma Adele retreated to her bedroom for a nap. I hunkered down on the carpeted floor of the living room to read the Sunday paper. We ate dinner, and when I'd finished washing dishes, Simon called. He was going to Georgia Tech in Atlanta in the fall to study architecture and we had already talked about my visiting him there and waiting for each other. He had not proposed. But I knew one day he would. Yet Simon really didn't know who I was.

We argued about what movie to see that evening. I relented, agreeing to see *Die Hard With a Vengeance,* mostly because a few weeks earlier he had agreed to see an Italian movie with me although he hated subtitles. I'd go with him to see something mindless and numbing as long as he'd accompany me to see a film in which, if someone died, they expired the way people do in real life, with a quiet distress that the ones they love can never forget.

I had told Simon only lies about my mother. He didn't even know she was coming back. When Simon said he'd pick me up at seven o'clock, I wondered if there was time in the two hours I had left to assemble something that sounded like the truth.

We had met the previous summer while I was sitting on the grass

on the banks of the Potomac River, near Georgetown. I wasn't working, and sometimes I walked from George Washington, where I was
taking an extra credit summer school class. I'd sit and watch people
fish, pulling croaker, spot, and bass from the tranquil, muddy river. I
liked the area a lot because nobody ever bothered me as I sat writing
in my journal. The fishermen, the health nuts in their sleek, form-
fitting spandex suits, pedaling past, drenched in sweat and spurred by
the belief they'd live forever, even the few people I couldn't catego-
rize, they all left me alone. But Simon sat down beside me one day as
though I had been merely waiting for him.

"What're you writing?" he asked. Actually, I had smelled him
before he spoke. He plopped down next to me on the grass, and
the scent of tar and nicotine and metal rose, staining the air. Before I
even looked at him I slammed the large black notebook with cream-
colored lined pages shut so hard, I figured the sound would scare him
away.

When I turned, I saw the face of a redbone. His skin was light,
with a sallow, slightly tan tinge, and his cheeks and the bridge of his
nose were home to an explosion of freckles. If you looked at them hard
enough, they'd create a map that would lead wherever you wanted to
go. His coarse, burnt reddish-brown hair was the color of October
leaves. At the sight of it, I smelled smoke, not like something was on
fire, but like something was getting warm.

He'd been running and wore a T-shirt with the arms off and
shorts that stopped just below his groin. His thighs were muscular
tree trunks.

"It's private," I said, straightening the folds of my skirt, pressing
my ankles tighter, reining in my body, of which I was suddenly
distressingly aware.

"You come here a lot."

"I've never seen you," I told him.

"That doesn't mean I wasn't here." He grinned mischievously, as if he'd scored a point. "Besides, you're off in your own world most of the time."

"How long have you been watching me?" I asked, my hands nervously picking clumps of dull, dry grass.

"I haven't been stalking you, if that's what you mean."

"I didn't say that."

"Sure you did." He laughed again as though he knew me better than he had any right to.

We were quiet for a while. Simon stretched out beside me, leaning on his elbows, alternately looking at me, or staring at the sky, which that day was a slate of eggshell blue, flat, cloudless, promising nothing.

"You live around here?" he asked, sitting up, his long redbone arms flung over his knees, his hand clutching his wrist.

"Nope."

"I do, in one of the apartment buildings on L Street. I'm a maintenance man. I fix things. You know, leaking faucets, broken pipes. I replace windows, toilets, doors. You name it."

"I'm a student at G.W."

"I thought you were a writer. That what you want to be?"

"Not really."

"Got a lot on your mind?"

"Yeah."

"That doesn't scare me," he said.

After high school Simon had worked as his father's assistant maintaining the L Street building. When his parents were killed in a car accident, Simon was hired to take his father's place. He took the job, he said, because "I had a free apartment, was making decent bread, and figured in a couple of years I'd have enough saved so I wouldn't have to go into hock to go to college."

"Where do you want to go?" I asked him.

"Georgia Tech to study architecture. They've rejected me twice. I'm gonna give them one more chance."

"But you've wasted almost six years already," I told him.

"No such thing as wasted time. I've been doing more than fixing broken toilets. You think because you've taken all those courses and read all those books you know more than me."

"I didn't say that."

"You don't hear yourself when you talk, do you? You don't even listen to what you say."

"I'm sorry," I said, only slightly surprised at my apology.

"There's forty-eight units in the building. What you learn look-ing at how people live, what gets broken and how! And man, people are lonely. Women know you're scheduled to check the noise the refrigerator's making and come to the door all dressed up or half naked. And then because you're there to fix something, man or woman, they'll just about tell you anything, all their business. You put on a uniform and you're not a person. I listen but don't hear a thing."

He looked at his watch, stood up, and asked me, "When you plan to be here again?"

"I don't know," I lied.

"I run every day at this time. You're usually here on Wednesday and Friday. I'll see you next week."

Simon's building was one of those generic, characterless modern structures that possesses not a glimmer of individuality. The tenants were mostly the kind of people who, when I came to visit Simon and passed them in the hall or saw them coming out of the elevator, strained to avoid having to exchange a word with me.

His apartment was a spacious two-bedroom unit at the end of the first floor. He and his sister, Linda, he told me, had grown up in the building. I didn't really know Simon very well the day I went to his apartment. Still, I felt absolutely safe as I followed him through the door a month after our first meeting. We'd had several conversations on the banks of the Potomac. He had described how, three years earlier, a fire truck rushing to a burning apartment building on O Street had skidded on a patch of ice while making a right turn and jackknifed, landing on top of his father's Jeep, which was stopped at a red light. "They didn't know what hit them," he'd said the day he told me the story. "I could tell that when I saw the Jeep. They didn't even have time to get scared. Maybe that's the best way to die."

A profusion of family photos were gathered on a small table near a window that looked out on Twenty-third Street. Simon showed me a picture of his father, a heavyset man whose barrel chest was draped in a bright Hawaiian shirt, sitting at a picnic table in Rock Creek Park. Terrance Mack's hands, resting on the table before him, were like large, inert animals with lives of their own. They were coarse, scarred testimony to years of maintenance and his sideline career of making cabinets and shelves and cradles for scores of tenants. In the photo, Simon's father was smiling, a slightly tipsy, crooked smile, induced, I could tell, by the revelry of that day.

Simon's mother was a tiny woman, holding her grandchild, Linda's son, a week after his birth. She sat posed, almost as though called to attention, ill at ease in the rocking chair, the child in her lap, the same rocker I saw that day in the living room near the stereo and television set.

"Do you ever not miss them?" I asked Simon, placing the photos back on the table.

"No. And I wish they had lived to see me go to college. The first one in the family."

"What about your sister?"

"She went to the police academy right out of high school. She works undercover."

Simon managed to live in the present, and yet his parents were always with him. Had they cosmically loosened their grip, or had he struggled and finally broken free? I yearned to ask him this that day but lacked the courage to hear the answer. Simon studied buildings. We'd drive all over Washington and he'd point out the Egyptian influence in buildings from one end of the city to the other, from the Egyptian-inspired carvings on the doors of the Library of Congress to the Washington Monument, which Simon said was nothing more than an obelisk "ripped off, stone from the pharaohs." We must have gone to the East Wing of the National Gallery of Art twice a month just so he could stand and meditate on the cavernous yet oddly inti- mate marble building, all curves and angles and mystery and space. He had stacks of blueprints he had done, and we spent hours talking about the buildings he wanted to design.

After a while Simon's apartment became a kind of home to me, for there I could pretend. I told him my mother was away at school, the same story I had told other people. I embellished the narrative, my nervousness inspiring me to talk longer, to tell more, to lie more elaborately than was necessary. When I was through, he shrugged and said, "Okay," informing me clearly that he had not believed me but that the lie, neither its magnitude nor length, would change our relationship just then.

For a long time we did everything but have intercourse. Simon was twenty-four and he respected my decision to remain a virgin. Still, he touched me. I touched him. He kissed me. I kissed him, all in ways and in places as intimate and as deep as real sex could ever be. But as long as we did not actually do it, I felt intact. I already felt ripped apart emotionally most of the time. My virginity was literally a shield. I couldn't bear for my body to feel like that too.

But a few months before my mother came home, I gave in. She still had several months before her release, and I was obsessed with doing something, anything, to stifle the power of her attempts to reclaim me. When we went out on the weekends, Simon had to get me home by one o'clock. One night we were lying in his bed, looking at a detective show and necking. His fingers were inside me, had rummaged beneath the crotch of my panties, and he had pulled down my bra. He was ravenous at my breast. By then we both knew how far to go. He could come, for example, anywhere but in me. It was ridiculous, painful, sadistic, and when Simon drove me home to Ma Adele's, we sat next to each other trembling so, I wondered why we never once smashed into another car. But that night, in the middle of all the fumbling, the sweat, the opening and closing of buttons and zippers, I stopped and I took off the blouse that was open, the bra that was half off, removed the skirt he'd unzipped, and stood before him beside the bed, despite my actions, grateful for the dark. Now that we were naked, I was unsure what to do next. But he knew. And even in his arms, delirious, on fire, laughing silently in my mother's face, I whispered in his ear, "Where's your condom?"

"There's no such thing as safe sex, Teresa," he moaned. "If it wasn't dangerous, we wouldn't want to do it."

He reached into the drawer of his bed stand and put on the condom anyway, with practiced, skillful hands that made me wonder about the women who came to the door half naked when he repaired their refrigerator or stove.

Despite the initial pain and my surprise at how much the actual thing resembled an act of aggression, when it was over I felt not fractured, as I had feared, but coherent and relieved. I saw the clock. It was three-thirty. I knew Ma Adele had probably gotten out of bed, put on her robe, and was waiting for me in the front room, a lecture and punishment resting on the tip of her tongue. I didn't care.

My mother was coming back soon and Simon was going away. Georgia Tech had accepted him. The same day he showed me his acceptance letter, he showed me his savings account passbook. The worn blue book Simon cradled in the palm of his hand as he turned the pages recorded six years' worth of at first modest but steadily increasing deposits made twice a month. He even had relatives in Atlanta who were going to let him live in their renovated basement for next to nothing. I was happy for him. Really I was. Why wouldn't I be?

When I hung up, I went downstairs to tell Ma Adele I was going out.

"Is this Simon the young man you told me about?" my mother asked, coming into the living room.

"I'll be glad to meet him. Or would that be too much to ask," she said, sitting down beside Ma Adele, who was doing a crossword puzzle in the *TV Guide.*

"No," I told her, my mind blossoming with possible scenarios that I swore would never happen.

"What did you tell him about me?"

"I said you were away at school. In California. At Berkeley."

"Berkeley? Why didn't you just say I was exploring the surface of the moon?"

"Lena," Ma Adele admonished her without gazing up from the magazine.

"No, really. I mean, if she put me on another coast, why not go all the way? Another universe wouldn't have been a stretch. Did you know about this, Mama?"

"Lena," Ma Adele said wearily, "you can understand, I'm sure."

"Was I supposed to tell him the truth?"

The question stalled her outrage, landed like a blow to the face. "I just need to know who I'm supposed to be."

"If you don't want to talk about it, don't," Ma Adele said, looking in dismay at my mother and me. "Fabricating stories big enough for a history book when all you really need to do is tell people, 'I don't want to talk about it,' or, even better, 'It's none of your business.' "

"Mama, you're old enough to get away with that. I'd get fired or else lose every friend I have. People need to know something. Teresa has just proven sometimes anything will do."

"Well, I don't like it, all this lying. What happened was a tragedy, not something to fill us with shame. I don't know how either of your souls can rest, misleading people so. Everybody on this block knew what happened. I didn't lose one friend."

"Mama, this block isn't the world."

"Well, it's enough of the world for me."

I stood listening incredulously to their debate. Now I'd never be able to tell them how proud I was of my ability to lie, how adept I had become at masquerading, how the self I had constructed was someone I loved and did not want to relinquish.

My mother was out in California, and I'd spend summers with her out there. I was living with my grandmother until my mother finished her studies. When I visited her in California, sometimes we'd drive across the border to Mexico. She spoke Spanish and I was picking up some too. My mother was really quite hip, a woman who believed everybody should go back to school every twenty years just so they could keep up with a world that changed so much and so fast. She and my father were divorced but were still good friends. I was an only child. Once I had a sister, but she died when she was really young of a rare disease. There was nothing the doctors could do. This was the autobiography I'd crafted in the years of my mother's imprisonment. I'd come to see it as an extension of the stories I'd made up and committed to paper. This was a story too, but one that found its most tantalizing, powerful life in my head. But more than that, this was who I'd come to believe, in some sense, that I was. Who would choose to be the real me instead? I went upstairs to change my clothes. I was almost dressed when my mother appeared in my doorway.

"Can I come in?" she asked hesitantly.

"I don't care." I shrugged.

She sat on my bed, watching me, and I knew that momentarily she would say something that I would hate, something meant to fortify us that would only tear us further apart.

"How involved are you and Simon?"

"What do you mean?" I turned to face her. I wanted to see her when she made her blunder.

"I mean, well, are you having sex?"

"Mom. How could you ask me that?"

"I have a right to ask."

"Do you have a right to know?"

"In a sense, yes."

"I don't think so." I shook my head belligerently. "You've been out of my life all this time and now you want to come home and get in bed with me and my boyfriend."

If she had slapped me then, I'd have accepted it. But she didn't. Moments after she stood up, her arm flinched, jerked reflexively toward me. But then she let it drop to her side. I couldn't believe the quiver of disappointment I felt. I didn't want my mother to hit me. But maybe I hungered for some articulation of what I had yet to reveal. If she struck me, I could hit back. Then I could tell her everything, more than she could stand, more even than at that moment I knew.

My mother didn't hit me, but she made a promise: "I'll give you what you want. You can have your life. Free of me."

Of course what she'd said was a lie, impossible, an impotent curse, and yet when she left the room, slamming the door behind her, I stood despising the gift I'd been given.

The darkness of the low-ceilinged mall parking lot induced in Lena a potent panic. Driving past row after row of cars, following a winding route through the structure that led them six stories down, the sight of a single open space struck Lena as a miracle. As Adele parked, Lena clung to the door handle even as the thought of leaving the car filled her with dread.

"Are you all right?" Adele asked, removing the key from the ignition. With a firm yet gentle grasp she turned Lena's face to hers. "What's wrong?"

"Nerves, that's all. You know I haven't been in one of these places in a while. They always gave me the creeps."

"You don't look good to me. Not at all."

"It's nothing. Once I get out, walk around a bit, I'll be fine." Lena began bustling, hurrying out of the car, all to avoid Adele's concerned stare. When Adele came up behind her, Lena reached for her mother's hand and smiled, too broadly, too archly, saying, "I'm fine, Mama, really I am."

The two women linked arms as they walked up the steep incline to the parking lot elevator.

"I know you're not sleeping at night. I hear your television on at three A.M.," Adele said.

"I don't mean to disturb you. Don't worry about me."

As they entered the elevator's claustrophobic, nondescript space, Adele said, "But I am worried."

An aggressive cheeriness, a profusion of lights, colors, shapes, and objects attacked Lena's senses as she and Adele walked through the heavy glass doors leading to the mall. Excess was the prevailing aesthetic in this shopping center that was at once gaudy and tasteful, spacious and overcrowded.

"There's a sale on at Macy's, let's go there first," Adele said. Lena dutifully followed, but the stores and displays oppressed her so that several times she had difficulty breathing. Overwhelmed by the feeling that everyone around her was moving with a speed and concentration she could not match, Lena slowly trailed behind Adele. How, she wondered, did the plants and trees stationed so gracefully around the mall survive in the sealed, ruthlessly manipulated environment? Outside the entrance to Macy's, Lena told Adele that she needed to sit down for a few minutes. They took the escalator to the lower level and sat at a small café.

The waiter, a young Black man with orange hair and small hoops in each ear, wore a striped silk bow tie and a starched white shirt and black vest. While Lena scanned the menu, she peripherally saw the waiter wink and pucker his lips at a blond, blue-jeaned teen at a nearby table. The young boy reminded Lena of the men who advertised expensive men's briefs on the pages of blindingly colorful magazines. The pages were odorous with the fragrance of overpriced, nearly toxic cologne. The models were posed sullen and preoccupied, bulging and drenched in subtle disdain for anyone who desired them. The blonde blushed and thrust his fork into a slice of German chocolate cake so sumptuous, Lena wondered if he would overdose. The menu

listed twenty different kinds of coffee, a dozen teas. More than anything, Lena had longed to be able to choose. Now she sat numbed by
the prospect.

Handing the waiter the menu, she told him, "A large decaf and a
croissant."

"I'll have the same," Adele said, then asked Lena if she wanted an
aspirin.

"No, I feel a little better already, just sitting here. It's just that at
Farmingham everything was so bland. I was used to the sameness of
things. Walking into a place like this unnerves me." Lena spotted a
group of young Black boys wearing oversized baggy jeans that
drooped nearly down to their groins and T-shirts emblazoned with
profane declarations. The boys dramatically and loudly assessed several young girls who passed them laden with shopping bags from the
Gap.

When the waiter brought their orders, Adele said, "I was thinking maybe at Thanksgiving we'd drive down to Wilson to see Ned
and Betty and their kids. They asked about you the whole time. They
said they'd love to see you."

"I can't."

"Lena, please."

"Mama, it's too soon. Can't you understand that I feel like everybody who looks at me can see who I am? That's with strangers, how
could I face family?"

"And who are you?" Adele asked indignantly. "You're my daughter, Teresa's mother. That's who you are."

"You know exactly what I mean," Lena insisted in exasperation.

"And that's why I'll have none of it. Why did you come home if
you didn't want to start over?"

"I can never do that. There's no forgetting. No forgiving."

"There's never enough of that for anybody. That never stopped me. It doesn't have to stop you," Adele announced, wiping her lips with a paper napkin, pushing her coffee aside. "We can talk about this some other time."

The sadness was always present, puncturing any calm Lena tried to improvise or claim. Her mother's house was a country she had once known well but whose borders had always been too close. Ingraham Street's pervasive nighttime quiet left her more on edge than the nights at Farmingham, nights in which she heard Fay patrolling the halls in her sleep, cursing the husband she had stabbed in a fight over ten dollars worth of heroin, her voice a wild, mangled cry that infiltrated Lena's own dreams. And the first night back in her mother's house, as she felt Teresa's fingers probing her face, Lena had not opened her eyes because to do so required more courage than she had ever known.

Inside Macy's, Lena saw few clothes that she liked. Finally she chose three dresses to try on mostly so that Adele would not feel that her offer to buy her several garments was not appreciated. In the dressing room Lena was dissatisfied with the fit of the clothes. As she replaced the last outfit on a hanger, she turned to face the three-way mirror again.

Her breasts spilled forth as she lowered the straps of her bra. Stretch marks tattooed the skin of her breasts and even the dark wide orb of her nipples.

In the kitchen some weekday mornings after Teresa was born, Lena leaned over the sink squeezing milk into several baby bottles that she would store in the refrigerator for the sitter to use later in the day. Ryland sometimes surprised her at the sink, plucked the bottle from her hand, and began nibbling her breasts. He was gentle and slow at first, holding Lena around the waist, his grip quieting her reluctant, whispered protests that she would be late for work. When his teeth grazed her skin, it hurt, but not too much. By then her plentiful feelings set her groaning, unable and unwilling to speak as he opened her robe and fumbled to grab a kitchen chair and pull Lena onto his lap.

Greedily matching her husband's movements, Lena was grateful for the rough pull of his hands on her shoulders that joined them close, but still not close enough. Pleasure was grasping for life inside her, and when she could finally open her eyes, Lena saw her milk leaking onto Ryland's cheeks, neck, and staining his beard.

But her breasts now lay against her chest defeated, aged. Lena massaged her body as if attempting to fill it with life once again, then removed her panties and her palms rested against the stomach that despite exercise persisted in protruding. Several gray hairs were tangled in the mass between her legs. Her thick thighs narrowed into slender legs, the one feature of her body that she did like.

Naked, wondering but not caring if the security cameras were filming her, and whose eyes were behind the lens, Lena felt the first tremor of tranquility she had experienced since coming home. Briefly, boldly, she thought of striding out of the dressing room as she was.

A forty-seven-year-old naked Black woman, walking quite calmly, hips jiggling, breasts bouncing, abdomen sagging through blouses into designer suits. The image of Adele's horrified eyes, the security guard frozen and unsure whether to arrest her or look the other way, pierced Lena with a glee so wrenching, she doubled over, melted onto the floor, gripped by a catharsis she had thought no longer possible.

That her laughter, uncensored and stark, brought no salesladies scurrying to investigate, or startled inquiries from nearby stalls, Lena accepted as her due. On the dressing room floor she nestled on the heap of her own clothes. Her laughter subsided and she slowly drifted into a deep and dreamless sleep, waking without a glimmer of surprise twenty minutes later. The reflection of her disheveled hair, her nudity, her attempts to gracefully rise from the floor, induced no surprise. Lena did not leave the dressing room unclothed only because she had nowhere to go. The room she inhabited in her mother's house was another cell. If she walked out of Macy's naked, Lena wanted to be marching to a room of her own. Farmingham had been a womb. That was only one of the things no one else would ever know, that she could never tell because she didn't know how.

When Lena reentered the women's dress department she saw Adele at the cash register, her worried gaze scanning the department.

"What took you so long?" Adele asked, panicked and clearly troubled as Lena approached her.

"I just wanted to make sure that they fit."

"Do they?"

"Yes, yes, I'll take this one," she told her mother, handing Adele a nearly ankle-length light brown linen shift with a scoop neck in back and front. "Let me put these back," she said, hurrying to turn away from Adele's eyes upon her, eyes that silently asked if the daughter she had known before would ever return or was, indeed, gone for good.

Lena was just starting out as an accountant when she and Ryland met. The profession was never just about numbers for her, for she felt that the beauty of the process lay in creating a statement that could be read as precisely as a book. As one of only a handful of Black women accountants then, she was lonely in the Big Eight firm she worked for. There was so much to prove. Every day. All the time.

Her first apartment was modern, efficient, the walls off-white, the furniture solid but understated. She went on cruises with her girl-friends and shopped at Saks. It was clearly amazing, she often thought, that Ryland found his way into her life. But it was the boldness of his decision to live literally by his hands that she could not resist. The first time she saw Ryland Singletary dressed in a royal blue dashiki, his left ear pierced with a tiny diamond stud, Lena was intrigued and aroused. He awakened in her so much curiosity, sexual, intellectual, and emotional, that she ignored the tiny shiver of doubt evoked by his beard, so long it lay against his chest, making him look both crazed and like a prophet.

They met at an exhibition of Ryland's work. He was a friend of the brother of Constance Radley, who graduated with Lena from

Catholic University, where they both studied accounting. Ryland had returned a few months before the opening from a summer spent in Jamaica, where he had painted in a frenzy, conscious yet unconscious, color devouring his canvas as never before. The robust black, brown, tan, mulatto faces of the island's progeny carved themselves in the wake of his brushstrokes.

Before, his paintings were dark, uncertain, and he used a fixed set of shades for expression and discovery. Now he applied color promiscuously. The shades confidently justified their existence.

He had discovered a new way to look at color, and standing in the gallery that night, his work surrounding him on the walls, Ryland knew that he was ready for anything. The most unexpected thing might happen to him. He might even fall in love.

He was twenty-seven years old, a man who had chosen to make his living reimagining the world. He read too much sometimes and analyzed excessively. If there was any one thing he would give to himself if he could, it would be the life of a monk, cloistered, unsavaged by the onslaught of others' desires.

Ryland had read and savored the Egyptian *Book of the Dead* and believed in numerology, astrology, and voodoo. After his time in Jamaica, he had divined that if he revealed himself on the canvas he would not die. That was the moment he became an artist. Sometimes he went for days without speaking, unplugging the telephone, storing up enough food to last, staying indoors. Those times for him were a kind of spiritual oxygen, for he thought everyone talked too much.

Because of all this, of course, women hounded him with their longing for him, even though they could not really love him. Women considered the silences, which had nothing to do with them, a rebuke, waiting instead for him to reassure them with familiar lies they could hungrily latch on to and clutch in sweat-drenched palms like a rosary. He wanted to tell them the truth. That he had been born to paint, and that he was servant to this charge.

Family, marriage, children, he was sure would elude him. He had no money and was still young enough then not to really care. Painting had not yet become a career, something that could destroy him.

But lurking in the corners of his mind—for the silences, the marathon sessions he spent working, could never extinguish it fully—was the knowledge that he was a Black man of little material means. And he was, therefore, nonexistent to almost everyone he knew.

His father had painted houses for thirty years, creating in the process a small, prosperous enterprise and had sent Ryland and his two brothers to Morehouse, Howard, and Hampton, paying their tuition, he liked to say, "free and clear." Delbert Singletary could say, and often did, with conviction and bombast, "I'm one Black man whose wife *don't* have to work. But he considered his oldest son's life a waste. He had told him that.

Ryland knew that few people really saw him. Until the night he met Lena he thought he might always be the only one who could.

Stepping into the Nommo Gallery that night, Lena was in the grip, quite literally, of a premonition that "someone" was going to happen to her. It was seven o'clock and so she had five more hours to make the event she had sensed poised to claim her on that day, ever since she woke that morning, actually happen. That is how she thought. "I have five hours to make my destiny."

If Ryland was convinced that no one saw him, Lena could not imagine invisibility. She had chosen accounting as a profession because numbers were hard, definite, and manageable. She was a woman who loved tangible things, the glide of silk across her skin; she went to a studio on Connecticut Avenue twice a month for a massage, where the penetrating touch of Eljean reintroduced her to her body each time, convincing her that she was indeed alive; the sight of the balance in her savings passbook assured her she just might be able to handle anything; cheesecake induced in her a sense of ecstasy; and she loved the succulence of well-cooked lamb. Her job left her little time to cook, but when she did, she orchestrated five-course meals for friends, investing herself in every onion, carrot, or homemade crescent roll. In the kitchen, reading the recipe, tying the apron around her waist, her pulse rising slightly at the thought of the endeavor she was embarking upon, Lena cooked as though preparing the bread of life.

Her stock portfolio was sensible, a mix of blue chips and mutual funds and one or two risks, the computers everyone was saying would be the next wave. Lena never wanted anything to surprise her. But, of course, Ryland did.

Her father, Oscar Ramsey, died when Adele was four weeks' pregnant with her. Adele had not even yet suspected that she was pregnant, and so her husband did not die missing the child he would never see.

Nothing could ever make sense, Lena thought, unless she enforced her will upon it. She could not prevent her father's sudden aneurism that struck him as he slept beside his wife, whose back was turned to her husband and who snuggled close to him at one point for warmth, calling his name at three A.M. in her sleep, ten seconds after the aneurism struck, as she felt an odd sensation like something vital leaking from her body, and waking briefly but closing her eyes and convincing herself that it was indigestion, not some shift in the essence of her husband's soul.

Yet as much as Lena craved and valued things and objects because of their materiality—so unlike the immateriality of a father she had never known—she was determined, above all, one day to have a family.

So she had gotten out of bed the morning of the day she met Ryland, convinced it was the day of her fulfillment. None of her girlfriends, not even Constance, knew of this yearning, for their lives seemed evidence that what she sought was impossible, to make sense of her work and find meaning at home.

While studying for the CPA examination, Lena and Constance formed a support group with two other women. After ten-hour days at their firms, they pored over their texts at the Library of Congress several nights a week. In the year they studied together, Doris's husband left her, and Jeannette decided to get out of the field and have a baby to save her marriage. But Lena was determined to become indomitable and accepted the mantle of the exceptional life, lived, not merely pursued.

Of course Lena bought one of Ryland's paintings the night they met. She walked into the Nommo Gallery looking for her destiny and a sound financial investment.

And she asked Ryland to come to her apartment and bring his portfolio to show her what else he had done. Sitting together in Lena's apartment a week after the exhibition, they recognized each other as the completion of themselves. Ryland sensed that Lena saw him. The passionate volatility that her suits and heels, her briefcase and pocket calculator, could not hide made him a thousand promises. She enticed laughter, unfamiliar and welcome from him as she talked about her work, where she had traveled, her friends, Wall Street, her mother, jazz, the Vietnam War, the mask she wore on her job. Every word was intentional, saved, he felt, just for him. Now he knew why he had practiced and savored bouts of silence—as preparation for the seductive, irresistible act of listening to her. Sinking into the plushness of her overstuffed sofa, sipping peppermint tea, watching her toy with a glass of Chablis, Ryland was convinced he had finally met someone who did not talk too much.

Lena heard Ryland's esoteric, ascetic conversation and imagined him planting the seed of geniuses in her womb. Her appetites were strong, her sensual desire persistent and vivid. And yet he would teach Lena the beauty of affection, subtle and delicate. The hand clasped even as the bodies claimed separate portions of the bed. A sudden unexpected hug without warning. But Lena was a woman who could bring herself to orgasm through sheer imagination, without laying a hand upon herself. She was a woman lit by her own fire.

In all the looking back, the remembering and turning away from what she recalled, a process begun during the eternal days and nights at Farmingham, Lena could not remember when she slammed into the wall separating her from what she had thought marriage would be, confining her to the dry, tufted acreage of what marriage was. She had tried to pinpoint the moment when, breathless with pain at the disappointment, she knew it had all gone wrong, and wondered if Ryland felt it too. But living within the borders of her marriage, Lena knew three things, that she loved Ryland, that he had failed her, and that she would not leave him.

The silences, in time, were used as a weapon against her, not merely as a period of solace. Passion, which she had cherished, a tangible, reliable thing, was the very first casualty of their union. Ryland worked all day and sometimes at night and gave, Lena felt, his best self to the canvas. When Lena accused him of being passionless, he thought she just meant sex.

To remain married, she would have to die, some parts of her anyway. Lena told no one what she had realized, even when in the first years of their marriage she periodically suffered headaches, fatigue, and some mornings could not get out of bed. How to admit love isn't perfect, marriage isn't everything or nearly enough? To say it aloud would've brought her pain out into the world and made it a tangible thing. Sometimes she'd conclude that what she felt was inevitable, the result of the tension between two individuals and a construct at once hopelessly idealistic, ruthlessly pragmatic and impossible, but that held everyone's hopes hostage.

Then one day, as she and Constance drove to a suburban mall, it all came rushing out, everything rising rebellious and unashamed.

Constance laughed bitter and cynical, lit another cigarette, and confirmed that every married woman she knew was dying too.

But in the very worst moments Lena wondered not at her own disappointment, but at Ryland's. How had she failed him? What had he lost in loving her? But where was she to go? What was she to do? She loved him. By the time Kenya was born, Lena realized that the emotions she felt comprised the air of marriage. Sometimes it was heavy, choking; other times it lifted. Some days you could breathe. Sometimes it was so clear and clean, it broke your heart.

And she needed him, more than anything, his weight, his essence in her life, could not imagine, despite everything, a life without him. He had left the world outside their door for her to conquer and possess, but it meant nothing without him to return home to. Her ambition camouflaged a need of which Ryland was fully aware. Lena's nightmares consisted of the day that he used his knowledge against her, turned her flawed but undeniable affection against her, the day she came home and for whatever reason found him gone.

Kenya was a small child, tiny really, and she possessed a quality of permanent fragility. Born two months premature, my sister lived the first month of her life in an incubator. Kenya is lodged in the deepest pockets of my memory. I can remember being five and my father holding me in his arms outside the glass window that separated us from Kenya. Honestly, now I don't remember what she looked like, which tiny squirming baby was her, but I remember the glass window, the feel of my mother's hand clutching my leg, my father's index finger pressed against that glass, pointing to Kenya, telling me to wave. I remember the window as a wall. Of course remembrance is not truth. Perhaps at five it was only a window. But the passage of time and all that has happened has transformed it in my memory into a barrier. Finally my sister gained enough weight to come home. But something of those incubator days remained with Kenya. She was the smallest, the least robust among us. She bruised easily and there were times that as a big sister I thought that she would break. Of course I did not think that she really would.

I talked to her a lot after she died. My voice, whether a convicted whisper or a plaintive scream, ever in pursuit of my sister, myself. It is the incompleteness that terrifies me so, for it will never leave. I search for healing, knowing I will always be maimed.

My father had a studio in the attic of our house on Sycamore Street and he spent much of his time there. I always thought of the attic as his house within our house. For my father had furnished the space, which was unusually large, with a cot and stereo speakers, a shelf of books, all on the periphery of the large space dominated by his paints, easels, and other materials. Virtually from the time Kenya could stand, my father gave her free rein in his space. He had tried to develop an artist's eye in me, but I was never interested in the canvas the way Kenya was. My father would use one of his old T-shirts as a smock, put it on Kenya over her clothes, give her a brush, and wait to see what happened. Playful and unconscious of her talent, Kenya created dozens of pictures that revealed an apparent gift.

Since he worked from home, so unlike most of the other fathers on Sycamore Street, my father owned our house in a way that other fathers did not. I remember the small things most, the way he'd take me by the hand sometimes and say, "We're going to inspect our property." If the attic was where he was close to Kenya, it was in walks and outside that he and I found a closeness. We had half an acre of yard, back and front. And I'd ask him what do you mean, "inspect."

"Well, inspection is another way of looking at something, and when you own something, anything, you always want to see how everything is," he told me solemnly.

We'd walk around our house, me cautiously, slowly following my father, for I wasn't sure what he was looking for and I was not really sure how to look. How to inspect. I saw grass and trees, lawn and deck. But my father always saw more. His eyes discovered, investigated. Once in the summer when he was clearing a space for my mother to start a garden, my father saw a baby rabbit buried in the ground. Just as my rake was about to clear away some weeds, he told me to stop. He was staring intently at the ground, at the soil, seeing what I could not. There was a patch of color embedded in the soil, an almost microscopic white streak. My father stood gazing in a funny kind of awed excitement. I saw what was in my father's eyes and that incited a new vision in me. There were tiny slivers of movement, and a wiggling beneath the soil. Suddenly my father was on his knees, squatting, digging gently, clearing away the earth that had harbored the tiny rabbit. The animal barely filled my father's palm. I had never seen anything pulsing with life that was clearly so precarious. We put the rabbit in a shoe box filled with shredded-up newspaper and fed it drops of milk from an eyedropper. But a few hours later the rabbit died.

When we "inspected," my father informed me of the borders that separated our property from our neighbors. The boundaries were determined by the position of a tree, the length of a fence, a depression or slope in the land.

In the fall, as Kenya and I helped my father collect leaves from the oak tree in the backyard, a tree that unleashed a perpetual shower of foliage, we were assigned always to look for those whose color or shape was distinctive. These found their way, along with tender branches, into the collages my father often made.

On winter evenings my father turned on the floodlights and stationed Kenya and me at the window in his attic, where we gazed into the backyard. We'd laugh, Kenya and me, protest that there was nothing to see. But even in the barren nudity of the trees, the dormancy of the no-longer-green land, my father saw pictures.

"The trees look unhappy. They look cold," Kenya complained.

"They're protected from the cold," my father explained.

After two or three winters spent at the window with my father, a tree stripped of foliage but muscular and stoic in the winter chill became more beautiful to me than the blossoms of spring. I could recognize beneath a full moon and a dark sky their slim shadows falling across icy, snow-packed backyards as a masterpiece, because my father had taught me how.

My father looked at the world through a painter's eyes. I learned from him how to see what was hidden, and sometimes what wasn't even there.

I thought then and believe now, despite what happened, that my sister and I were loved children. Until the day of her death I had treasured our sheer normalcy. Sometimes things were reversed in our house, but I thought that made us a more interesting family. Like during the tax season, from November to May, when it was my father who really ran the house because of the long hours my mother spent at the office, where she was an accountant. My father turned grocery shopping into a thrilling three- or four-hour expedition, driving all over the city for exotic ingredients for the recipes he made from one of my mother's cookbooks. He'd let Kenya and me help make turkey tetrazzini or fettuccine Alfredo, dishes with strange-sounding names and pungent, unusual flavors and spices that in time I grew to love but which Kenya nearly always refused to eat. My father would have to open a can of tuna fish or spaghetti for her. And after dinner we'd all load up the dishwasher and then my father would make us do our homework. And just after the dishes were done my mother would enter the house, her arrival anticlimactic yet awaited by us all.

In time I began to sense that my parents lived in different zones. I could tell that my mother's world was deemed more important. She spent a long time each morning deciding what suit and heels to wear to work, leaving the house color-coordinated and crisp. I always imagined her leather Coach briefcase filled with secrets as valuable as those the government might covet. She took me to her office once, one Saturday morning when she had a meeting with some other members of her auditing team. I was disappointed, for the office did not reek of subterfuge or mystery. I saw computers, lots of papers on the desks. She told me to wait in her office for her to finish her meeting in a conference room down the hall. We were going shopping when she was through. She gave me a bound report with graphs and charts and numbers to look at when I asked her to show me something she had done. I looked at the pages, expensive, some colored illustrations, the typeface serious and imposing, and tried to read the story the words were telling. I couldn't figure it out. I tossed the report aside and looked instead at the photos on her desk of us at Disney World in Orlando and a striking side shot of my father at the breakfast table. My mother's world seemed dense and indecipherable. And yet there was a tangible quality about it that was impressive to me even at eleven, the age I was that day.

My father's world was different. He worked to music, all kinds, reggae, classical, pop, R and B, as he painted or drew. His hands were activated not only by his imagination but by the rhythms pulsing through the rooms of our house. He'd start shortly after my mother left for work. Then he'd stop around noon and watch one of the soap operas while he ate his lunch. One February day when I was home from school with a cold my father and I sat, me bundled beneath the covers of my parents' bed, him sitting in a chair nearby, both of us eating chicken noodle soup and watching *The Young and the Restless*.

"This stuff just gives my brain a rest," he told me, laughing in mock horror at something outrageous and totally unbelievable one of the impeccably dressed characters on the TV had just done. Then he'd work until around four, when he'd start dinner. My mother spent all day in a world that, it seemed to me, she was subject to. My father, it appeared, was master of his.

I didn't know then, of course, that my father's life was even more cruel than my mother's. For once he had finished a painting, he had to convince someone they couldn't live without it. When he illustrated a book jacket, he had to cross his fingers that the author and the publishing company thought his design was definitive and irreplaceable. My father could take nothing for granted. He depended on the vigor and uniqueness of his vision, but galleries, agents, people he did not know and sometimes would never meet, could extinguish what he had done by a decision made in thirty seconds.

Twice a year my mother threw a party to which she invited friends and clients, parties designed to show off my father's paintings. At those parties my mother proudly flaunted him. His canvases crowded the first floor like members of a family reunion. But my father was uncomfortable, awkward, enduring the parties more for my mother's sake than for himself.

One night after a party, I was in the family room, watching television. My mother was beautiful that night, dressed in a black and gold caftan, her hair a mass of long, elegant braids tied in a black velvet ribbon.

At the sound of their voices I ran and stood in the doorway, seduced by the sound of impending turmoil.

"Look, I don't want to go through any more of these parties," my father said, scraping plates and putting them in the dishwasher.

"I'm just trying to introduce you to more people. Get you out of the attic and into the world, Ryland. You've got to network, make connections," my mother said, her back to him as she poured leftover sauce into a plastic container.

"I'll do that my own way, in my own time."

"I haven't seen any evidence of that."

"Are you looking for it?" my father asked, slamming the dishwasher closed.

"Why not?" My mother shrugged, turning around to face him.

"All right, here it comes."

"Here what comes?"

"The old I'm-shouldering-the-whole-load routine again."

"Ryland, I said that once, and I told you I didn't mean it," my mother said, placing a silver tray with a few remaining canapes on the counter.

"You meant it. You mean everything you say."

"What's my crime? Wanting you to be successful?" She began to dig in, to position herself before the stove as she answered my father, crossed her arms at her chest.

"Forget it. Forget it."

"Don't worry. I'll never give another party for you," she sneered, closing in on my father, walking slowly around him, assessing him with obvious distaste. "Sulking in the corners, barely speaking to anybody. I guess they wondered if you were crazy or we were in the middle of a divorce. No wonder nobody wanted to buy anything."

"Ungrateful? So I'm ungrateful. I guess I would be to you, somebody who puts a dollar value on everything."

"If I did that, I'd have never married you."

"Why, because you knew I'd never amount to anything?"

"You're always twisting things around."

"You make me feel like a tenant. This is your house. You made that clear."

"I never said anything like that."

"You didn't have to."

"What is it you want?" My mother moaned, clutching her stomach and writhing in anguish as she stood before my father, as though his charge had been an assault.

"I want you to leave me alone."

"I'm your wife."

"Right. Not my manager. Not my agent," he shouted. "You think you're helping. I feel like you're drowning me."

"You're drowning yourself."

Clinging to the walls, both spy and victim, I didn't see who landed the first blow. I saw them run out of words and take refuge in violence, easier, more potent than words when they arrived at this twisted arc, the corner turned, the precipice neared. It always happened in a flash. The possibilities escalated. Everything was at stake. This was where they were headed all along. I closed my eyes, and when I opened them my voice was gone, tongue useless, and since I could not speak, I had to see. I watched my mother as she ran from the kitchen and tripped over a footstool and fell on the floor a few feet from where I stood. My father was on top of her, trapped in an action I choose to believe he dreaded fueling but could not stop. My mother bit his ear and then he pushed her against the floor, held her there with his knee against her breast. Vanquished by his greater strength, my mother's breathing was a ragged, ravaged, horrible sound. I fled the room. To watch them rise from the floor, avoid my gaze, the seizure of hatred dissolved into shame, might kill me.

I lay in bed that night, wondering why my father didn't realize the house belonged to us all. Why did my mother want my father to be more than he was? He was enough for me.

Was love a wicked, evil spell, I interrogated the darkness in my room, holding myself tight in my bed in the aftermath of their fights. I felt most ashamed of and betrayed by my father. His reticence and gentleness, his careful measuring out of words, the genius of his silence, should have made what I witnessed impossible. But I know now that silence can be a form of tyranny, that the measured, hoarded word can be a weapon. Maybe the fights were, after all, the easy part.

Once, on some other night, I thought of calling the police. I lay in bed and heard their fear unraveling below me in the kitchen, first the charges hurled like stones so often used, so familiar they never missed their mark, and then the sound of chairs and tables pushed, shoved from their station by my parents locked in a tango of despair.

I went into their bedroom. I turned on the light and stood staring at the phone on the night table beside the bed. It was so easy. I could dial 911. There'd been a story on the news the week before about a three-year-old who had dialed those numbers after her mother collapsed on the kitchen floor in the throes of an epileptic seizure. A three-year-old had done it. Why couldn't I? But what if the police really came? What if they took my mother and my father away? That thought drove my fingers to the light switch, and the room was dark again.

In the hallway I found Kenya standing at the top of the stairs, leaning against the banister, clutching her blanket and teddy bear, hungrily gazing down the stairs although there was nothing from that angle that she could see. I quietly walked up behind her and reached for her hand and pulled her down the hall and into my room.

When I turned to look at her in the dim hallway light, she was still looking behind her, trying to find, it seemed, where the sound of my parents' voices began and where that sound would one day end.

I know they went into counseling, spent almost a year once, going every other week to see someone. My mother told Kenya and me, announced it almost casually to us one night as we prepared for bed. We were in the bathroom. I was brushing my teeth, and my mother was drying Kenya off after a bath.

"Your father and I are going to start seeing a counselor," she told us. "So we can stop arguing and start loving each other again." But I heard fatigue rather than optimism in her voice as she toweled my sister dry and then suddenly hugged her, held her close, and looked at me.

"You mean like a psychiatrist?" I asked after I'd rinsed out my mouth.

"I know it may seem like it sometimes, but we aren't crazy." She grinned sheepishly. "We'll see a marriage counselor."

"Then you and Daddy won't fight anymore," Kenya said, offering the words as a commandment and not a question.

"That's what we want, baby," my mother assured her, handing her the lotion and her nightgown.

When Kenya left the bathroom, I asked, crossing my arms at my chest, leaning against the sink in flagrant judgment, "Do you think it'll work?"

The bluntness of the question caught her off guard. Her only response was to gather Kenya's clothes from the floor and walk away from me.

Every other Saturday they'd head off in my father's Land-Rover to some office I'd never seen, my father as though being dragged to punishment, my mother determined and stoic. A few hours later they'd return, burdened, it seemed, with more knowledge of each other and themselves than they could possibly survive. They sometimes went away together for the weekend, taking the trips like a homework assignment, and over dinner or breakfast I could feel them tapping down the anguish that previously they would merely allow to explode. They were careful and cautious, polite with one another. I almost longed for the arguments, for then I knew what they felt.

The truce didn't last, and when my father left he'd leave at night. Then it was my mother's job to explain his absence. He always left quietly, an odd counterpoint to the fierceness of the battles that preceded his departure. Reaching for cereal in the cabinets or cooking eggs at the stove, my mother would say offhandedly, "Your father's gone away for a few days. But he'll be back soon." And when she'd announced this to the kitchen stove or the refrigerator or the sink, she'd turn and look at us. In squalid bloom on her face was an expression I never learned how to read, so subtly did she camouflage her pain. Kenya crumbled into tears. And I sat staring at my mother, grateful for the tranquillity that would reign in my father's absence, contemptuous of them both. We all played our parts no matter how often he left. In memory I can conjure no specific number of departures. I recall only the stillness that permeated our house when my father wasn't there, the way I'd imagine the sound of his key unlocking the front door, him coming heavily down the stairs that led to his attic work space, the premonition I had, more than once, that one day he would leave us and never return.

We never knew, Kenya and I, where my father went when he left. Asking my mother would merely confirm the origin of my heartache. Knowing too much might be lethal, catapulting me from innocence into conspiracy with my parents. For what they knew would then become my property and my burden. I loved my mother too much to ask where my father went when he left us. She loved me too much to even offer to tell me.

There was never any need for my father to transition back into our lives when he returned. Just as we had awakened to find him gone, other mornings we rose to find him back, sitting in the kitchen mulling over *The Washington Post,* munching a whole wheat muffin spread with butter and strawberry jam.

Even Kenya stymied her curiosity, swallowed in a huge gasp the questions that should have erupted at the sight of our father once again in our midst. Perhaps to her it was a game. But I know it was not. Too many nights she crept into my parents' bedroom, crawling beneath the spread, positioning herself against my father as he slept.

"So he'll stay," she told me one morning over oatmeal when I asked her, after my mother left the kitchen, why she did it. "Or, if he goes again, he'll have to take me with him." Watching my sister wolfing down her cereal, I envisioned her love for my father as some amazing adhesive that might actually accomplish what she desired. This was the way we lived. Nobody ever said a mumbling word. How could we? Silence and deception was our shelter and our friend. Like all the houses on Sycamore Street, ours was built on shifting, unreliable sands.

Back then I never even wondered if my mother had been the one to leave, would forgiveness have been her right? Would there have been a statute of limitations on our love for her? My father never had to earn or prove anything once he came back home. If my mother had knocked, would we have opened the door?

Kenya was the first person to hear my stories, to know that I wrote and to suspect how much the writing meant to me. I was reading Judy Blume and Nancy Drew and the Babysitters Club a few years before I was "supposed" to. I started writing my own stories as a way to design a counter world, one opposed to the one I inhabited with my parents. I began writing when they began to argue the first thing in the morning and the last thing at night.

Nothing like that happened in the stories I wrote. My feisty heroines who relied on common sense more than brilliance made everything come out all right in the end. This was fiction after all. And as I turned more and more to writing, Kenya and I grew closer.

By the time I was twelve, my parents felt I was old enough to watch her for a few hours on my own. Kenya was used to getting most of the attention in the house because she was so frequently sick. Sometimes she'd do awful things, rummage through my drawers and throw my clothes all over the floor or scatter my small library of books all over my room, hiding them in the house, where it took me days to find them, just to provoke a response. She'd stand excited and nearly dazed by her own power in the midst of a mess she'd made, twitching her reed-thin frame, her arms folded at her chest, sublime and confident that there was nothing I could do to punish her.

Once my parents went to a movie and I was determined that I would control both the events of that evening and my sister. I decided to read Kenya one of my stories. It was a typical tale of ghosts and haunted houses and hairbreadth escapes—but I set it on our street, in our neighborhood, and made the characters like people we knew. We sat in the family room, Kenya bundled at one end of the sofa, me at the other. I read the story in a melodramatic voice, took on the qualities of the characters, even stood up and ran around the room to dramatize. Kenya sat astonished and hushed. When I told her I had made the story up, she didn't believe me. But then I asked her to draw pictures to go with the story. We went upstairs to my room, closed the door, and sat on the floor. I'd read a section and then Kenya would draw a scene to go with it.

After that day, sometimes when we'd hear my mother and father arguing in their bedroom or in the kitchen, Kenya would come in my room and hand me one of the books we had made together, holding it out to me and whisper mournfully, "Let's read." We never told anyone about the books we made, about a dozen in all. Those "books" which we stapled together—Kenya's pictures were glued onto construction paper out of which she had also made covers—were ours, our bulwark, our fortress. I think we were afraid that if our parents knew, their knowledge alone might change the stories. They wouldn't belong to us anymore.

Saint Mary's Girls' Preparatory School occupied an entire block of Wisconsin Avenue. Behind an iron fence, the campus sprawled pastoral and complacent. Ma Adele enrolled me at Saint Mary's when I came to live with her. I think she thought that a Catholic school would provide me with an armor against further calamity. The Sisters, the required uniform, the celebrated Catholic discipline, even the infusion of a faith she did not honor, convinced my grandmother that at Saint Mary's, if nothing else, I would be safe. Disaster couldn't touch me there.

Saint Mary's is where I met Jennifer Marshall. Of the dozen or so Black girls, some were on scholarship like me. The rest were girls who had attended private schools all their lives. Girls like Jennifer, whose thick black hair was worn in a long braid in school but combed out at the bus stop on the way home, whose gray eyes seemed transparent as icicles, who even at sixteen was statuesque and seductive as a diva. And it turned out that Jennifer wanted to be my friend.

The effort required to pretend that I was normal, that my life was as conventional as everyone else's, exhausted me. I developed a reputation among the other girls as a chameleon. Depending on the moment I was approached, I might be in the throes of either a full-blown bout of paranoia or a yearning to talk that was as merciless as a physical craving. I harbored the secret wish that in the process of talking I would discover someone who could make me stop wanting to disappear. I had watched Jennifer with the other girls, and seen them become a galaxy united by the gravitational pull of her charm. I did not relish such a fate. I was a renegade star, orbiting on my own course, teetering, sometimes tumbling through my own private darkness.

I was in the library studying one afternoon when Jennifer announced herself by saying, "The school's got a counselor, but nobody goes to see her about anything important. She tells everything you say to the Sisters." I looked up from my copy of the complete poems of Emily Dickinson and stared into Jennifer's face. Up close I saw no conceit, no beauty notorious enough to reduce me to rubble. Why had I imagined Jennifer larger than life? She seemed even momentarily bashful, as though her pronouncement were a ploy to stall for time while she assessed my reaction and the safety of sitting across from me at the scratched wooden table. She stood hugging her books against her formidable chest.

"What?"

"I said if I had a problem a counselor at this school would be the last person I'd tell."

"What makes you think I have a problem?" I asked, my eyes nervously skimming the verses in the book. The anxiety that congealed in my stomach and often made me feel frostbitten and numb began to melt. Simultaneously the sensation began to regroup in a valiant effort to resist Jennifer. I wanted to gather my books and walk away, but beneath the table I kicked off my penny loafers and curled my feet around the chair leg. I wasn't going anywhere.

"I didn't say you did. I was just sort of warning you, you know, giving you advice, like in case you ever did have a problem you wanted to talk to somebody about." She finally sat down across from me.

"Okay, thanks."

"You ready for the test on Emily tomorrow?"

"I guess so." I liked the way Jennifer said "Emily," as if this dead white woman were someone she had talked to on the phone the night before.

"I kind of like her poems," she told me.

"Yeah, they are nice," I agreed.

I had imagined the assurance, I saw that now. Jennifer was large-boned, big-breasted. She sat tugging at the front of her blouse, which was too tight, her breasts taut against the material, straining, it seemed, to break free. In the chair she sat slightly hunched over, her broad shoulders rounded, in a clear attempt to flatten her edges. She was a big girl trying to make herself small.

It was study hall and Jennifer opened her notebook. While she pretended to review her European history notes and I thumbed through Emily Dickinson, we talked about the Sisters we thought were lousy teachers, how we both despised the too-small cliquish nature of the school yet cherished the familial sense that same insularity imposed. Then she said, "I tried to commit suicide once. Just to see, you know, if I could really go through with it."

"What happened to make you want to do that?"

"Oh, some family stuff, some real bad family stuff. Somebody I loved a lot died."

"Who?"

"My brother."

"How?"

"Of cancer. He was twelve. Leukemia."

"How'd you try to kill yourself?"

"Aspirin."

"Aspirin?" I tried to stifle a giggle.

"Can you believe that? Aspirin." Jennifer's own unselfconscious, astonished laughter unleashed my own. "I took about thirty-five, maybe forty. Counted them out and took them one at a time. It didn't work. Besides, my mom found me in time."

"She saved your life."

"Yeah," she said wistfully.

"Did you really want to die?" I asked, leaning forward, closer to her than I'd ever been. The three or four seconds she waited to answer were an unbearable millennium for me.

"I wanted to share something with my brother, I think, you know, feel what he'd felt."

"What happened to you?" she asked. And I did not even wonder, when she asked me this, how she knew. I did not curse the failure of my attempts to disguise my grief. I merely told her, "Some family stuff too."

Her curiosity was apparent in her hands fidgeting with the edges of the textbook as she stared at me, certain that soon I would break. Expectation shone like fireworks in her eyes. Finally my silence inspired her to say "I wasn't trying to get in your business. It's just that I can sort of sense things, you know, I can see when it hurts."

"Do you think other people can?"

"Probably not. Most people aren't even really looking at you."

"How come you are?"

"Ever since my brother died, it's like I see things in people I don't want to see. I can feel and just tell things."

If I told her I was gripped most days by the same symbiosis, the same weird connection to people who'd been where I was now, I'd have to tell her everything. I said nothing. I realized I didn't have to.

The bell rang to end study hall.

"Well, see you in geometry."

"Yeah. See you."

And so I drifted toward a friendship with Jennifer. Or was I pulled? I began to sit sometimes on the periphery of the circle that gathered around Jennifer in the cafeteria at lunchtime. I witnessed an intense, often embarrassing jockeying among the girls for a strategic position near her. These girls wanted to meet one of the many boys Jennifer was rumored to know, to get an invitation to her house, to get her help with homework because she was an A student, to say that she was their friend because her father was an appointee in the Reagan administration.

Jennifer bore all this with a humor that managed never to degenerate into contempt. But as I sat on the edge of the group, picking at overdone fried chicken and undercooked potatoes, Jennifer would catch sight of me, and the bored restlessness the others did not see, or ignored, faded for a moment. I didn't want anything from Jennifer. Maybe that's why we exchanged phone numbers and she called me. We talked for hours, mining over everything we already knew, sifting for truer colors and meanings, wallowing with passion and fervor in a steady flow of gossip and complaint. She'd wait for me at my locker at the end of the day and we'd walk to the bus stop. Jennifer's father was an economist with the Office of Budget and Management. She'd been to the White House and had shaken the hand of President Reagan. "He looks like he's already been embalmed," she told me. "Imagine a corpse that could walk and talk and smile." Jennifer lived in a majestic three-story abode that had once been an embassy on a street tucked off Connecticut Avenue. The rooms were large, wide, and high-ceilinged, designed, it seemed, for ballroom dancing and the kinds of intrigues that occurred to the strains of Bach while men and women waltzed and flirted in the stories of Thackeray or Tolstoy. I saw her father only once or twice, a tall, gray-haired man who spent long hours in his upstairs study when he was at home, and emerged from the room anxious and clearly worried. I wondered what he knew about the national deficit that nobody else did. Jennifer's mother was a large woman who, unlike Jennifer, managed to be graceful and even agile. She didn't work. I didn't know mothers who didn't work. She did volunteer work instead. A woman from El Salvador came in once a week to clean the house.

Jennifer's bedroom teemed with teddy bears. Stationed on shelves along the walls, the bears, who varied in size from mini to magnum, were dressed in baseball and football uniforms, tennis outfits; they were outfitted as an aproned mama bear baking cookies, like a majorette, a beauty queen, a schoolteacher, an astronaut, a policeman, a doctor in a white coat. There was even a bear dressed in kente cloth. The largest bears stared vacantly from the floor, where they congregated silently in a massive pile, their beady plastic eyes ghostly and inescapable.

I screamed in horror at the sight when Jennifer turned on the lights the first time I entered her room.

The wail quivered up from the bowels of an anxiety that had nothing to do with bears. Mrs. Marshall ran up the stairs only to find

Jennifer laughing and me agitated and trembling in the middle of the hall, trying to recover from the primitive sound of my own buried anguish.

"Do you think the Sisters are really celibate?" Jennifer asked, tossing me a bottle of nail polish called Rogue Red. We sat in our nightgowns on the twin beds in her room.

"To be celibate for life? Sure. Why not? I don't think it would be so hard."

"You don't?" Jennifer asked, wrinkling her nose in disagreement as she carefully painted her thumbnail.

"Now we're talking like, forever, Teresa, forever as in *never* having sex again." For emphasis, Jennifer looked at me, holding the nail polish applicator suspended above her beringed fingers as if awaiting my immediate verbal compliance.

"I know that."

"And you still think it'd be easy?"

"I don't think it would be the hardest thing in the world to do," I insisted.

"Well, I do." Jennifer announced this with such passion that I was afraid she was going to tell me that she had had sex. Since starting my period the year before, biological upheaval had become routine and colonized my body. I ached sometimes with a longing I could not name, that was unfamiliar and frightening. Fumbling in the dark in my bed, I learned how to still this completely original distress. Stumbling upon a form of pleasure so brilliant I knew it must be taboo, I told no one.

"Did you ever do it?" Jennifer asked.

"No," I mumbled, twisting the cap off the nail polish.

"I did . . . almost," she said.

"Almost?"

"He tried but he couldn't get in all the way."

Jennifer's brutal, entertaining honesty was a welcome refutation of the genteel, purposeful hypocrisy of the adults controlling my life. I cherished Jennifer because I felt that she would never lie to me. I was riddled with shame and had perfected subterfuge. Jennifer was obvious, so intentional, she achieved a precision in her observations that made her sound almost wise.

"There's like this skin, I forget what they call it, that the guy has to break through to really get in you. I sneaked over to his house after school one day. We did it in his bedroom. His parents were out of town."

"God, Jennifer, weren't you scared? I mean, they could've come back early . . . anything."

"Sure I was scared, but that sort of made it like more fun," she said thoughtfully. "Not fun exactly"—she was determined to arrive at an exact description of her feelings—"but more exciting. Anyway, he tried to get in me for what seemed like nearly an hour. Then I got tired. I was raw down there and hurting and thought maybe I was deformed. You know, if he couldn't get in me."

"Who was it?"

"Calvin Franklin, he's a senior at Archbishop Carroll. He was my boyfriend then but he kept nagging me after that to try it again." She was waving her hands in the air to dry her nails. "It seemed like that was all he wanted to do. So I quit him." Jennifer blew lightly on her fingertips and placed them in her lap. "Damn, like we hadn't even done it and he was trying to turn me into a sex slave or something. Can you imagine if he'd got in there?"

"You'd still be in his bedroom right now, whether his parents had come home or not."

"Right," Jennifer roared. "I think he enjoyed it anyway. He had me take his thing and rub it, you know massage it until he came. I didn't like that. It's like I wasn't even there when I did that to him. I could've been anybody. It took forever for him to come even with me doing that."

"Did you love him?" I asked, more as an obligatory inquiry than that I thought Jennifer would say yes.

"Nope . . . I thought I did . . . I told him I did."

"I don't know about the Sisters, but *I* can sure wait."

"They always think I've already done it."

"Who?"

"Boys. Because I'm big. They think I've done it a thousand times. Sometimes that's really all they want." Jennifer said this as though stating that the world was round. But before I could decide whether the hollowness I heard in her voice was sadness or defiance, she began humming some Whitney Houston song about love and misery.

When our nails dried we watched a video Mrs. Marshall had rented for us. It was boring, and we started talking, and Jennifer asked me, "How come you live with your grandmother?"

"My mom's away at school. Did you ever tell anybody else at school about the time you took those aspirin?" I asked quickly, to change the subject.

"I never told anybody but you."

Now it was my turn to seal our friendship with the sharing of a terrible truth. Jennifer sat waiting, expectant, her breathing stalled in anticipation. But what could I say? I had never encountered words bold enough to withstand such a venture.

"I just wondered," I said, and then reached to turn off the light beside the bed.

The months we spent waiting for my mother's trial to begin introduced us to our collective punishment. The law intervened immediately after my sister's death. I was not allowed to remain in the house on Sycamore Street and so became my grandmother's ward. The day after my sister's death there was a small article in the morning paper. What happened to my sister competed with a story about Medicare fraud in the suburbs, the city's fiscal crisis, and the overnight shooting of two teens.

The article gave my mother's name, our address, and designated my mother as someone who had killed her own child. It detailed what my mother was alleged to have done. The words were about my mother. But I knew they were about me too.

Over the next week, Ma Adele's house was filled with people who arrived in waves. Their shocked, garbled mumbling floated up the stairs and filtered into the room where I lay fraught with a knowledge I dreaded sharing, vowed not to, and felt I must.

Some evenings when my grandmother's friends left, after they had sat with her to prove that she was not alone, Ma Adele knocked on my door and, at the sound of my voice, strained and feeble, she entered. I could feel her crying, her shoulders shaking as though she might fall apart.

I had seen what my mother did. In response, I had made myself minuscule. The me who had seen it hid someplace inside me where even I could not find her. But when Kenya was buried, finally I cried, standing beside my father. Clutching his hand, I cried, because if I didn't I could not live. I fainted at the funeral and woke up several days later, groggy from the sedatives the doctor had prescribed to calm me.

One night after she had entered my room, several days after the funeral, Ma Adele fumbled for me, patting the spread with her hands to locate me in the dark. My grandmother's heavy palms, sprawled across my chest, confirmed and resurrected me. "The Lord doesn't give us any more than we can handle," she pronounced with a weary conviction.

I hated that platitude, had heard my grandmother say it in the past, and I wondered if she really believed it. I wanted to ask her how you knew something wasn't more than you could handle. And what if it drove you crazy or killed you or made you feel as numb as I felt then? But I didn't. I merely held on to my grandmother, smelled her talcum powder and the odor of the fried chicken Odelle Anthony had brought on a plate covered with aluminum foil. I sat up and hugged my grandmother.

"I want you to pray not only for your sister, but for your mother." When I said nothing, she asked, "Did you hear what I said?"

I told her I had.

I slid out of my grandmother's embrace and slumped back beneath the spread, my eyes wide open, afraid to close them. If I did, I would see only Kenya's face, innocent and shocked, the moment she realized she was tumbling backward, falling down the stairs. My eyes had become curtains that raised on that scene endlessly.

"I'm afraid to go to sleep," I whispered.

"Afraid to sleep alone?"

"No, afraid to sleep at all."

She left the room and came back with a glass of water and she pressed a tiny pill into my outstretched hand. She did all this in the dark, as though turning on the light would be a sacrilege. Then she sat on the bed with me, silent, as shattered as I was. Tossing and turning, I battled the sight of my sister's face. And finally the drug pushed me down, deep inside, beyond the realm of Kenya's reach.

During the nine months we waited for my mother's trial, the court decreed that we were only supposed to have supervised visits. Another judge might have left what remained of my family intact. Judge Alice Wexler decided not to.

In the aftermath of my sister's death, the hushed subterranean voice of a crank caller had spit out the words "child killer" over a dozen times when my mother or father answered the phone. Someone left a shoe box on our front stoop with a chubby plastic Black doll whose head had been broken off. My father and I drove most Saturdays or Sundays from Ma Adele's house to Sycamore Street in silence. But it was a silence that contained a union of grief. Words seemed superfluous. My father gained weight and appeared perpetually haggard when he came for me. I could only guess at the life he and my mother lived in our house. But when I looked at my father, I knew that my mother endured his judgment every day.

For several weeks after the funeral I did not see my mother. I did not want to. But one day, sitting in a geometry class at school, I yearned, terribly, totally, for her. I felt a longing only she could fill. At lunchtime I walked out the front door and caught the bus to Sycamore Street.

I still had my key to the house. I carried it with me every day. When I turned the corner onto the block, I was momentarily afraid, suddenly wary, fearing a flashback that would immobilize me in public, where everyone could see. But it was the middle of the day and the street of large, sprawling houses set a comfortable distance from one another was placid, unsuspecting. I approached our house and walked up the steps.

I opened the door and found my mother sitting in the den, the small room where we'd usually watch television, where she did needlepoint, where Kenya's drawings were always scattered and my books proliferated. She was sitting on the sofa with her feet on the coffee table. From where I stood I could not tell if my mother was awake or comatose. I saw her in profile as she sat staring ahead of her as though she were looking at something only she could see. She did not move when I closed the door behind me. I bravely gazed at the stairs and at the floor at the base of the stairs. The flashback burst through. I stood before the front door, my eyes closed tight, my hands covering my face, sweat and fear and tears overwhelming me. I parted my lips to howl and stuffed my fist into my mouth instead. All this lasted only a moment in real time, but I felt that I had aged as the sensations released their hold. Wiping my eyes and face with the sleeve of my blouse, I longed to sit beside my mother. As though watching myself do it, I threw my backpack onto the table beside the door the way I always did when I came home from school and walked into the den.

When my mother turned, and saw that it was me, she appeared not to be surprised, as though she had just been sitting there, waiting for me to come home. I sat beside her and lay my head on her shoulder, which felt hard and angular. She had lost weight. And she smelled bad; I could tell she had not washed. I wanted to say something familiar, something easy, for her sake and mine. After we sat there for a while, just the two of us in the den, my father's paintings around us on the walls, I asked if she had eaten lunch. She said she hadn't. And so I went into the kitchen and opened a can of soup. I poured it into a bowl and heated it in the microwave and put it on a plate with some crackers and took it to where my mother sat. She had not moved. I gently prodded her legs from the table and placed the soup before her. She reached for it but I could tell it was too heavy, for she nearly dropped it. I went into the kitchen and brought her a tray and sat watching her eat. While she ate I told her about the new school.

When she finished eating, my mother wanted to see my homework. I brought my backpack into the den and pulled out several papers. She looked at them approvingly. Then I told her that she didn't smell too good. She smiled grimly. I told her, because I knew I could, to take a shower. Then I watched her walk slowly, with difficulty, upstairs as I took the tray into the kitchen.

While she showered, I lay on my parents' bed. I had passed the guest room on my way down the hall and I saw my father's clothes there. So I knew that my mother slept in this bed alone. The door to Kenya's room was closed. I did not go inside. Taking refuge in my parents' bed, the sound of the shower made me slightly drowsy.

When my mother came out of the bathroom, she was wearing a white slip. I winced at the sight of how thin she was. I did not want to look at her body, and so I looked at her face but found there the same absence, the same diminishment.

"Mom, what's going to happen?"

"There'll be a trial. More than that, after that, I don't know."

"Do you sleep at night?" I asked.

"Not much."

"When I try to close my eyes I see Kenya," I told her.

She looked at me as though she were going to say something but stopped and went to her closet to find something to wear. While my mother rummaged through her closet, I looked at the portrait of us that sat on the chest of drawers near the window. My mother had paid a lot of money for the black and white picture, which was taken at a studio in Georgetown. In the portrait, we sat on a hardwood floor before an off-white background that was really just a huge wide sheath of paper hung from the studio's ceiling. My father was sitting Buddha-style, my mother was leaning against him with her hands on his shoulder. Kenya sat on my father's lap and I lay stretched out on the floor in front of them, my head propped up on my hand, smiling wistfully into the camera.

We spent much of the afternoon in the studio that day dramatizing family happiness, and we were exhausted when we were through. Several months later I passed the studio while riding the bus and saw our portrait, blown up and placed in the window. I stared at the photo and had not felt that it was really me or any of us. I looked at my family as though I did not know them. Lying on my parents' bed, I wondered what the photo meant, what could it mean now that Kenya was dead and I lived with my grandmother and my parents no longer shared this room.

My mother tied a wraparound dress around her waist. We heard my father's Land-Rover pull into the driveway and we looked at each other as though we had been caught in a moment of dangerous conspiracy.

I strained to hold on to the sense of something I knew and loved that had come over me as I huddled in the folds of the sheets and blankets. My mother and I sat terrified, yet lucid and intuitive, both knowing what would happen. My father entered the house. The den was below my parents' bedroom and I imagined my father seeing my backpack, my shoes beside the coffee table. When we heard him coming up the stairs, not a breath passed between us.

He stood in the doorway, as depleted as my mother, yet gaining some necessary strength because my mother was so weak.

"Teresa, why aren't you in school?"

"Ryland, she just came to see me."

"You stay out of this," he snapped at my mother in an alien, murderous voice.

"Let's go," he nearly whispered, the summons choked and halting, informing me that he really wanted me to stay.

But I didn't move.

"Teresa," he said, coming over to the bed, standing between my mother and me, stalwart, silent, lost as were we. I rose from the bed and walked past him.

"Go downstairs and wait for me," he said. I looked at my mother but she sat, mute, as though collapsed, folded in on herself. I left the room but clung to the walls outside their room.

"She's still my daughter. I don't care what any court says. She's mine," my mother told my father. "They can take her out of this house. But she's still mine."

"She's mine too," my father said, "and you aren't supposed to be alone with her."

"How can *you* say that?" she shouted.

"How could I say anything else?"

My father drove me to Ma Adele's, and when he parked in front of the house, before I got out I asked him, "Why don't you sleep with her anymore?"

"Did she tell you that?" he asked, remnants of the tone I had heard him use with my mother aching in his voice.

"I saw the guest room."

"That's between your mother and me." He clutched the steering wheel as though steadying himself.

"It's because of Kenya. You think she did it on purpose." He waited so long to answer that I had prepared myself to accept the truth of my assertion.

"I think I miss my daughter. And I want you back," he said, turning to me. "And I don't know what happened or what to feel except anger and pain. And since that's all I know, I can't sleep with her."

Then I asked him what I had asked my mother, what I asked myself over and over, the question a tape playing underneath all my conversations and thoughts, even beneath the awkward stumbling flow of sleep I sometimes managed.

"What's going to happen?"

"I don't know, baby, I just don't know."

I kissed my father on the cheek and left the car quickly because I could not bear that he did not know, could not guarantee or promise some sure path out of the morass that had trapped us. Nobody knew and that meant the worst would happen. Nobody knew. But even then I was sure that they knew. They just couldn't bring themselves to say it. They were no better than me.

What did my mother feel in those first days and
months after my sister's death? I was repulsed by and
drawn to the sight of her, wan, thin, her brown eyes
growing bulbous, protruding like searchlights in her face as she lost
weight. I watched her lay in bed for hours, not moving, so still I could
hardly hear her breathe. She would not have been able to maintain
disbelief in the face of what had happened, what she had done.

She'd seen my sister in a casket, had been interviewed by the
police, and she'd had to talk to the lawyer Ma Adele hired to defend
her when she was formally charged with my sister's murder. There
would have been no region of fantasy or escape for her.

She must have wondered at the audacious betrayal of her hands. I
saw her sometimes examining her fingers, her palms, staring at them,
then shaking her head, finding those hands insoluble, perplexing. She
would have wondered, because she was essentially a person of courage,
if she had indeed wanted my sister dead.

Separating herself from herself as she lay wrapped like a mummy
in the stale sheets in a room she prayed never to leave, my mother
would have asked the impossible. For even one infinitesimal moment
had she wished her child silenced forever? If she had not, how had it

happened? That fatal laying on of hands, she would have argued with herself, must have risen from some subterranean impulse so dangerous that until the moment of its eruption it had been impossible to face.

My mother would have tried and sentenced herself more perfectly than any court ever could. My sister would have fallen again and again behind my mother's closed eyelids and before open eyes that could see nothing else.

By the third month after Kenya's death, I had begun to openly defy the court order and my father's reluctant attempts to enforce it. I spent weekends with my parents, sometimes went there straight from school. I went back to Sycamore Street whenever I wanted to. Soon my father, just as my mother, welcomed me back home. I was his child, the one that remained, what else could he do?

I slept beside my mother at night on Sycamore Street, taking my father's place, loyal, loving, needing her despite everything. I lay next to my mother and listened to her sleep, partial, nightmarish, my sister's name breaking through her sobs. And as terrible as it was, there was no other place for me. She was my mother. I knew they would take her away from me. We would all pay for what she had done.

Somewhere beyond our house, now disturbed forever, in downtown offices and courtrooms, our fate was being designed. There would be a trial and then a decision. But I knew no matter what the verdict, we were already lost. If my mother did not go to jail, my father would leave, and this time for good. If she went to jail, I would kill myself. Already I had decided that. I had fantasized about pills and knives and ropes. The subtle implosion of my insides induced by capsules. The shocking, oddly glorious sight of my own blood. The tug of braided strands of hemp burning the skin of my neck. She was my mother. I could not live without her. No matter what she had done.

In time my father assumed a gentleness with my mother I had

rarely seen. One morning I watched him bathe her. He roused her from sleep, although she bitterly resisted opening her eyes. With her eyes clenched shut, she fought my father, her bony arms flailing like clumsily wielded sticks. Finally he lifted her from the bed.

She was limp in his arms. My father motioned for me to follow him into the bathroom, where I filled the tub as my father sat on the toilet, holding my mother's body in an awkward yet resolute embrace. I saw no pity, no affection on my father's face. My mother could have been a stranger he'd rescued from the side of the road. I turned away from my father's impassive stare, my mother's slight body, her eyes blotting out me and everything else, and sprinkled bath salts into the water.

When I looked at them again, my father had stripped my mother of the gown she'd worn for a week. Stretch marks girded her pelvis and thighs. The sight of her pubic hair, wild, massive, startled me. My father shook her gently, told her he was going to put her in the tub. He kneeled beside the tub and slid my mother into the water, which rose, hungry, welcoming, around her. She opened her eyes and watched my father soap the washcloth and rub it over her wasted body, washing her so gently, it seemed as though he had never made love to her or filled her with his seed. My mother bore all this unflinchingly, unfeelingly. Although her eyes were open, I cannot imagine what she saw.

The minimum security women's prison, officially called a federal correctional institution, was almost hidden within the grandeur of the West Virginia mountains. As with each mile we journeyed higher into the sprawling wild elevation of the mountain range, I remember thinking that we would soon stand outside the door of heaven.

The first visit was the hardest. My mother had been at Farmingham two months. Ma Adele and I left Washington Friday, around noon, for the five-hour drive, and we stayed over in a motel that night to rest up for the next day. The prison was a sprawling, one-hundred-fifty-nine-acre campus that reminded me of Saint Mary's.

But just as I hadn't really believed for a very long time that Kenya was dead, I hadn't really believed my mother was in prison until I saw her there. The visitors' area was a small building just behind the main entrance. A huge television was perched on the wall and two admitting officers were stationed at the front desk.

All the women we saw that day looked neat and healthy. Some were even fashionably dressed in regular clothes. My mother was wearing jeans and a turtleneck sweater and an army fatigue-type jacket she'd been issued by the prison.

That day there were many other women receiving visitors, all of them huddled together on hard Formica chairs in small groups, recreating and mocking the family circle. Small children, restless and bored, chased one another around the room.

"Are you all right?" Ma Adele asked as soon as my mother entered the visitors' area and sat down with us in a corner near the door. It was the same question she asked when she talked to my mother on the phone, the same one that hovered over the lines of her letters. I was surprised that she looked the same. She looked like my mother. Indeed she was my mother. I had expected prison to immediately alter her. But there was nothing like that. And I knew she was the same when she told us about the prison, at first I think to assuage our fears. Then the more she talked, I could tell, she felt that all the information, the facts, the figures, made sense of what none of us could understand.

My mother told us about working in the textile factory sewing gloves and navy swim trunks that earned her twelve cents an hour. "Before it's all over," she said brightly, "I could even have my own room." As a relatively new inmate, she was still sharing a large room with eleven other women. You had to earn the right to move into a smaller cottage or dorm. Her fellow prisoners were women who, like her, had committed unspeakable crimes. The woman who tried to shoot President Ford was in there with my mother, as was a woman who had killed a dozen elderly patients in the nursing home she managed, then stolen the money from their bank accounts.

Sitting before us, my mother strained to achieve a sense of acceptance I could not believe.

"There's the commissary, the chapel, educational programs, the library," she said, as though her imprisonment was a much-needed vacation, or a monastery where she could replenish her soul. Her attempts to make prison sound like camp clearly left my grandmother unassured. She sat beside me, relentlessly massaging her hands, sighing audibly and gazing around the crowded, nondescript room to avoid looking at my mother and to keep from crying.

"If I didn't have a college degree, I could earn one here."

She sounded like a commercial for the army. What did any of that have to do with her? I tried to imagine her sitting at a sewing machine, making gloves all day long, my mother, who engaged in discussions with my father about black holes in space and had dreamed of traveling to the Fiji islands and Australia and taking Kenya and me along. What, really, was she trying to say?

The room was warm with the mass of bodies. Because I couldn't bear my mother's attempts to be brave, I looked around the room, and I saw only women and children. Where, I wondered, were these women's husbands, these children's fathers? But I quickly and brutally squashed the thought, for it reminded me of my own father's absence. Some of the women had boarded a special bus in downtown Washington that brought them to Farmingham because they didn't have cars. They came laden with coolers, picnic baskets, bags of clothing, and tapes. Some came faithfully each weekend and stayed all day. You could eat lunch or dinner with the inmates. And on Sunday you could attend church. Ma Adele and I never did any of those things. The women prisoners sat before their visitors as casually as though sitting in their living rooms at home. I heard laughter and snippets of convoluted stories of family affairs, a lost job, an unexpected pregnancy, a death. The apparent adjustment to prison that had been made by the people surrounding us horrified me so, I turned back to look at my mother. Suddenly it seemed easier to witness her awkward struggle with assimilation into the prison culture than the result.

I sat and watched Ma Adele and my mother talk, as though they were trying to say all the things they had not before. My mother listened patiently to gossip about our neighbors on Ingraham Street, and the latest activity of Ma Adele's sorority, the Deltas. Then I got up and went outside to a small area where there were picnic tables and you could really see and feel the mountains so close, it was like they were inside you. I stood out there a long while, feeling almost content that my mother and grandmother were inside talking, inside laughing, even if it was here.

While I waited outside, a black-haired young white woman approached me. Her face was long and angular and her cheeks were as sunken as deep crevices. Her sallow skin was pockmarked. I watched her walking steadily toward me, her feet plowing through the piles of autumn leaves. The prison uniform she wore seemed too big for her skinny frame. When she stood a few feet from the picnic table where I sat, she smiled, a large, unselfconscious grin that revealed two missing teeth on the upper left side of her gums.

"I'm Kelly," she said, extending her hand. I stared at her hand, the knuckles red, as though bruised, the skin so pale I could see the veins, the hand trembling in expectation. When I didn't move or say anything, she let her hand drop, whisked it away, and hid it, jamming it into one of the deep pockets of her camouflage jacket.

"You Lena's girl?"

I finally found a way to speak and told her that I was.

"You got a good mama," she declared, staring at me with tiny gray eyes, pensive and hopeful, digging into the leaves with the toe of her boot.

I didn't know what to say, unsure whether to feel assaulted by the judgment Kelly had foisted upon me or grateful for what might be an offer of friendship, so I hid any response at all and continued to look at Kelly as though I had never quite seen anyone like her.

"My mama named me after the actress Grace Kelly," she told me. "I never knew why she didn't gimme the Grace part instead."

She sat down across from me, and I felt her unbearably close, although the table was quite wide.

"Lena told me all about you," Kelly marveled. "I got kids too. Wanta see 'em?"

Kelly quickly pulled out her wallet and showed me a photo of a girl and a boy in one of those posed color school photos. The boy, younger than the girl, had Kelly's sunken cheeks, and his smile was mirthless and unconvincing. The girl, big-boned and husky already, seemed prepared to wrest from the world anything it didn't want to give.

"My mama's got 'em," she explained when I handed the photo back to her. She looked at the photo and smiled at the faces in the picture as though they could see her smile and said, "She won't let 'em come see me."

"That's too bad."

"Near 'bout everybody here is somebody's mama." She laughed, the sound rumbling with a wicked edge. Again she looked at the photo of her children as though engaged in a conversation with them, not me, as she returned the picture to her wallet. "We s'posed to be some of the worst women in the world, but we still somebody's mama."

"Is my mother your friend?"

"I'd be proud if she said she was."

"Do you know what she did?" I asked.

"Uh-huh. And she knows why I'm here. Ain't no such thing as a secret at Farmingham. Everybody knows your offense 'fore you get off the bus."

"What did you do?"

"I killed my boyfriend. My boy's daddy."

"Why?"

"He was gonna kill me." Her pronouncement was simple, self-evident. I knew she'd told me something vital about her world. I didn't think I could stand to know more, so I asked her, "How'd you know who I was?"

"Your mama showed me your picture."

"Lord, let me rescue this poor child." We heard Eve Bennett's voice before we saw her approach us. A tall, buxom woman dressed in wool slacks, a silk blouse, and a three-quarter-length suede jacket, Eve batted her false eyelashes in mockery as she approached us. Her curly hair was streaked with white, and in a pair of soft leather ankle-high boots she walked through the leaves as though striding across a red carpet awaiting her approach.

"Forget you, Eve." Kelly laughed, the sound deep and guttural inspiring a spasm of dry hacking coughs from which I wondered if she would recover.

"Not only is she full of it, she's catching," Eve pronounced, sitting beside me.

"You look just like your picture," Eve observed as she reached in her pocket for a pack of cigarettes.

"Now, I'm sure Kelly has bored you with photos of her young ones. But I don't have any children. I have a cat. He's staying with my sister until my sojourn here is over. His name is Raleigh, you know, like Sir Walter."

"Why are you here?" I asked.

"Embezzlement," she said, releasing a long drag on her cigarette.

"They call it stealin' where I come from," Kelly said, making a dismissive sucking noise with her tongue and teeth.

"It's a long story, dear," she said, patting me patronizingly on my shoulder, "and although it involves money, believe me it's R rated, so I won't unload it on you. But remember, crime doesn't pay."

I saw my mother walking toward us. I stood up eagerly, walking quickly over to her, wrapping my arms possessively around her waist, looking at Eve and Kelly as I did this, hoping just by this display to weaken their claim on my mother's allegiance. We walked away from the two women, and before I could ask my mother about Eve and Kelly, what they meant to her, she said, "I don't want you and Mama to come up here too often."

Her voice was poised, composed, trying to soften words I feared would be fatal.

"I don't like the idea of Mama driving so far. And I don't want you to get used to seeing me in jail. Can you understand what I'm saying, Teresa? I don't want you to get comfortable sitting in that room back there. I don't want you to get comfortable because I've sworn I won't ever be comfortable being here. I just don't want you coming a lot. We'll keep writing letters. And you can call me."

"It won't be the same," I said, tightening my hold on her around her waist.

"Honey, nothing will be the same, not even when I come home."

"When will that be?"

"I don't know. But I can probably get out in four years."

I would be in college, eligible to vote, to get married. To her the time seemed finite, manageable. To me the announcement was an apocalypse, pure and simple. We walked toward the center of the prison grounds, the open space solemn beneath the burnished autumn sky.

"I want you to help Mama out as much as you can," she said, stopping to sit down on a bench outside one of the cottages.

Clusters of women passed by. They stood milling about, congregating, smoking, laughing. Some of them stood apart, waiting, for what I did not know and could not imagine. One of the women waved at my mother. Several looked at me closely and then at my mother, trying to affirm, I could tell, that I was her daughter.

Gently touching my chin and turning my face back to her, away from the women whom I was following with my glance, my mother said, "Send me your papers from school, and pictures of you, send me some of those poems you're always writing. When you get a new boyfriend, send me his picture, too." She grinned.

Those women had seen aspects of my mother that I never would. Everywhere I looked, I saw women in small or large groups, joined by something I would never, could never, know. And like my mother, most of the women I saw did not look like criminals. I didn't know then, even with what my mother had done, that evil and danger often look benign before they strike, and that we are often more comfortable in their presence than when surrounded by good. Beside her on the bench I bitterly watched the other women. This place, these women, were my mother's punishment. She could not modify or escape it. And she could not come home with me. I knew that much. But still I told her, "I miss you, I want you to come home."

"Teresa, stop." The craziness in my voice inspired her to quickly, desperately, kiss me on the cheek. She stood up, then began walking fast, furiously, away from me. She had said four years, and I knew she couldn't guarantee that. Her word in this place meant nothing. I watched her walk away from me and then I ran, ran behind her faster than I had ever run in my life, and I caught her. I gripped her arm, dug into her sleeve, held her, and screamed from somewhere so deep inside me that I literally shook, *"Don't go."* And then I fell on my knees. It had rained the night before and the ground was still damp, and the mud was soft and a bit gravelly against my skin and I grabbed her leg and said again, "Don't go."

"Teresa," she pleaded, coaxing me, urging me to release her leg. But I just gripped her tighter. Then my mother kneeled down and she reached in her pocket and pulled out a tissue and wiped my eyes and my nose and she held me and said, "Honey, we can do this. The worst is behind us, baby, the worst is over."

She sat there on the ground with me and rocked me. Over her shoulder I saw Ma Adele coming toward us. My mother whispered in my ear, "Honey, the worst is over." How could she have known then, that day, how could either of us have known that the worst hadn't even started.

Within six months after my mother began serving her sentence, my parents decided to sell the house. This was done through lawyers and official-looking papers and signatures. The one thing my mother could do from prison was to dismantle what she had left behind.

My father told me that some of the money from the sale of the house had been put away for my college education. My future, he implied, was safe, secure. "So what?" I wanted to ask. My father told me this as though it would make up for the loss of my sister and the family we had once had, the life we had lived on Sycamore Street. Our life had not been perfect. But it had belonged to us. For that reason alone, I wanted it back.

Behind the door of the loft apartment he moved into, my father quickly exhausted the possibilities of the canvas. The "meditations," as he called them, the collages, drawings, sketches, even carvings and small sculptures of my sister, erupted without warning. Inside apartment 312 West, my father imagined with color and cloth and photos and wood and glue and ink and paint, a life for Kenya that was definite and clearly impossible. Early on, he sped past ordinary grief. His grief was extraordinary. There was no other kind.

My sister came back to him as she sometimes came back to me. He told me that for a while he was so relieved that she had returned, that she was with him, not just at night when he tried without success to sleep, but that she had become the outline and foundation of everything he did, that he consigned his hands, in the beginning of it all, to stillness. It was enough that Kenya had come back to where he was, where they could speak the same language. But then he grew afraid, terrified really, that one day she would leave and neither memory nor prayer would retrieve her. My father turned to art to capture what remained of my sister, and all that he could never forget.

The works evolved and sometimes simply burst forth. Always, he was an instrument, whether the concept of rendering Kenya as mother to her own child, using wire and cloth, filled his fingers first and set him to creating without thought, but conscious of design, or whether he brooded for months on what colors to use on a canvas before he picked up the brush. My father was servant to Kenya's unextinguished formidable will. My father painted and he could live. He rummaged all over the city for materials for a collage and my sister's death was no longer utterly absurd. He completed a canvas in which Kenya was actual, so coherent he sometimes told me, that he sat staring at her face, indulging in lush, satisfying conversation with her. The sound of Kenya's responses convinced my father not that he was mad, but rather that he might one day remember his daughter with more than only pain.

The walls of the twelve-hundred-foot studio space in which he lived and worked were clamorous with Kenya's face. The framed, unframed paintings, small, massive, hanging in the kitchen, even in the bathroom, were scores of different women, all versions of my sister she would now never be.

My father and I talked on the phone two or three times a week, and he'd often stop by and have dinner with me and Ma Adele.

Sometimes I'd visit him in his apartment in a huge building the city had bought and renovated just for artists, where they could live and work. I'd hang out with him, just be there with him, often reading or studying while he was working. He was teaching part-time at the Corcoran School and at Howard and lived like a monk, dedicated to his paintings and uninterested in the world. Every time I came to see my father there were more pictures of Kenya, more objects and artifacts dedicated to her. It was a little frightening at first, walking into my father's space, surrounded by images of my sister. But it was in my father's apartment, sitting with him, watching over time, the proliferation of his ode to my sister, that I learned that I didn't have to forget Kenya, that I could live and still hold on to her too. Although some people thought my father had gone crazy, all those paintings were really making him well. I came, in time, to feel that maybe my father was the bravest one among us. For he militantly refused to grieve quietly or with discretion. The canvases were a scream my father dared the world to try to silence.

I knew that my father wasn't visiting my mother at Farmingham. We even talked about it once. We had gone to the movies and had bought Chinese food on the way back to his apartment. I knew they were legally separated. Neither he nor my mother had said anything to me about it, but Ma Adele had.

"Will you ever go to see Mom?" I asked after we'd opened the cartons and begun eating.

"Maybe, I don't know."

"She told me she didn't want me to come to see her too much. But I don't think she really meant it," I told him hopefully. "She was just saying it. I mean, if I was there, I'd be lonely. I'd have to be."

I picked over my vegetables and rice, looking at my father now and then, trying to gauge his response. He gave up nothing.

"Maybe when you go see her I can go with you?"

"I don't know when that will be," he said wearily.

"But you'll do it sometimes, right? I mean, you have to. How could you not ever go see her."

"When I go, I promise I'll take you."

"I can tell you don't mean that."

"Look, it's more than I can do right now, Teresa. I just don't have the energy," he said, plucking a sliver of broccoli from a plate of moo goo gai pan.

"Why not?"

"I don't know if there's anything left. Holding us together during the months before the trial took a lot out of me."

The chopsticks he had taught me how to use so skillfully quivered in my fingers.

"I've done my part and then some," he insisted. "There's too much I don't understand. That I'm unsure of."

"But that's all the more reason why," I said, letting the chopsticks slide from my fingers.

"No, it isn't, Teresa. I can't nail or glue us back together, especially not now."

"You found someone else because Mom isn't here."

"There's no one else."

"Then why'd you have to separate?" I shouted.

"Did she tell you?"

"Why didn't you?"

"She signed the papers," he said smugly, continuing to eat, refusing to let my outburst defeat his appetite.

"But you sent them. You were already separated. Why'd you have to make it legal?" I was near tears. "You wanted to hurt her. You wanted to punish her even more, that's why."

"Do you blame me?" my father asked, pushing his plate aside and leaving the table.

As long as my parents were still married, I'd felt somehow there might be a way out of the remnants of what had happened. I was old enough to know better, but I had daydreamed about my father visiting my mother at Farmingham, faithfully, and often. I had fantasized that there, in that strange place, in the hills of West Virginia, they would fall in love again. My father forgave, my mother was redeemed, and when she came back to us we were a family once more. We were the family that even with Kenya with us we had never been. Now my father had made that impossible.

I heard him in the kitchen opening the refrigerator, pouring something into a glass. I got up from the table and went into the kitchen.

"It's like Kenya is the only one you love."

"Teresa, that's not true. You know it."

"That's how you make me feel."

"Look, calm down."

"There won't be anything left. Nothing at all," I screamed. "And you don't care. You never did."

I was backing away from him, out of the kitchen, as he kept moving closer to me.

"She'd visit you. She would. I know." I bumped into the table where we'd been eating and he grabbed me, held me so tight in his arms, I couldn't move or run or break free.

My father stilled my flight, held me and rocked me as though I were a baby. In his arms that's how I felt. This was all he could give me, and momentarily it was enough. I held him too. I closed my eyes and felt my tears stain my cheeks and imagined them mingling with the dried remnants of the colors on his T-shirt, some color that maybe he'd used to highlight the image of my sister's eyes. But more than anything I wanted to hear him say he still loved my mother. It did not matter that there were days on which I promised to hate her forever because of what she had done and we all had lost. I wanted my father to swear that when she came home we'd be a family again.

That's all I needed to hear. They were only words. How much could they cost? But he said nothing, just held me. And as soon as he released me, slowly, in stages, freeing up first my shoulders and then my waist, as though I were some animal he had trained and trusted that had turned on him, I pushed him away.

"She'd visit you no matter what you did," I screamed, grabbing my pocketbook and running out of the door.

My father had given me a key to his apartment, and a few days later I went there when I was sure he wouldn't be at home. I had come armed with a pair of scissors I'd sneaked out of Ma Adele's bedroom the night before. Inside my father's apartment I sat on his bed, sat there with the image of my sister as the only witness to what I was about to do. Reluctantly, without the passion I had imagined, I pulled the scissors from my backpack, stood up, and opened the drawers of my father's chest and the closet.

I could hardly see for the tears. I cut his shirts, ripped his ties, tore his pants. The revenge I had sought was fleeting, a tremor that sprinted so quickly from fingers ripping cloth and cutting pants legs in half, I hardly knew if this transgression possessed even a glimmer of satisfaction. But when I was through, my father's clothes bunched in a colorful heap at my feet, I could see, even through the tears, that for the first time since everything happened, as futile an act as it was, I had done something real. I had done something back.

L ena was awake when the cramps started. This time the fault line of pain, plowing across her abdomen, did not rip her from sleep. She was already awake and thinking about Kenya, who came premature, and too small, her breathing almost inaudible, at one and a half pounds and three days old, was hooked onto machines, encased inside an incubator, more wish than real, more hope than fact. Born in the fall, it was winter before they could bring her home. And always there was the fear they would lose her. Asthma attacks stole her breath in the middle of the night, on the playground, and at school. "Breathe, breathe," Lena would whisper, holding Kenya in her lap in the backseat of the car as Ryland sped to the hospital. "*Breathe, breathe.*" Kenya's breaths, thin, tremulous, whisper-anemic, whistling wheezing a terrible awful song, threatened to Lena's ears to be the last ever. Nobody died of asthma, she convinced herself. Not now. But they did.

Once in a panic, home alone with Kenya, she'd tried mouth-to-mouth. She brought her back, saw gratefully the fluttering eyelids, the groggy movements, felt the flow of a resilient will in the warmth of her child's body, electric, shocking, filling her own fingertips, quieting her rampaging heart. And in the aftermath, in the quiet house, watching Kenya finally sleep, Lena's ears listening to each breath, swearing silently she would never lose her again.

Lena perpetually assessed and studied Kenya, watched her at play, could close her eyes and conjure the imprint of her palm, the color of her iris, the curve at the back of her neck. In case she lost her. If one day she could not catch her breath, then she would exist embedded in memory as she had once been rooted in the womb, tangible, existent, breathing.

One Sunday April afternoon they were sitting on a bench at the zoo. Lena had bought Kenya cotton candy after an hour of visiting elephants, tigers, giraffes, and bears. She'd had to look away from Kenya, for her pocketbook was at her side.

But when she turned around, Kenya was gone. At first, of course, she did not panic. She was sure Kenya was just a few feet away, wandering again, perhaps toward the giraffes, whose height and necks had fascinated her. Lena took a three-hundred-and-sixty-degree turn on the bench and saw nothing, not even a flash of the lime-green shorts or yellow top, or the sickly pink wad of cotton candy she'd had to have taken with her. The sloping grassy knolls that encircled the park had become impenetrable woodlands in Lena's suddenly fevered imagination. The Sunday-afternoon families, with children, toddlers, balloons, carriages in tow, teemed, a massive threatening throng hindering Kenya's discovery. There was color, there were shapes everywhere Lena looked, made indistinct, unrecognizable, by her fright. She turned around once again to look at the bench, and saw not Kenya but a few strands of the cotton candy glazing the air as they dislodged from the wooden splinters and were carried away by the wind. Lena sat dividing her vision into blocks, her peripheral scanning everything, everyone at the sides, her frontal vision honing in on every face, every body that passed or approached. Wobbly, faint with fear, she rose from the bench, imagining already, some man, his hands inside Kenya's underpants, between her legs, behind the monkey house. The dull, final thud of a car door Kenya could not unlock filled her ears. Standing up made it worse, for then the park was suddenly a swirling world of faces and bodies. It hadn't seemed this crowded before they sat down to rest.

If she ventured too far away from the bench and Kenya came back? If she didn't at least look down some of the winding circuitous paths that made up the zoo, which now struck Lena as an obscene maze, what could she do? She had to look, she couldn't just stand there. Tentatively, carefully, looking three ways at once, she walked a few feet from the bench, searching so hard, peering at, probing the people in line for hot dogs and streaming into the animal houses and standing before the bird cages, that she could feel a migraine forming, clawing from a vein at the base of her neck, into her temples. She was looking but not really seeing anything, bumping into people, whispering, "Excuse me, excuse me," each time, looking but not seeing, for she felt inside her the void, excavated, hollow, the absent place on the bench where Kenya had once sat. Quietly hysterical, Lena roamed the park, crying—she did not know this, could not feel the tears, she was so disassociated from herself, so hungry for, focused on, Kenya. She did not even see the odd, clearly frightened stares of the people she brushed against as she passed, as she wandered, looking, looking so hard that it all became a blur and the void inside swallowed her. When her wanderings finally led her back in the direction of the bench, because there was no place else to go, down the hill that led to where they'd sat, she saw, thought she saw, maybe it was a mirage, a snippet of lime green, a haze of yellow. Though she was sure Kenya had vanished, was invisible, defaced by what she feared had happened, she ran, pushing past clumps of parents and children, ran, stumbling, almost falling, ran, feeling herself becoming with each step, visible again, to Kenya, sitting on the bench next to a young girl maybe two years older, who wore a pair of plastic blue sunglasses, swinging her feet as she sat patiently beside Kenya, waiting for Lena's return. The girl had found Kenya in the reptile house, eating cotton candy, alone and in tears. Kenya has been gone twenty minutes that lasted an eternity and Lena promised never to let her out of her sight, never to lose her again. Driving home, turning her gaze from the traffic every chance she got just to look at her daughter for verification and sustenance, touching her arms, letting her palms rest on Kenya's slender thigh, her angular shoulder, hearing her dazed silence, punctured by the intermittent wheezing of what Lena feared was an asthma attack brought on by fear, Lena knew that from that moment on they were a new and unfamiliar mother and child.

A riff of pain played beneath the line of these memories as Lena's body relived the tremors of Kenya's birth. Psychosomatic, the doctors told her. Each birthday, since it happened, in her mind she delivered Kenya all over again. And by the time it was over, Lena could only limp to the bathroom at the edge of the hall and shower, the vigorous flow of water absorbing her screams.

When she returned to her bedroom she saw the sheets and pillows on the floor, bunched and twisted, as though she had fought within their folds for her life. She dressed quickly, grateful that neither Adele nor Teresa was yet awake, and left the house. It was Saturday morning and already the sun was bristling and prickly. Lena had no idea where she was going. She wasn't in her mother's house. She wasn't in prison. She wasn't even in her room. So, she reasoned, she must at least temporarily be free. Maybe she could walk far and fast enough and Kenya couldn't catch her. Stoking this belief like a fire, Lena walked, past still-slumbering houses like the one she had left behind.

Kenya would've been fifteen today. At fifteen, Lena kept a diary hidden beneath her mattress, its pages filled with conversations with the father she had never known. At fifteen she felt herself to be blessedly indistinguishable from her two best friends with whom she camped out in the rain in front of the Howard Theater to be the first in line for tickets to see James Brown, friends with whom she talked by phone each night, discovering like hypersensitive child artists, dread, passion, possibility in the mundane.

And at fifteen, someplace deep, hidden inside her, she was prepared for anything, knew that as the daughter of Adele Ramsey she had to be the best. She was not beautiful. Did not have light skin, shoulder-length hair, a barely discernible nose, but thank God she was smart. And even then, unconsciously, in some subterranean region of herself she'd decided to make being smart her weapon. And when she realized years later as a wife and mother and professional that she was indeed beautiful, her attractiveness manifested in the frankness in her face that was carved in determination and desire, she hardly thought that looks mattered anymore.

At fifteen, what would Kenya have been? Conjecture, projection, hurt too much. Lena allowed herself to believe the asthma attacks would have subsided. Kenya would have taken breathing and life for granted. That would have been enough. For Kenya had remained small, delicate, never recovering from her premature birth. Strangers often thought she was two or three years younger. To be well and strong and breathing freely, easily all the time at fifteen. That would have been enough.

When Lena stepped out of the taxi at Lincoln Cemetery, she was almost surprised to find herself there. Standing at the partially opened gate, Lena heard the driver speed away after she failed to respond when he asked her if she wanted him to wait. The large cemetery was pastoral, even surrounded by a residential neighborhood and several apartment complexes and a shopping center. The cemetery occupied its own separate geography, seemed spiritually segregated. As Lena walked through the gate, the cemetery around her was still, quiet, and utterly frightening. The linen dress Adele had bought her exposed her neck, and the sun branded her arms and shoulders. There would be no need to stop in the cemetery office. She knew where her daughter was buried.

In another two hours the grounds would fill with late Saturday morning and afternoon mourners. Walking the cement pathway, Lena prayed she wouldn't have to witness any funerals.

She started out from the top of the rise where the gate led into the cemetery and had to walk downward as the road twisted around the long, grassy stretches of land filled with headstones, punctuated by flowers. The headstones, some immense and ornate, others smaller, stood as committed as sentries to their task. The sky above her was billowy, cloud-filled, and serene. Her shoes clicking lightly on the pathway was the only sound save the warbling birds Lena could spot perched near several plots.

It took her ten minutes to reach Kenya's grave, which was marked by a flat, rectangular metal marker, now surrounded by other markers that had not been there before. Lena had brought no flowers, no mementos to be placed on her daughter's grave, only the gift of herself. Lena slumped onto the ground and let her fingers trace the letters of Kenya's name, then rest on the cool metal of the marker.

The grave was well tended, for Adele came often. Lena touched her lips with the fingers of her right hand and placed them on the marker.

The day she arrived at the abortion clinic in Alexandria, protesters were lined up outside. A dozen men and women, hooded and bundled against the nearly glacial chill and the lightly falling snow, marched in a tight circle before the building's entrance on that January afternoon. An elderly Black man was among the picketers who carried signs reading BABIES KILLED HERE and placards with pictures of blood-drenched fetuses.

Driving down King Street, Lena had seen the protesters as she turned to enter the garage across the street from the clinic. And at the first sight of them she had resolved not to be moved, not to be terrorized into changing her mind. Not until she had parked, walked out of the garage, and stood on the corner had she doubted what she was going to do. She could easily enter the building from the back, but suddenly she could not move. No one else knew she was pregnant. No one would ever have to know what she had done. But watching the pickets walk slowly, methodically, in a tight circle of conviction, Lena felt the burden of her deceit. She had not expected guilt, had envisioned a swift, efficient determination of all their fates inside the doctor's office. But standing on the corner, watching others cross each time the light turned green as she held back, Lena wondered how she would hide what she had done. If she did not confess, the crime would be transparent. Ryland was her husband. Surely he would look at her and know that she had killed his child. She stood on the corner so long, a policeman approached her and asked if anything was wrong. She assured him she was fine and headed for the garage.

When she entered the house, she could hear Ryland in the kitchen, and Coltrane's "Alabama," mournful and languorous pouring from the stereo. The house was fragrant with the deep, hearty aroma of vegetable stew. In the hallway, Lena removed her coat and boots slowly. She felt shell-shocked, numb. Thoughts of what she had almost done had burrowed so deeply within her that she felt as if she had gone through with it.

"Hey," Ryland called as she entered the kitchen.

"Uhm," she mumbled, going to the cabinet on the other side of the kitchen, reaching for a bottle of red wine on the middle shelf. She was cold, could feel herself trembling as she had standing on King Street in the snow. Her hands gripped the bottle but it still slid too easily through her fingers. Ryland raced over to her side in time to catch the wine rolling off the counter, heading for the floor. Clutching the bottle of Beaujolais, he asked, "What's wrong?"

Lena gazed placidly at the wineglasses on the shelf and reached for one, then gently lifted the wine from his hand. Removing the cork, pouring the wine slowly, measuring the deep burgundy liquid with her gaze, she asked, "What do you mean?"

"You never come in and go straight for the wine cabinet. What happened today?"

Lena lifted the glass, took a sip, closed her eyes, and savored the solemn texture of the wine. Finally she turned to face her husband and looked at him, taking him in as she had been afraid to do, not for what she would see in him but what he might detect in her. The yellow apron he wore, with WORLD'S GREATEST CHEF inscribed across the front, was stained with tomato sauce and the aroma of onions, parsley, garlic, and beef mingled with the fragrance of his skin. His eyes rested warily upon Lena, unsure, prepared to worry.

"I'm pregnant."

In a matter of seconds a procession of emotions unfolded on his face. Surprise and the glimmer of fear washed over him first, but was almost instantly consumed by the sliver of a smile that at first merely flirted with the possibility of existence, then relinquished doubt and claimed every part of him.

"When did you find out?"

"Today," she lied, placing the glass on the counter and looking away from him, finding the happiness her words had induced, a kind of affront.

"You're upset?"

"More than upset. I'm afraid." She whispered the words bunched like a fist in her throat. The admission inspired her to walk over to the kitchen table, clutching the wineglass like a charm, and sink heavily into a chair.

"Afraid of what?" Ryland asked, not following her but standing his own contented ground leaning against the counter.

"Everything."

"Everything? What does that mean? We're not talking about everything. We're talking about a child. Our child."

"How would I handle another baby, Ryland? I'm swamped at work. But I don't want to give it up. There's no time for a baby!"

"There was with Teresa."

"That was five years ago."

"We did what we had to do."

"I'm in the middle of a twenty-person audit for the Department of Transportation now. I head the team. How many teachers' conferences and PTA meetings have you had to attend alone?"

"None of that matters."

"Yes, it does." This was the argument she had feared, these were the words she would never have heard if she had done it.

"Are you even listening to me?" Ryland's plea sliced through the fog of rumination and regret.

"Of course I'm listening," she lied again.

"You're a good mother."

"Are we good enough? As people, as a couple?" she asked, turning around to look at Ryland. Sometimes they argued terribly over the smallest thing, over nothing really. But of course it was over everything that they wanted from each other with all their hearts and knew they would never get because they were human and horribly real and not the fantasy they had vowed to love until the end. Ryland once didn't speak to her for a week. Once she threw out all the clothes she had bought him, which was half his wardrobe. They had never hit each other, not yet, they had never gone there, sunk, crawled, dragged themselves to *that* place, but what if?

"We were good enough for Teresa. We're not perfect. Who is?"

"But that's the way I want it to be." Her voice was truculent; she heard herself whining like a cross, irritable child.

Ryland walked over to the table, stood behind Lena, and rubbed her shoulders. His thumbs massaged the pressure points in her neck.

"Lena, we can do this. We've got enough love, enough of every-thing for another child." Ryland massaged her in silence for a while, then sat down across from her.

"I haven't been as successful in my work as I'd hoped I'd be. If that's what's worrying you."

"You don't have to say this."

"I'm working on some projects that will pay off soon. Lena, be-lieve in me enough to give our baby a chance."

"I do believe in us."

"Maybe what I'm really asking is for you to believe in me."

Lena said nothing and drained her wineglass and told him, "I'm going upstairs to change clothes."

Ryland found her in the bathroom and held her. The tip of his tongue licked her tears. He removed her bra, fumbling with the snaps in the back, asking huskily, "Do you think it's a boy or a girl?"

"Ryland, I don't even want to think about that now." The sight of Lena's breasts, tender, large, warm, nearly hot against his palms, made Ryland shudder. He fell to his knees, pulling her panties down to her ankles, placing his ear against her stomach. His beard scratched the soft flabbiness of her abdomen.

"I can hear him. He says I'm a boy."

"You're crazy, you know that?" Lena felt laughter fomenting somewhere inside her.

"About you," he said, looking up at Lena from the floor. The lips that had urged Lena not to be afraid kissed her between her thighs and wandered into the place where their child would find its way home. Lena slid onto the long, carpeted bathroom floor beneath Ry-land, who was undressing with one hand and holding her with the other.

She willed herself to forget the lies of that day. This moment—swift, hard, greedy, and generous—was the truth. Welcoming and claiming her husband, circling his waist with her strong legs, her feet resting on his buttocks, her thighs a chokehold of love pressing him against and into her, washed away her guilt. Each movement of flesh upon flesh and him inside her erased her sin but not her doubt. Could she love another child?

Slick as seals they lay in each other's arms, their heads against the pink porcelain of the huge tub that was also a Jacuzzi, and Ryland told her, "This baby is our magic, Lena, our miracle." His hands stroked her body as though to calm her fears, and she lied for the third time that day, saying, as she rested her arm on his chest, "I won't be afraid."

As Lena watched a caravan of cars driving slowly along the road- way and further down the hill—the funeral she had feared—she felt Kenya, smelled her, sensed her. This was not a memory, but Kenya actual, real and alive. She arrived sometimes foisting herself so fiercely between Lena and a moment, an action or thought, that Lena could only endure the moment hoping her daughter's return would never end, yet afraid to give herself up completely to this startling verisi- militude. There she was, standing a few feet from her own grave site, substantial, even poised. She was the darkest among them, her young skin a glorious near-ebony that made the daring, the pensiveness that lived always in her gaze, a warning and an enticement. There she stood, heartbreakingly thin, her legs and arms jutting from a match- ing blue short suit. Teresa, when angry with Kenya, teased her, call- ing her "Skinny." And one night over dinner as Teresa continued the insult, Ryland had told Kenya, "Your sister's just jealous. You're built for life's surprises. Being so slender, you can run faster than the rest of us, hide where nobody would ever think to look, and reappear when nobody expects you." Kenya had smiled in triumph across the table at Teresa shouting, "See, I told you." There was a hole in the toe of the sneakers she was wearing and the small gold cross on a chain around her neck that a Catholic friend at school had given her was plastered, in the heat, to the skin of her neck. Lena heard her daughter's breathing raspy and labored. The summertime pollution had forced her often to remain indoors. Lena knew that this was real. For Kenya's eyes were not empty. They rested upon her brimming with expectancy. Did she imagine or actually see love? If Lena rose from the ground, would she vanish? Maybe if she held her breath, Lena thought, moved carefully without seeming to move, like a breeze or a benevolent phantom, Kenya wouldn't be frightened. And this time she'd stay. What if she touched her and Kenya vanished, what if she spoke and Kenya responded? What if Kenya asked the only question she could? Lena's fingers traced the letters and the date on the metal marker as a hot, harsh wind sliced through her dress, blistering her skin, swallowing the vision of Kenya whole. Closing her eyes, she yearned to stay. A few moments later when she left, she did not say good-bye.

From the cemetery Lena took a bus back into Washington and then found herself wandering aimlessly around downtown. She sat in the park across the street from the White House for several hours, watching tourists gathered outside the gates, snapping pictures. It was her daughter's birthday, and she sat in Lafayette Square in sunglasses, a spectator, a stranger looking in on the world. Later she wandered into the Grand Hyatt Hotel and ordered a drink at the bar, where she got into a conversation with a white lawyer from Seattle who offered to buy her dinner. Demurring politely, Lena told him she was meeting friends for a concert at the Warner Theater and left the hotel and the man, abandoning the business card he had given her beside her empty wineglass on the marble counter.

Then she took the subway to Union Station. A minute but perceptible emotional lift always overtook her upon entering the ninety-six-foot-high main hall of the station, with its white facades, its domelike ceiling, and columns, its overbearing sense of gratitude and homage to Rome and Greece. The huge promenade space held several restaurants and two white marble circular fountains. The overall sense was one of expectancy, as passengers hurried to board trains or shoppers browsed in the stores along the halls of the three levels.

Entering America, Lena followed the maître d' up the winding staircases past the muraled walls onto the third level, where she was seated in an area whose tables looked through wide columns onto the main hall below. Thirty-six statues of Roman legionaries ringed the level she was on as well, seeing what she saw. And even when she had finished dinner, starting it with a glass of white wine and capping it with two glasses of sherry, Lena left Union Station and continued roaming, walking, restless and morose, along slowly darkening streets, hoping there was someplace she could go and not feel Kenya there, waiting for her.

At midnight Lena walked back into her mother's house. In response to Adele's puzzled, clearly worried stare that greeted her as she closed the door behind her, Lena went upstairs to shower. She did not want to see in herself what had prompted Adele to open her mouth to speak and then turn away at the sight of her. So she undressed in the bathroom in the dark. Lena sank slowly to the floor of the stall, hugging her knees, the water a dense, steady consolation.

When she entered her room she found Adele sitting in a wicker chair beside her bed. She had placed a small glass of sherry on the nightstand. "I thought it might help you sleep," she said.

Lena settled on the bed, wrapped in a terry-cloth robe. The sherry was dry and she sipped it slowly, gazing into the glass as she said, "Mama, I'm sorry. I never said that to you. I'm sorry for all of this."

"Maybe I should let you get some sleep."

"I can sleep anytime, Mama," Lena said, terrified Adele would leave her alone.

"I saw her today."

"Where?" Adele asked without a trace of surprise. Several times a year Kenya visited her with so much accuracy that days after, the texture of the child's hair and skin still tingled on Adele's fingertips.

"At the cemetery."

"So you went."

"I actually thought she would stay this time."

"Lena."

"If she would just come back."

"One of the women from Farmingham called while you were out today. I think she said her name was Eve."

"You met her, Mama."

"I don't remember," Adele insisted. Lena said nothing, content to participate in her mother's willful amnesia, appreciating after this day her need for it.

"I wonder what I'd have bought her. What would she have wanted?"

"Lena, this doesn't help."

"She would've wanted to live, Mama, that's what she would've wanted."

They sat wordlessly in the small room. At midnight Adele rose to leave, stifling the urge to speak, watching Lena hugging herself, her knees and her body gathered in on themselves, rocking back and forth.

In her bedroom, Adele turned on the small Tiffany lamp on her nightstand and sat down heavily on her bed. She removed her dress, slip, and panties and then reached beneath her pillow for the white seersucker cotton nightgown Teresa had given her for her birthday. Plumping up the two layers of pillows against the headboard, satisfied with their thickness, Adele slumped back and closed her eyes. She knew she would not sleep until Teresa came home. She never did.

Everything about that day had consumed her. The heat wave raged on, implacable and invasive. She woke that morning to the sounds of Lena scrambling, hurrying out of the bathroom, back to her room and then out the front door. The sound of the hasty, clumsy movements, the opening of her closet, the sudden closing of drawers, initially alarmed Adele. But since her daughter's return, Adele had learned to expect anything.

Today was Kenya's birthday, and her daughter had opened her eyes and the first thing she thought to do was take flight. Adele had hoped they might all go to the cemetery together. Now Kenya's birthday was here, pressing in on them, and Lena had chosen to honor the day alone. Adele turned on her side, knowing as she did that she could not sleep in that position. But she hugged the pillow anyway and closed her eyes.

Several months after Kenya's funeral, when Adele found that despite the comfort of her friends she remained bereft and unhealed, she sought out a support group.

The group met in the basement of a northwest Unitarian church. They were a bus driver whose son was killed by a gang that drove onto their normally quiet block, randomly spraying gunfire as the boy washed his car; a nursing student whose five-year-old daughter was killed by a hit-and-run driver; a computer salesman whose wife died of a heart attack; and a female police officer whose daughter was raped and beaten to death.

After the first meeting, Adele vowed not to return. The awful stories of loss and tragedy gave her no relief. The knowledge that she was not alone provided no catharsis. But she returned, because in the small basement, which during the day served as a day care center, sitting in a circle on a folding chair, sipping stale coffee from paper cups, amid the innocent preschool decorations, was the one place she felt safe. All they really did was talk. Sometimes there was even laughter, which she had not expected, but which she greedily reached for and indulged in as swiftly as the others. They sat in a circle and broke the silence the world had decreed was all they had left.

Finally the night came when she had to tell her story. Adele had composed a neat, articulate rendering. Neither Ryland nor Teresa would attend the meetings with her, and so she felt as though she had

been given a gift every other week of a period of solitudinous reckoning. Nearing the church that night, Adele thought the words sounded
perfect in her head. She would tell them what happened and she
would not lose control. With the telling of the story she would purchase membership in this fellowship that had saved her life.

There was always a period of settling in, pouring coffee, sharing
the events of work and life that had taken place since the last meeting.
In theory, a counselor who attended the church, and who had a private
practice as a therapist, led the group. But Walter Symington, who
favored bow ties and tweed jackets and who was perpetually fragrant
with the odor of the pipes that cluttered his pockets, seemed more
spectator than leader. His presence was more steadying than di-
recting, and Adele wondered as she watched him, his gangly legs
crossed, seeming to jut in front of him, how he bore the accumulation
of all the stories he had heard. Why, Adele wondered, was he not
crushed by the weight of others' sorrow? Who healed him when he
broke?

During the moments before the meeting began that night, Marlene, the nursing student, had come up behind Adele, who sat a little
apart from the others and whispered, "The time will go by faster than
you think it ever could," squeezed her shoulders, and took her seat. A
few minutes later the circle formed.

I still don't know what happened, she began. *I don't think any of us do.
But my daughter, she killed my granddaughter.* Adele paused for the look
of disgust to shroud their faces. She saw only patient, impassive waiting. She was so warm beneath her blouse that she wondered if she was
having a hot flash and wiped her brow with a small sheer handkerchief. The words didn't sound the way she had planned. *I've often
thought, prayed really, for some way to go back to that moment, to take my
granddaughter's place.* The sob lay in wait, pacing and eager to devour
her. But Adele fought back. *And now my daughter is in prison. So I've lost
her too.* Shifting in her seat, breathing in sharp and deep, Adele beat

back the painful cry. *She's not a killer. I mean, they say she is. And Kenya is dead. But to this day I know what she told me, what came out in court. And I still don't understand.* Adele was gazing at the walls through most of this, at the calendar the children had made, the oversized rabbit carrying an Easter basket symbolizing the month of April. She was so weak she felt as though she had run a marathon. She couldn't believe she was still talking. The time wasn't passing fast at all, not like Marlene said it would. *I mean, if she had died a natural death. . . . One day we're all going to die. I know that. But my grandbaby wasn't supposed to die first.*

"Why does love hurt, Grandma?" Kenya asked her several months before it happened. They were in the kitchen at Adele's house, Kenya eating a slice of sweet potato pie, waiting for Lena and Teresa to pick her up.

"Why what makes you think love hurts?" Adele asked, turning away from the sink, where she stood washing her hands, to see her granddaughter's skeptical eleven-year-old face, the eyes cunning and discrete, waiting, it seemed, to catch Adele in some trivial, unnecessary moment of deceit.

"Mommy and Daddy."

"What do you mean?" Adele asked, moving to the table, where she sat across from Kenya.

"Why does love hurt them? Why does love hurt me and Teresa?" she insisted, her thin, sharp voice warped by so much knowledge and impatience that Adele was convinced once again that her granddaughter just might be the oldest spirit she knew.

"Sometimes grown-ups don't do everything well, even though they're grown. Love is just another thing they have to learn to do."

"Does it have to hurt, though, for it to be love?" she asked as she reached for the glass of milk beside her saucer, her eyes impertinent and precise, unflinching as they watched Adele over the rim of the glass.

And at that moment Lena's key had slid into the front door lock, the sound encouraging Adele to push Kenya's inquiry aside with a noisy, bustling rising from the table that set her nearly running into the hallway, where she greeted Lena and Teresa. And Kenya's question had throbbed, ached really, inside the onslaught of conversation with which she overwhelmed Lena and Teresa as they entered the house.

She was always asking questions like that, so facile and penetrating you were terrified to answer, for no response seemed worthy or true.

She would have been their conscience. Kenya would have been the one no one could face or deny. Teresa wanted to be a lawyer. Her sister had been born, somehow, a judge.

Adele heard a car door slam in front of the house. She got out of bed and pulled the curtains back and looked out her window and saw Teresa getting out of Simon's car. Now she could sleep, she thought, getting back into bed. Or at least she could try.

At Farmingham, with a genius for survival bred sometimes by desperation, women formed families that were, for some, the only ones they had ever known. In these complex, all-encompassing entities, women acted as mother, grandmother, father, sister, even brother, husband, and wife. These female clans were ruled by conventions as rigorous as the codes imposed by blood. Sometimes families were carefully constructed, with women choosing the members of their grouping more cautiously than they had ever chosen a job or a mate. More than once, a younger inmate for whom Lena composed or wrote a letter, or assisted as a part of her job in the law library, began calling her *Mom,* saying the word with a nearly rapturous joy, imagining Lena as antidote to a mother who had been absent, abusive, or never known. It did not matter that Lena had been sentenced to Farmingham for the murder of her own child. The women listened to the careful, modulated tone of her speech, overheard her conversations, filled with a sumptuous knowledge of things, and were inflamed with a desire for her protection. If Lena became their "mother" at Farmingham, they thought, in some hidden place beyond reason, they'd be raised right this time. They'd never end up here again.

Lena had joined no families, but there was Eve Bennett, who had stolen two hundred and fifty thousand dollars from the investment accounts managed by the Richmond, Virginia, bank for which she was an assistant manager. At Farmingham, Lena had not found the intricate narrative Eve shared appalling. The tale of greed and arrogance had been merely one aspect of Eve's past.

The crimes that had landed the women at Farmingham often became the least interesting thing about them. Lena had wondered not so much at the avarice of Eve's actions, which took place over a three-year period, but at her boldness, her determined implementation of a plan.

On Friday nights, no matter the weather, Eve often strode into the dances in the recreation room, wrapped in a shimmering, full-length mink coat and she regularly reinforced her sense of superiority over the other women by showing off color photos of herself and a lover twenty years her junior sprawled on the beaches of Bimini. The muscular, tawny-skinned youth was named Geraldo, and Eve told a table of women in the cafeteria one evening that his nickname was Good-for-What-Ails-You. The photo of Eve, all two hundred pounds of her, wearing a scarlet silk bikini, broad sun hat, and dark glasses, earned her the nickname BB, for "bad bitch."

Each woman's crimes imbued her with a mystique. Those who had stolen money on their own, unaided by men, became heroines, were seen as women possessing nerve and bravado and sometimes a manic craziness. As a high-tech thief, someone who didn't even use a gun, Eve had occupied a relatively high place in the pantheon of Farmingham heroines.

She chose Lena as "partner," her definition of their relationship, because Lena was one of the few women she thought was smart enough to spend more than five minutes talking to. Farmingham was home to women who were illiterate and who had Ph.D.'s, and Black women so bourgeois they were called "Miss Ann." Lena wasn't the smartest woman at Farmingham, but Eve made her feel that way. With her bravado and facile answers that sounded like wisdom behind prison walls, Eve had been for Lena refuge and bulwark.

The day Lena received the separation papers from Ryland, after dinner and before lights-out, she visited Eve.

"Well, what did you expect?" Eve shrugged from her bed, where she sat, sewing buttons on a bright orange knit jacket.

"I don't know why it surprised me."

"You been daydreaming, that's why," Eve observed in chilling disdain, more for Lena's emotional response than Ryland's actions.

"You see any men coming up here on the bus every week to visit us? Damn near every woman in here's got a kid by some man out there, and I can count on my left hand the number of men I've seen on visiting day since I've been here."

Lena thought of the insecurities that raged among and within so many at Farmingham, how the women had sold themselves for men, how one young woman named Princess had chosen her babies' fathers because they had straight hair and light eyes, and was proud that she had supported the children until she was arrested, selling drugs, not asking either of the boys, one of whom had three other babies, for any money for his child. Princess boasted that she didn't want to be dependent on "no men no way," not even thinking that while she might not need the men in her life, the children did. The fragile sisterhood that sometimes bonded the women could be shattered in an instant, sometimes violently, by an accusation or the wrong interpretation of a look or a word spoken in jest. Were the women who sat there, waiting for men to visit them, Lena wondered, really any better than the men who'd written them off, abandoned them, or managed to escape the women with their lives? And what would she have said to Ryland if he had come to see her? Lena had no idea. He had wanted to leave. Now he could. He had not visited. She had not called.

"Let me see the papers," Eve said.

Lena walked over to the bed and handed Eve the Federal Express envelope. Eve spent several minutes reading the papers, then handed them back to Lena, who sat at the foot of her bed.

"You still want him?"

"I know I didn't want this, not here, not now. Why couldn't he wait?"

"For what? With you here," Eve said, snapping the thread and shaking out the jacket, "he had the upper hand. That's what they always want."

"Not all of them," Lena insisted.

"Everyone I ever met."

"Eve, I can't imagine you allowing anybody to be the boss but you."

"Can I help it if I wrote the book on assertiveness training? But you know I'm a pussycat beneath all this."

Lena gazed at her, unconvinced.

"Really!"

"Whatever you say."

"I say it's low down what your old man did, but no more than can be expected."

"Maybe if we hadn't sold the house," Lena said wistfully.

"Why'd you sell it anyway?"

"He said he couldn't live there anymore."

"That was the first step. You should have known this was coming."

From Teresa and Adele, Lena knew about Ryland's paintings of Kenya, his grief and bitterness and how the brave show of competence he had marshaled to get them through to the trial had dissolved when she was sent to Farmingham. And Adele had told her how Ryland had at one point left the city for three months. He'd spent the time in Barbados, where he knew no one, rented a cottage on the beach and slept and swam and looked into the horizon sometimes for days at a time. He came back gaunt, his beard and hair flecked with more gray, his body an iridescent bronze from the sun, his movements slower, more cautious, both ready to live and afraid to.

Lena walked over to the window and looked out onto the prison grounds. In the distance she could see lights in houses ringing the mountains. Eve walked up behind her and whispered, "Go on, cry if that's what you need to do." The charge released and summoned up everything. Even when she felt Eve's hands on her shoulders, stationing her in place as they caressed her, and Eve's pampered, manicured fingers outlining her body, Lena welcomed the sensation of desire, piercing the sadness, muffling the pain. Eve turned Lena around to face her and cradled Lena in her arms. Lena held on to Eve with her eyes closed tight and her heart open. That night, they made a kind of love in Eve's bed. Eve was more gentle than Lena had thought possible. Lena gave more of herself than she had thought she could. None of the pleasure that engulfed her in Eve's arms surprised Lena, even as her head teemed with thoughts of Ryland as she felt Eve's lips on her nipples, her tongue slide across her navel. Lena thought bitterly how inevitable this moment was and wondered how she would fill the emptiness that awaited her once day broke and this night was through.

In the middle of the night, as Eve lay beside her asleep, her arm resting on Lena's breasts, Lena slipped out of bed without waking Eve and went to her own room down the hall.

In the cafeteria the next day, Lena carefully avoided Eve, because now she could see more in Eve than she had ever wanted to, and she did not know what to think of what she now knew of herself. Eve whispered in her ear as they stood in line for lunch, "Honey, I know you've got your image to protect. If you want to, we can just agree that last night never happened."

E ve met Lena at the door of her apartment dressed in gold lounge pajamas, a corpulent, disdainful Siamese cat perched on her shoulder. She paused for several seconds, her hand clutching the door, seeming to strike a pose satisfying and self-congratulatory, one practiced just for that moment.

"Is this Raleigh?" Lena asked, gazing at the cat masking its curiosity about her behind an elegant yawn.

"The one and only. Come on in."

The small apartment overlooked the harbor, where scores of boats and yachts were docked. The furniture was cream-colored, as were the walls. Only the dark brown hardwood floors gave the room warmth and depth. Eve had curled up on a love seat across from Lena, who sat on a sofa facing her. A decanter of red wine, a fat hunk of Brie cheese, and wafer-thin crackers were lined on a teak tray on the table between them.

"So how've you been?" Eve asked as she inhaled deeply from a joint.

"What can I say?" Lena shrugged.

Eve extended the cigarette to Lena, who surprised herself by reaching for it. More than once since her return she had craved the easy oblivion of the high that blocked out feeling and thought at Farmingham, risking punishment of three days in solitary if caught. Eve had chided her that she thought too much, was "too damn serious." Still, Lena had thought that seeing Eve again would make her feel better. Instead, she sat holding the joint, sitting across from the woman she had once incredibly thought was her friend, not knowing what to say, where to begin, wishing she could stand up and head for the door.

Lena gazed longingly at the joint and then placed it in a nearby ashtray and watched Eve stroking the body of Raleigh, who sat perched between her legs, eyeing Lena disinterestedly.

"So what's this bookstore crap you told me about on the phone? Come on, Lena, you can do better than that."

"I'm what they call a sales associate. Really, it's not bad."

"Come on."

"You wouldn't believe it, the number of people who come through the store every day. The store does over a million dollars in sales every year. Besides, it's low stress, not much responsibility. I'd be afraid right now to handle too much."

"Yeah," Eve said, yawning, clearly uninterested.

"You bounced back," Lena observed, changing the subject and looking around the apartment.

"Honey, I'm fifty-two years old. That year and a half at Farmingham is a blip on the screen of my history. Actually, I'm subletting this place; it belongs to a friend who's in L.A. till the end of the year."

"What's this consulting contract you told me about?"

"You'll love this"—Eve grinned conspiratorially—"a firm hired by my old bank, which is now owned by this bank in Chicago, approached me about doing some freelance security work for them."

"Security work. You?"

"They want me to design a system to prevent what I did from happening to them."

"Oh my God." Lena laughed.

"Ain't that nothing?"

"Does the bank, I mean your old bank, know?"

"I'd be working kind of off the books, like, you know subcontracting."

"Will you do it?"

"If the price is right."

She had laughed, but when the laughter subsided Lena felt inexplicably agitated. She had never judged Eve before; why did anything matter now? Lena poured a glass of wine, hoping to drown the sense of loss overtaking her.

"How's your daughter?"

"I can't seem to find my way back to her."

"That's gonna be a tough one. I can't help you with that," Eve said, lifting Raleigh from her lap and pressing the cat against her cheek.

"I didn't think you could," Lena said, a flash of anger stunning her. "I was just being, you know, honest."

Eve turned on the television with a flick of the nearby remote and they sat listening to the evening news, sipping wine, nibbling on the cheese and crackers. Finally Lena asked what she had come really to discover. "How'd you get through the first weeks? I can't seem to get it together."

"Stayed high." Eve laughed, the sound brusque, a grunt that shook her large breasts and broad shoulders.

"You couldn't stay high."

"Who couldn't? That feeling you're talking about, sure I had it for a while when I first came out. Know how I solved it? I stayed indoors. I'd come home from the shitty secretarial job I got just so I'd have a gig to satisfy my parole and holed up at my sister's for six months and didn't go nowhere except my parole officer. And him and me got a deal. Believe me, my urine's never dirty."

Lena drained her wineglass and sat on the edge of the sofa, slightly tipsy.

"You know the hardest thing for me so far?"

"What?" Lena asked, although she did not want to know, had no interest in ever knowing anything about Eve again.

"To be intimate. Sexually, I mean. I thought I'd pounce on the first man that showed interest. But it was hard for me to open up that way. It was hard. I don't know why."

"I haven't thought much about that."

"You must be sicker than I thought."

"It's just that I feel like everything's changed. And I'll never fit. One night I went through my old phone book, thought about calling some old friends. I got scared and threw the book in the trash."

And a week earlier she had nearly been hit by a Jaguar as she bolted into the street a few blocks from the bookstore when she saw a manager from her old firm a block away heading toward her. Peter Mathis had been her mentor and friend, and that day he clearly didn't even see her, as he walked along M Street in khakis and a sports shirt, clutching a bag from an expensive men's store. But the fear that an instant of recognition would force them to speak drove Lena to thoughtlessly bolt into the street, the green Jaguar screeching to a halt a few inches away from her. She had run for several blocks, bumping into people and not caring, their curses dogging her flight. She had come to tell Eve about that as well, but that prospect now struck her as somehow useless.

"Kelly wrote me. She gets out in a few months," Lena said.

"What's her plan?"

"Plan?"

"Yeah. What's she gonna do, go back to Dogpatch?"

"Eve, come on. She's going to try to get custody of her kids."

"I don't know, her mama might be doing Mom and kids a favor, keeping them apart. I'm sorry, I mean, it's not like with you. Your case is different. You aren't a flake."

"I don't think she has much of a chance."

"She's a white girl," Eve said.

"A poor one, from West Virginia. Hell, she's a nigger too."

"Tell her that." Eve laughed.

"I'm sure somebody already has."

"Whatever." Eve shrugged. The two women sat finally confirmed as strangers. Then Lena asked, the odor of the reefer infusing her with an easy carelessness, "What happened to the money? The money that you stole."

At Farmingham, the money had seemed symbolic, almost unimportant. Sitting before Eve now, it loomed monumental in Lena's imagination.

"You don't need to know," Eve told her, stroking Raleigh methodically, attentively, as though she never planned in this lifetime to do anything else.

"Maybe I do."

"It was my money."

"No, it wasn't, Eve, you just thought it was."

"Who made you judge and jury, Miss Thing?"

"My little girl."

"Well, look in the mirror sometimes."

"That's all I do."

"Freedom's sure made you a bitch."

"Who knows?" Lena said. "Maybe I always was."

That night in her bedroom Lena picked up the phone as she had done scores of times since her return to call Ryland. And in the end she could not. It had all come undone when he left the last time. She had carried in her head, ever since she was a child, a paradigm for happiness, and each time Ryland left her, the construct crumbled. Each time he left, in her mind she was reduced to rubble. All she had ever wanted was a home like the one she had never had. Her father dead before she was even born, her mother so dedicated to work and raising her and, it seemed, nothing more. Everything she had done, the good grades in school and then college, her ambition, transforming herself into a new-breed, new-world Black woman who could fit comfortably in an office at a Big Eight firm and a Black man's arms, had been inspired by the yearning for a home and family. And once she got it, she had vowed never to lose it, no matter what.

When Ryland left, an unspoken etiquette sprang up between them. She'd let him alone for some time, for she always knew he had gone to the small studio space on R Street, the place where he'd been working when they first met. Ryland had refused to give up the studio even after they moved into the house on Sycamore Street, where he had more than enough room to work, had all the space anybody could ever need. It was then that she knew she'd never really have him the way she wanted. He'd always have someplace else he could go. She had a key to the studio, and when he'd leave home she'd go there under the guise of taking him his mail, and he'd make her feel like an intruder. Standing outside the door to the studio, one of four in a former warehouse, preparing to slide her key in the lock, Lena prepared herself each time to find him lying on the small cot tangled in some other woman's arms.

And when she'd enter, unannounced, for that was where her power lay, she knew he was hers again. Entering the huge, drafty, drab space that he refused to let her decorate, the brick walls splotched with paint, so profuse it resembled evidence of a crime, she'd ignore his studied refusal to acknowledge her or his threats to change the lock. Of course he never did, which meant that he wanted her to always find him.

"The girls miss you almost as much as I do," she'd begin after she had placed the mail on the cot and heard the echo of her heels against the dingy cracked wooden floor, nearly growing faint on the odor of paint, wishing for the hundredth time that he'd let her give the place a good cleaning. His hair would be matted, and he'd look like hell maybe from painting twenty-four hours straight, without a break. He did his best work when they were most anguished and angry. And she could tell that like her, he hadn't slept much. She'd strip off her coat, toss it onto the cot beside the letters, and ask him when he planned to come back home.

Once she fell on her knees before him in that room, her silk stockings tearing because of a splinter in the floor. She couldn't re-member what she had said. But she had begged him. Begged him to come home. How many ways are there to do that? And on her knees she kept hoping he'd lift her up from the floor, release her from this moment, but he didn't touch her, just let her stay there on her knees before him. She couldn't remember what she'd said, because in the midst of it she had wondered why she felt such a mixture of horror and shame when she was on her knees out of love. When you loved someone, there was no difference, was there, between asking them to stay or to come back standing or prostrate. Wasn't there something in the Bible about love knowing no shame or vanity? She could feel her hands reaching out to him, preparing to grip his legs, hold them tight, root them to her. There was no vanity here nor any shame. But why did she feel so sick inside?

But he had turned away from her. She didn't know what was in his eyes, lacked the strength to look there. But, of course, she had to see him turn away and walk out of the studio, slamming the door behind him so hard the room shook, the floor beneath her knees rumbling slightly. And she convinced herself that it was the tremors of the walls, the ceiling, that toppled her, in a heap of silk and cologne—for she had stopped by on her way home from work—onto the floor, not anger or fear.

He came home the next day. But the last time he left, Lena knew he was gone for good. And because she could not get to him—he was miles away in Michigan—for the first time in their married life there was nothing she could do. And every day that he was gone she was suddenly six years old again, hearing Adele tell her why she had no father, hearing Adele tell her how Oscar Ramsey had died in his sleep, hadn't even known she had been made. But what she really heard was that her father had not loved her enough to stay. And every day of Ryland's emigration from her love, she was once again, the same age as Kenya, and the moment Adele left the house to run an errand or to go shopping and left her alone, entering Adele's bedroom and opening the drawer where she kept her lingerie, fingering the folds of rayon and silk and cotton, her fingers finding once again the photo of her father. In the picture, cracked and fragile with age, she saw a big-faced brown-skinned man with a mustache and flight in his eyes. She sneaked into Adele's room and looked at the photo so often, she grew drunk, dizzy, on the image of her father. As she grew older, she saw a sunken sadness in the smile that years earlier had seemed so innocent, held the photo up beside her face before the mirror so that they both looked at her, and with her hands searched for Oscar Ramsey's imprint on her nose, in her skin. Lena recalled the stories her father's brothers and sisters told her about him each time she looked at the picture and saw her father through the screen of their remembrance and her own longing.

But what the picture had taught her, what her father had told her during all those hours she spent clutching the picture, the sweat, the acid from her hands eating away at the photo, erasing what remained, was to never let go.

Once I went with her to see her parole officer. She had to present herself every two weeks in a small office downtown. I'd allowed myself to think that she was free, but they still held her accountable. She couldn't even leave the city without permission. A unique vocabulary defined and controlled my mother's life. Many of the words I had been unfamiliar with, had not needed to know. But I became aware of their power. I had found language alluring before, but the words that constructed the boundaries of my mother's existence were menacing. Soon I attained a kind of fearful respect for language, drilled into me by witnessing how a word could close options or obliterate possibilities.

My mother was found guilty of involuntary manslaughter. I looked up those words in the dictionary and tried to mesh them with what had happened. I made the connection, but the definition seemed to possess a calculated objectivity that was almost cruel. I looked up the word *parole* and discovered that "on condition of continued good behavior" was part of the definition. I wondered how good my mother had to be for her parole not to be revoked, or for it to end. Maybe if she never kills again that will be enough, I thought sometimes, but the authorities demanded much more than that.

Since my mother came home, Ma Adele liked to eat in the formal dining room, the room that usually sat as composed as a mausoleum. We'd usually eat in the breakfast nook in the kitchen. But the formal dining room, with its ceiling-high china closet and brocade curtains and its wide, cushioned dining chairs poised around the mahogany table, this is where my grandmother insisted that we have dinner several times a week. Because of my mother.

My mother passed Ma Adele the macaroni salad as she told her, "I have to see my parole officer tomorrow, so I'm not sure what time I'll be home."

"Can I go with you?" I asked. The desire had been brewing for a while, but I'd had no plans to act on it until that moment.

"Now, why on earth would you want to do that?" Ma Adele asked, so agitated she stopped eating to glare angrily at me across the table.

"I'm just curious," I said, quickly filling my mouth with salad so that I would not have to answer any more questions.

"I think that's a terrible idea," she went on, looking at neither my mother nor me, confident that the sternness of her pronouncement would impose correction. "It even sounds like an invasion of privacy."

While Ma Adele bemoaned the impropriety of my request, my mother had methodically lifted each serving plate from the table, gently placing a fish fillet and an ear of corn beside the macaroni salad. She didn't look like someone who'd just come home from prison anymore. The tasteful yet deliberate application of makeup transformed her face everyday, and she had even gotten a new hairdo, a close-cut curly permanent that made her look young and virtually unscathed if you didn't look too close.

"Mama, it's not such a bad idea," she said finally. She had filled her plate and then she stared across the table at me.

"If you want to go with me, meet me in Thomas Circle at six

o'clock. But you can't sit in on the meeting. Is that what you wanted?"

"She doesn't know what she wants," Ma Adele said in disgust.

"I just want to see what it's like."

"You could just ask me."

"But I want to see for myself."

When my mother finally began to eat, I asked, "So I can go, you don't mind?"

"I mind, but you can come."

The entrance to the building faced an alley and the whole structure huddled behind the new chrome and marble buildings that occupied Fourteenth Street a few feet away. My mother was already there, waiting for me in the lobby, when I arrived, and we silently took the elevator up to the fourth floor. When we entered the parole office, which was really no more than a large, open, barnlike space stretching the length of the building and separated by room dividers, she introduced me to the secretary at the front desk, who sat doing a crossword puzzle. They chatted briefly but pleasantly, almost like old friends. From this outer section we could see my mother's parole officer, whose desk occupied a corner section. The walls around his desk were plastered with sentimental framed inspirational sayings printed in flowing calligraphy against backgrounds of incandescent sunsets, footprints in the sand, and bold, happy sunrises. He hung up the phone and waved to my mother as she told me to wait for her and to sit down.

Joe Hardy was rotund and middle-aged rumpled. He was bald and you could tell that he'd had a receding hairline and just decided to shave his hair off rather than wait to lose it. His protruding belly strained against his shirt buttons, and he wore a small African-style fez atop his bald head. He strode toward us before my mother could leave my side.

"This must be Teresa," he said. My mother introduced us. Because he was used to looking at the faces of criminals or at least people who had been convicted of a crime, he smiled at me and I was afraid he could see the crimes of omission I had committed against my mother.

"I've heard a lot about you." I smiled unconvincingly but said nothing.

"Don't worry, all of it's good."

They went back to his desk, where they talked for nearly half an hour. I had expected a grim interrogation, but while I could not hear what they were saying, I saw Joe Hardy lean back in his swivel chair, his fingers laced behind his head, nodding at whatever my mother was telling him. He'd lean forward, hunching over a pad on his desk, scribbling, doodling, but still listening intently to my mother. She talked for a while and then he began to speak, using his hands as fluid, muscular punctuation to his words. Joe Hardy was the most powerful person in my mother's life. I was amazed by what seemed to be a strange, benevolent conspiracy of respect between them. I was bored, fidgeting, ready to go, when I saw him give my mother a small plastic container. She reached for it and stood up and went into a small room a few feet away that I guessed was the bathroom.

I imagined my mother pulling down her panty hose and panties, sitting on the toilet seat after she had placed toilet paper on it to protect herself from germs, holding the plastic cup and waiting for the urge to pee. Everything they had said, no matter how positive or pleasant, could be obliterated by dirty urine. I knew there was no possibility of that with my mother, but sitting there, I wondered about the other women whose bodies betrayed them, whose insides could not keep a secret. Drugs could send my mother back to Farmingham. But there was no test for her to take that would reveal the presence of guilt. And if there were, would it be a trace, a stain, or a tumor? There was no test to gauge how scared my mother was of me or herself. But looking back, I think, maybe that's what the drug test was, a gauge of fear. You were afraid and so you smoked, snorted, or shot up. Drugs made you forget, feel good. Then they sent you back to jail just because you got scared.

I looked at my watch. It had been ten minutes. I was sure that my mother was finished. She had peed on command and she had closed the container, washed her hands and looked in the mirror over the sink, and recomposed herself. My mother would convince herself that the plastic bottle full of her wastes had nothing to do with her.

When she came out she gave Mr. Hardy the container, now inside a plastic bag. I could see them looking at what I guessed was a calendar on his desk. He wrote something in it. Then my mother told him good-bye. When we arrived in the lobby of the building, stepping out of the elevator, I asked, "How can you be so friendly with him?"

"He's not my enemy."

"He could send you back to jail."

"Only I can do that," she told me with a vehemence and a kind of pride I had not expected.

We took the subway to Connecticut Avenue because we weren't ready to go home and strolled past the Mayflower Hotel and the ritzy clothing stores my mother once shopped in, and we found ourselves facing the park in the middle of Dupont Circle. It was ringed by blocks of commercial businesses, bookstores, record shops, banks. It was a classic Washington, D.C., summer night, sweltering, nearly tropical beneath the cover of slowly emerging darkness. In the park-like space, a cluster of men huddled around a chess game. The chess players were a muscular, T-shirted Black man with a goatee and a baseball cap on backward, a toothpick perched between his teeth, staring down a young white boy in a plaid shirt who had a cherubic, pink-cheeked face. The game was surrounded by a circle of quiet, patient spectators. Throughout the park, male homosexuals walked

hand in hand. A young woman in another part of the park in flowing
African dress played bongos beside a man playing a flute. We stood
looking and then walked around the park. We bought a sorbet from
an ice cream shop and walked back to the park and sat down.

The presence of strangers, the encroaching night, melted some of
the edginess that seemed to bloom like static between us and I asked
my mother, "What was the worst thing you saw?"

"One of the women hung herself. I saw her body dangling from a
shower rod." I was quiet for a while, for the image momentarily
stalled the barrage of questions backlogged in my mind.

"How did you not go crazy?" I asked, folding the plastic sorbet
container in my palms, wondering if she had ever tried to kill herself.
Hoping I would never find out if she had.

"I did go crazy," she said solemnly, staring ahead, choosing not to
look at me for this admission.

"Do you ever miss any of those women?"

"Sometimes," she said, wiping her fingers and lips with a small
napkin and stuffing it into the pocket of her skirt.

"But why? I mean, they weren't really your friends." I sat beside
my mother, interrogating her, because questions were easier than
conversation. I knew no other way to reach her except through curiosity.

"I was there long enough for some of them to become my friends.
I got a letter from Kelly last week."

"Will you write her back?"

"Sure."

"So those women will always be a part of your life."

"I don't know."

"You'll never belong just to us completely like you did before.
You'll belong to strangers too."

When I visited my mother in prison, I'd convinced myself that
she was not like Kelly and Eve and the others. Prison had never been

my mother's destiny. Something had gone wrong. A cosmic mistake
had been made. At Farmingham I looked at the other women and
could often see, ground into the flesh of their faces, the fists that had
slammed them, the love they never had, the stupid choices they had
made, the cruel twists of fate that had ushered them onto the grounds
of the prison. I knew, as well, that not all of them were guilty. Life
and the justice system were both tragically, horribly flawed. Not
everyone there had gotten what they deserved. When I looked at my
mother I saw someone who had given birth to me and who I refused
to believe was as unlucky as the women she lived among. But if she
had become friends with women at Farmingham, she was not so
different after all. But I would never be able to discover what united
my mother to the woman who wrote her or the women she admitted
that she still thought about. I was her child. My eyes had not been
designed to possess a vision that charitable or forgiving.

"They weren't so different from me," she said as though she were
clairvoyant. "And in many ways I was just like them. Teresa, when
you came to see me you saw only a group of women in fatigues and
jeans who all looked like they belonged there. Some of them did,
some of them didn't. But they were individuals, not numbers. That's
how I became their friend."

I asked her other questions that night, sitting in the park, equally
illustrative of how many bad prison movies I had seen and of how
much I had not seen or come to know when I visited her at
Farmingham. But I could not know then, that night, what I know
now, that my mother could not really tell me the story of her imprisonment. If we had sat until dawn, even if she had decided that I
owned the story, that it was not only hers, she could not really create
it for me. But I wanted the story, because while Farmingham was her
story, it was my story too. She had asked me once what it was like
living without her, living with Ma Adele, living away from my father,
without my sister. But it was as difficult for me to tell her as it was for

her to recreate her days and nights in jail. My sister's death gave us competing yet complementary chronicles. I thought if I could possess my mother's story, the story itself would replicate familial unity. But some stories, I have discovered, you don't tell because you can't. You lived it. And that is more than enough.

She was a good mother, a normal mother until that day. I believe that. I have to. But what do those words even mean? You don't look them up in the dictionary, you carry their definitions inside you, embedded in every breath you take, everything you feel. She was a good mother. I couldn't be her daughter and believe anything else.

When she came home in the evenings, my mother could change into a sweatsuit as fast as Lynda Carter became Wonder Woman in the reruns I saw sometimes on cable. As she bathed Kenya I heard the water splashing and Kenya's sharp, clear laughter from behind the bathroom door as I sat finishing homework in my room. When they were done Kenya streaked naked and wild through the hallway, a tiny yet robust whirlwind, screaming in glee or just in recognition that Mom was home, or that she was six or seven, a child, and alive.

My mother would check my homework, complain about the state of my room, and I'd try to tell her absolutely everything that I had thought or felt or that had happened to me that day. Once she took Kenya and me to New York for the weekend. We stayed in a hotel overlooking Central Park, saw *Les Misérables,* and to the delight of Kenya and me had room service deliver breakfast on Sunday morning before we caught the shuttle back to Washington.

Then I turned thirteen, and my spirit was hijacked by alien hormones and genes that had been storing their power, priming their energies for the precise moment of attack. I became pathologically secretive. I hated my mother and my father and had no idea why. Each day when I came home from school I stormed into the house, ran up the stairs, locked the door to my room, and bundled myself under the comforter and sheets of my bed, where I wallowed in fits of crying, the certainty that the two people who had given me life did not understand me and never would again, daydreams of premature death, and, most frightening of all, the fear that I would never be kissed or asked to dance at a party. My father steered clear of me, taking the line of least resistance. But my mother wanted her little girl back, refusing to believe such a feat was impossible. The tension between us escalated measurably each day. My sarcasm and willfulness provoked punishments that I chose to ignore. If I couldn't use the phone, she'd come home in the evening to find me calling a friend long distance.

One evening when my father was out, when she found that one of Kenya's teachers had called a week earlier to discuss problems Kenya was having with reading, she asked, "Why didn't somebody tell me this sooner?" As I headed to the dining room with a wooden bowl filled with salad, I blurted out snidely, cruelly, "You're never here." The lethal charge bubbled up from my subconscious. My hands were trembling as I placed the bowl on the dining room table.

When I turned around, my mother loomed over me. Without the slightest trace of emotion she slapped me so hard I fell against the table, my arms flailing over my head, noisily overturning water glasses and scattering cutlery and plates. I lay sprawled before her, feeling my cheek throbbing, already swelling. But I refused to cry. I would never let her see me do that. My mother thought she could win. I'd prove to her I could. "Don't you ever talk to me like that, do you hear," she shouted. My silence inspired her to shout again, "Do you hear me?"

"Yes," I said bitterly through a mouth aching so, I could hardly open it.

"Get up," she screamed. The anguish my words inflicted now pulsed in her voice; tears stabbed the corners of her eyes.

I locked myself in my room and I never told anyone about that night. It remained our secret. I kept it a secret because I thought if I did I'd never see her look at me or at Kenya that way again.

One evening when I came home from work, Simon was there. Ma Adele was in the kitchen, inspecting an array of vegetables she had brought in from her garden. The collard greens filled a wicker basket, their color dark and hearty. The tomatoes were sumptuous, and so red it almost hurt to look at them. The crisp, pungent smell of the string beans promised satisfaction. I loved to eat tomatoes like fruit, wash them quickly in the sink and bite into them like plums or peaches. So as I placed my pocketbook on the counter and greeted my grandmother, I scooped up one of the tomatoes, whisking it from beneath Ma Adele's proprietary glance. My grandmother took gardening seriously. I had seen her stand over a table laden with vegetables she had grown, eyes closed, hands outstretched, mouthing a silent prayer of thanks.

"We've got company," she told me as I stood at the sink, washing a robust beefsteak tomato that filled my palm.

"Who?"

"Simon's out back, talking to your mother."

I turned around to look at Ma Adele as though looking at her would change what she had said. "He didn't tell me he was coming by."

"He doesn't need to. That young man's always welcome here." Ma Adele sat down at the table and began shucking corn, her hands efficient, nearly ruthless in the speed with which they stripped off the husks, revealing the rows of gleaming yellow kernels.

"How long's he been here?" I asked, still holding the wet, dripping tomato in my hand, aware now that I would not eat it. I had no appetite.

"Almost two hours."

"He knows what time I get home," I said irritably, placing the tomato on the counter.

"He didn't come to see you," Ma Adele said, clearly enjoying the gradual unfolding of this secret. "He came to see your mother."

"How do you know?" I moved from the sink and sat across from her, the vegetables heaped between us, struggling to dampen the panic in my voice.

"That's what he told me when I opened the door for him." The corn was now stacked in two neat rows before her.

"How did he know today was her day off?"

"He didn't. He said he decided to just take a chance that he'd find her here."

"He never mentioned a word about this to me."

"I think it shows he's got home training," Ma Adele concluded, taking the corn to the sink, where she washed each ear and dislodged the remaining silken hairs.

"I wish he'd told me."

"Why, so you could've stopped him?"

"I wouldn't have done that."

"He probably wanted to meet Lena without you getting in the way. And I think it shows respect."

"For her maybe, but not for me."

"If you were as smart as you think you are, you'd realize just how much respect it shows." My grandmother told me this, her back still to me, the water running in the sink, her hands cradling a dozen ears of corn. She had not looked at me, had not trained her impervious glance over her shoulder, but I sat at the kitchen table, squirming anyway.

Simon had sat and talked with my mother for two hours. What could they have possibly said to one another? As I stood up and walked toward the door that led to the backyard, Ma Adele warned me, "Don't go out there and start any mess. Leave well enough alone."

I said nothing and was relieved to stand on the screened-in porch, where I could see them sitting in a small brick patiolike area beneath the oak tree that reigned over the backyard, several feet away from the fenced-off garden. My mother lay on a padded chaise longue. Simon sat in a chair a few feet away from her. He was wearing beige Bermuda shorts and a purple T-shirt. Everything about him seemed more pronounced. From where I stood, his arms bulged muscular and irresistible, his legs and feet struck me as more substantial than I'd noticed before. Leaning forward, his elbows on his knees, his hands clasped, it seemed he wanted to make sure that my mother heard every word he said. A pitcher of iced tea and two glasses sat on the latticed iron table between them.

In the cool shade of the porch, I wondered what Simon now knew about me and about my mother that I had not had the courage to reveal. Had my mother told him imaginary tales of her time in California or confessed to things even I didn't know about Farmingham. Simon was a stranger, and so the possibility was quite real that he now knew the truth. My mother had nothing to lose if she told Simon what she had done, for she was not bound to him by blood, love, or expectation. He could not cast her out from a place she did not inhabit in his heart.

Dazed, intoxicated by fear, somehow I managed to leave the porch and walk over to them. Simon had allowed me all this time to live what he suspected was a lie. His visit to my mother intercepted my control over when and how I'd decide to transform falsehood into truth. As I neared them, I strained to hear what they were saying but knew it was too late. Simon stood up and met me halfway, greeting me with a gentle peck on the cheek.

"Hey, baby," he whispered as he held me in his arms.

"What's this all about?" I asked, my arms clutching his waist more tightly than they ever had before.

"Don't get paranoid," he said, laughing, flashing his bright smile that this time did not quicken my pulse.

"I'm not paranoid. I just wondered why you didn't tell me you were coming by."

"Because I didn't know. Not until today. Not until this afternoon. I was driving back from Hechinger's and decided to stop by to talk to your mom."

"You knew I wouldn't be here."

"And?" he asked, belligerence suddenly rising in his voice.

"Nothing, forget it."

When he came by to take me out, Simon and my mother had exchanged quick, formal pleasantries. My presence, I knew, censored the nature of their exchange. That was the way I wanted it.

How had Simon's curiosity about my mother escaped me? The gentle laughter and the energetic sound of my mother's voice that I'd heard while watching them from the porch appalled me.

"Nothing? You sure don't act like it's nothing. Your mother and I were talking, that's all."

"About what?"

"Where's this coming from?"

"I don't want to argue. But see what effect she's having already?"

"Teresa, come on," he said incredulously.

I reached for his hand and we turned and walked to my mother, presenting, I hoped, a united front.

"I was telling Simon how surprised I was to find him here," I explained, sitting on the edge of the chaise longue so Simon could take his seat.

"He was a pleasant surprise," my mother said, lying in the shade of the tree as sublime, it seemed to me, as an empress inspecting her subjects.

Simon settled in his chair and told me pointedly, "I didn't know your mother was an accountant."

I looked at him blankly.

"We've been talking about the professions, about hitting glass ceilings and surviving when you're the only person of color in the room," my mother told me.

"I was telling her that I want to start my own architectural firm and make an end run around all the bullshit," Simon said as though giving me an oral report. He sounded suddenly uncomfortable.

"The downside of working for yourself is that there are no days off," my mother said. "You've got to show up sharp every day. There were lots of days when I was with Maxwell and Jeeter that despite my title and salary, I was on cruise control. There were enough people working under me that I could get away with that sometimes."

"Yeah, but at least I'll be building my own thing," Simon said, rubbing his hands together as though he planned to build his company at that moment brick by brick.

"But you could learn a lot from an established firm. Put in a few years there and figure out how you'll be different, how you'll be better as well as how the system works."

They sat talking as though I weren't even there. The innocence of the conversation did not fool or comfort me. Soon made irrelevant by their banter, I announced I was going to help Ma Adele with dinner.

"Okay," Simon said, not even looking at me as I rose to walk back to the house.

Simon stayed for dinner, and as I listened to him and my mother talk over the barbecued ribs, corn on the cob, and beans and rice I'd helped Ma Adele prepare, I realized that there was more to my mother's past than the crime she had committed and the price she had paid. She could talk to Simon all night long and never once mention Farmingham and still render a sense of a life lived fully and completely.

I had listened to Simon's career plans with an unfocused but apparent generosity. My mother knew exactly where Simon wanted to go, for she had already been there. Before my eyes my mother became guide and mentor to the man I loved.

Over dinner my mother regaled us with tales of the three months she spent in Europe before she met my father, auditing banks in Switzerland, London, and Amsterdam and staying in four-star hotels in every country. Her performance was spectacular. She was at ease, and more relaxed than I'd seen her since she came home.

"How old were you?" Simon asked.

"Young enough and old enough," she said coyly. "I was a Black woman in Europe and I felt like I belonged to and could conquer the world. I even thought sometimes about trying to stay there, get a position with one of the banks I was auditing."

"Why?" Simon asked, surprised, his eyes locked into my mother's casual gaze.

"They seemed more in touch with themselves and the things that mattered. Sure, I was different. But I didn't feel like I was a shock to them. Not in the way I felt entering a meeting at the branch office in Manhattan."

"Humane?" I sneered. "Surely you don't mean that. They didn't have slaves, they had colonies instead."

"Your mother knows that, Teresa," Simon scolded me irritably.

"I just felt something, a way of being"—she shrugged, looking into her glass of iced tea—"that I'd never felt here."

I watched her gently place her glass back on the table and rest her chin on her hands, clasped before her face, and by this action impose a silence we all instinctively respected. If she had remained in Europe, I thought, I would never have been born, my sister would not have been killed. The thought of my possible nonexistence filled me with curiosity rather than grief. I looked at my grandmother, pushing her plate aside, Simon digging into his second slice of lemon meringue pie, and then my mother, pensive in the wake of the personal history she had unleashed and revealed. We were cosmic puzzle pieces. Remove one and all else was altered or erased, suspect and incomplete.

Quite suddenly my mother breathed in deeply and said, "And while I was there, in my free time I discovered an African aspect to European history we never hear about here, the Moors, the Black Madonna. I wasn't a stranger there. They'd seen me before."

"Why'd you get out of it?" Simon asked. "Did you reach a point where you couldn't go any higher? Were you burned out?" Simon asked eagerly, waiting almost breathlessly for my mother's answer.

Ma Adele and I looked at each other so that we would not have to look at my mother. Could she lie as deftly as me? I wondered. Then I recalled that she'd been lying in a sense all day if she hadn't told Simon about what she'd done.

She pushed her pie aside as though it had suddenly lost its taste. I could sense her calculating, testing all the possible fabrications in her mind, weighing them for believability and impact.

"My life changed," she said slowly, lifting her gaze from the table to look at Simon. "Something terrible happened to us all." She looked at me and then at my grandmother as she said this. "My husband, Teresa's father, and I separated. Everything fell apart. The job got lost in the debris."

"Oh, I'm sorry," Simon said.

I couldn't believe that she'd outsmarted me. She had virtually told the truth.

The hush that descended threatened to swallow us all, and Ma Adele began collecting the dishes, scraping the remains onto a platter. Simon stood up and helped her. My mother sat quietly stunned. I didn't move but sat with her at the table and listened to Ma Adele and Simon talking and cleaning up in the kitchen. Before I could say thank you, my mother stood up and went upstairs to her room.

When we entered Simon's apartment that evening, he headed for the refrigerator and brought out two Cokes. He tossed me one and drank his quickly, guzzling it standing in front of the fridge, then he tossed the can into the wastebasket beside the sink and raised his arm, smelled himself, and grinned, saying, "I stink, let me take a shower, then I'm all yours. You want to join me?" he asked.

"Go on, just hurry up," I said, faking a nonchalance I did not feel.

I sat down in the living room, wishing I could write the necessary words, not speak them, for then I would know what to say. I could construct with words a building like the ones Simon wanted to create, and I'd live in it and find shelter there. But I couldn't pass Simon a note. A letter would be simply another lie.

It was all so muddled. I had told the truth when I should have lied, had lied to hold on to what I no longer had. I hated my mother. But I hated myself more. For before anyone, before even she admitted guilt, cast aside forever the possibility of innocence, it was I who said what happened. It was I who told what she did.

The policeman had the aura of someone you could trust. He was a weary veteran, concealing whatever horror he felt at the sight of what he saw entering our house that day. His interrogation of me was rigorous yet patient, and he was as detached as a priest in the confessional, as concerned as someone who loved me.

I told him what I saw, told him what my mother had done. The tears that erupted moments after I said the words were for me, for my damned, unfaithful heart, still burdened but now able to beat because I had spoken.

And at the trial I was a hostile witness, hostile to the sight of my mother, hemmed in, imprisoned already, it seemed, behind the wide oak desk, her lawyer at her side; hostile to the truth they made me tell, the truth I could not escape. The truth which would not set us free but would guarantee I would lose my mother and, I was sure, whatever love remained.

And what did I witness? What did I see? My mother's malevolence or simply a twisted, inexplicable moment when an angel fell from heaven. How could I be sure? I told. At first unwillingly, and then bitterly, but I told. No one, not even Simon, could love a child as worthless as I.

Finally I went into Simon's bedroom to wait for him. When he came out of the bathroom he lay on his bed and looked at me and said, "Tell me what happened. And this time tell me the truth."

"My mother killed my sister."

Disbelief turned Simon's gaze upon me into a laser, and I could nearly read his mind, I saw it unfolding on his stunned, nearly pained expression. I knew he was trying to imagine the woman he had spent the evening with committing such an act. He said nothing for a while, a time for which I would always be grateful. Finally he asked, "Why didn't you tell me?"

"How could I? I didn't want you to pity me. I didn't want all that between us. But I wasn't going to keep it from you forever."

"What did I have to do to earn the right to know?"

"My mother went to prison, we buried my sister, and my father lives in an apartment filled with paintings he's done of the daughter he lost. Do you think that's an easy history for me to share?"

"Did she mean to do it?" he asked me, now sitting up, propping himself up on his elbow.

"No, of course not," I said with an absolute shake of my head.

"How do you know?"

"I don't. But I know what I believe."

Simon leaned forward, staring at me. "Was she angry when it happened?"

"Yes."

"What about?"

"Everything. Our whole life. The way it was then."

"But not at your sister?"

"When it happened, she was mad at her."

"Why your sister, why not you?"

"It was what my sister was going to do that set her off, that made her snap." I sat on the hassock near the bedroom window, my thoughts reeling through a morass of memory.

"You wouldn't have made her snap?"

"I knew her better," I insisted loudly. But did I? Would I ever? Until that instant I had never thought that my sister's death might have been arbitrary, that it might have been I who died that day instead of her.

"I had to testify against her. I had to tell what I saw."

"What did you see?"

"I'm not sure. I don't think I ever will be."

"My parents used to hit each other sometimes. But it was never lethal. It was the way they were. I never thought Kenya or I would ever get caught up in it."

"Collateral damage," he said, rising from the bed and walking over to me.

"What's that?" I asked, looking up at him.

"That's what they call civilians killed by bombs or gunfire intended for military targets."

He touched my face, my head, my cheeks, then knelt before

me and kissed me. "Is that what I am to you, a casualty?" I asked.

"It's what she made you, not what you always have to be." I closed my eyes and imagined myself, finally, but even in my fantasy, only momentarily safe.

I don't know why my father's leaving surprised me. Perhaps I thought my parents would live together forever, eternally dependent upon the nearly dangerous tensions that fueled their love.

I was the one who arrived home first that day and knew before anyone else that my father was gone. He was usually there in the afternoons when Kenya and I came home from school, on the phone talking, usually about his work, to someone in another city. Or I'd hear him upstairs in the attic, his footsteps padding firmly across the ceiling, a sound that was always reassuring to me. But when I entered the house that day I felt his absence as a permanent part of the atmosphere of our home. The sensation was so unsettling, I was chilled, and though I didn't know why, afraid to be in the house alone.

When I entered that afternoon, everything was as I'd last seen it that morning. The comics section of *The Washington Post* lay on the floor before the television, where Kenya had eaten her cereal. A pair of panty hose my mother had hurriedly taken off when she discovered a run in them lay balled up on the sofa. But a discreet prophetic silence pervaded the house. The quiet was claustrophobic and unexpansive. If

I left the house, as I momentarily thought of doing, where would I run?

I walked up the stairs slowly, as though I were being pulled by necessity warped into awful desire. Clutching the banisters, I counted each step, reminding myself that I was at home, in our house on Sycamore Street. Nothing bad could happen to me here. Yet, as I climbed the stairs, I could smell the absence of my father like something cold and crisp and final in the air.

The closet in my parents' bedroom was open and one side of it was home to a few empty wire hangers dangling pitiful and alone. The drawers of the bureau chest were still partially open and mostly empty. Assorted mismatched socks, too-small shirts, out-of-fashion sweaters, were strewn on the bed. My father had been methodical and haphazard in deciding what he would take with him.

The sight of all this pierced me like a wild, blindly aimed incision. I thought briefly, fleetingly, of the attic. If he had taken his paintings too, I thought I would never see him again.

I descended the stairs the same thoughtful, unbelieving way I had walked up them. In the family room I sat on the sofa very still, trying to be motionless, trying really to erase everything I knew. Finally I saw the note, a white sheet of paper folded in half, with my mother's name on it. It lay in a flat green-and-yellow ceramic bowl that my mother had bought in a pottery shop in New England. The bowl held spare change, stamps, pencils, staples, safety pins, minutiae that looked like useless clutter but that nearly always rescued us in a moment of panic.

The paper was folded, but I could see my father's handwriting near the bottom. What, I wondered, could he have said that the empty closet did not? The sight of the note, the mere thought of it, was more final than the attic I had imagined with empty walls. If my father had chosen to write, that meant he was clear, definite about what he had done. A letter implied premeditation, not the haste I'd assumed in the bedroom. How long had he wanted to leave us? How long had he hated being here? And as much as I sat despising the letter, I reached out for it. The moment my fingers touched the note, I heard my mother opening the door.

My mother was carrying two bags of groceries, and Kenya trailed behind her with a six-pack of sodas in her arms. I stood up nervously as they entered. One look at me and my mother asked, "What's wrong?"

Kenya came back from the kitchen, where she had placed the sodas on the kitchen table and went straight to the television, sat on the floor in front of it, and turned on the raucous sound of afternoon cartoons. The noise demolished the artificial calm. Kenya passed by the table and the note from our father, oblivious, unsuspecting.

When I positioned myself in front of the bowl, that merely heightened my mother's curiosity. But she turned from me and strode quickly into the kitchen and put the bags on the table beside the sodas. She turned around to find me behind her, my hand out-stretched, offering her the letter. I had not opened it, for I did not want to cry then and there in front of her.

It took her only a few seconds to read it, and then looking forever, it seemed, at the paper, not at me, she folded the note into squares, making it smaller and smaller. My mother performed this task very slowly, turning the note into a tiny object and gently sliding it into the pocket of her suit jacket. When she did look at me, I could not read her feelings. I knew I would never see the note again.

"What did he say?" I demanded.

"We'll talk about this after dinner," she told me firmly as she unpacked the groceries, lining them up neatly on the table. Kenya's giggling and laughter filled the living room, in thoughtless opposition to the dreadful loss of the moment. "Help me put these things away."

"Why'd he go?"

"I said we'll talk about it later," she reminded me harshly. "Don't say anything to your sister."

After we finished putting the groceries away, my mother went upstairs and changed into jeans and a sweatshirt and came into the kitchen, where I helped her cook dinner. How had she changed clothes so quietly, so quickly in the room without screaming? My mother worked fastidiously, preparing a small salad, frying veal chops, cooking rice, saying nothing, moving around the kitchen with dervishlike speed. Out of habit, and as a kind of wish, I set the table for four. My mother said nothing when she saw what I had done.

"Where's Daddy?" Kenya asked after we said grace. I looked at her sharply, trying to stifle her bubbling energy. She sat vigorously pumping her legs back and forth beneath the table. Ma Adele had taken her to get her hair cornrowed over the weekend, and Kenya sat, shaking her head, her braids twisting and flying like winged toys around her face.

"Your father's going to be gone for a while. He had to go to a school out in Michigan to teach. He'll be back for the holidays," my mother said, her voice treading so delicately over a possible eruption of emotion from us that I knew she was lying about him coming back.

"Why didn't he say good-bye?" Kenya asked, her face collapsing in on itself in panic.

"He didn't have time, I guess."

"Where in Michigan?" Kenya persisted.

"You don't need to know," my mother snapped, staring at her plate.

"Why not?"

"Just eat."

"I don't want to. Why's he going to be gone so long?"

"If you can't settle down, then leave the table," she told Kenya, her gaze so angry and confused it was awful to behold.

"I will," Kenya screamed in churlish anger.

Kenya bolted angrily from the table, stomped out of the kitchen, and noisily ran up the stairs. I prayed she didn't look in my parents' bedroom, that she didn't open my father's drawers or closets. Rooted in my chair, I sat facing my mother, who had resumed eating. I could not move. This time the feel of my father's leaving was absolutely perilous. I sat staring at my mother, my hands clenched in my lap. She couldn't bear my gaze, and even though she had not finished, rose from the table and cleared the dishes.

A few days later my father called. We were in the family room, looking at television, when the phone rang. The transformation in my mother as she held the receiver informed me that it was my father. She clutched the phone tensely but said nothing, listening to my father for maybe ten minutes. Then she handed the phone to me. The sound of my father's voice erased my fear even as he said the kind of things I hated to hear because they seemed to mean nothing. Help your mother. Be good. Take care of Kenya. Hearing this charge, I wondered who was going to take care of me.

My father had gotten a visiting professorship at a college in Michigan. My mother had known nothing about his application for the job or his plans to leave. What we didn't know then is that we'd lose my mother too. She didn't leave us immediately, she took flight incrementally, over time, in small doses.

My father gave me an address and a phone number where he lived in Ypsilanti, Michigan. I wrote, choosing letters over the phone because even then I believed that the written word, sculpted and planned, simply held more power than any words I spoke. I feared he could ignore the plaintive tone of my voice, but surely not the summons inherent in every letter I wrote.

In the beginning my mother woke each morning, showered, dressed, supervised our preparations for school as she always had, waking at six o'clock, rising to subdue the day ahead. Before my father left, Kenya and I caught the bus to school. Now we left early so she could drive us. I don't know what that half hour in the car with us meant, but my mother honored it. She honored that time even as Kenya sat in the back sulking, entrenched within the grip of a determined mourning of my father's absence. There were days she fell mute, refused to say a word to my mother or me. She ran away to my grandmother's house, insisting that she didn't want to come home and wouldn't until my father came back. In the evenings her teachers called my mother, asking what was wrong. Just as she had lied to us, my mother lied to them too.

It was my father who told me the truth. One night he called to speak to tell Kenya and me good night, and before I called Kenya for her turn to speak to him, I asked him why he went away, and if what my mother had said was true, that he'd be home in time for Christmas. He told me he wasn't coming back to live with us. "I don't want to hit your mother again. I don't want her to forgive me again for doing it."

I had seen their fights. There were never black eyes, bruises, broken bones. The pushing, the throwing, the pulling, seemed an extension of their conversations. But I had felt and tended to my own internal injuries, inflicted just by being a witness. After each fight my body was numb, my senses frayed. I couldn't sleep. I was afraid to.

It was usually at night that I saw the signs of my mother's unraveling. She'd sit for hours in the family room with the curtains parted, staring out the window as though she were staring all the way to Michigan. She missed my father, she told me, and I wondered if she missed as well the blood-pumping fusillade of pain that joined them. She seemed purposeless without him and began to sit in the living room or her bedroom all night in her gown with the light on. She couldn't sleep after a while and lay on the sofa all night, watching television. She could get through the day at work fine, it seemed,

staying no longer than before. But it was night that trampled the day's display of competence. Night was composed of hours that were stubborn and mocking, hours that stopped, stalled sometimes at will. I wondered sometimes if the nights were as long where my father was.

Ma Adele came to see us often during those months, sometimes two or three times a week, and her visits always had the feel of a rescue mission. She was clearly worried about my parents' separation, for she had always felt a great deal of affection for my father, and despite the turbulence of my parents' marriage had hoped they would find a way to stay together. She'd come sometimes to the house before my mother got home from work, and under the guise of preparing dinner or supervising us, she'd subtly interrogate Kenya and me, asking when we had heard from my father, did we know when he was coming back. More than once she told us to call her if we saw something about my mother that frightened us.

Sometimes she'd even spend the night, and she and my mother would stay up late talking. I'd sit at the top of the stairs, after having crept out of my room at the first sound of their voices. This was the only way I could find out what I needed to know.

"He took our life with him, the only life I've known for more than fifteen years," my mother said one night.

"Lena, you hadn't been happy in a long time."

"What married people do you know who even use that word?"

my mother asked cynically. "He ran away from home. Like a child." I could hear her suddenly stand up from wherever she had been sitting and begin walking around the room in that feverish, excited yet melancholy way I had seen her do sometimes when she thought she was alone, pacing in her bedroom.

"You couldn't go on like that," my grandmother said. "Maybe what he did was an act of courage."

"Courage?" my mother exploded.

"Maybe he felt that was the only way he could leave."

"You always took his side, felt he was the victim, I was the monster."

"Lena."

"No, admit it. You always took his side." My mother's voice was hysterical, rising.

"He's my son-in-law. He always respected me."

"And you always sympathized more with him."

"Lena, you're exaggerating. And please, sit down."

"Admit it."

"He came to see me once and told me he wanted to leave but he didn't know how. He said he felt trapped."

"And you never told me."

"He asked me not to."

"I'm your daughter."

"I made a promise."

"He wanted to be the boss, that's all."

"Lena," my grandmother said wearily, "in a good marriage nobody's the boss but everybody gets what they need. He told me you always reminded him what you had done for him."

"I did a lot."

"He was your husband, the father of your children. He felt like in your mind that counted for nothing. And the fights, Lena, he wasn't that kind of man."

"Ask Teresa or Kenya whether or not he was that kind of man, ask them what they saw."

"He wasn't fighting alone."

Finally my mother sat down. Then I heard her say, "After we hit each other the first time, there was no fear. I wasn't afraid to do it again or to take it. I wanted it to be over once it started. But, Mama, I also wanted to win."

"And you really thought there was a way you could," my grandmother asked incredulously, "with your children watching it all?"

My mother said nothing. I left the stairs and went back to my room, wishing I had remained in bed.

Our house took on a different look and feel. My mother kept the blinds down when she was at home, as though she were afraid our neighbors could see her decomposing just by looking through the windows. And so it always felt like a tomb in a house that had previously been open and filled, drenched most days in sunlight. She'd fill a wineglass and I'd see the hunger in her eyes, the need to be numbed, to be healed and comforted when she reached for the glass filled with wine that she didn't sip anymore but rather guzzled greedily, trying to quench some thirst I could not identify but felt in my own way too. She left for work each morning sober and alert, but when she came home she'd pour a drink first thing, as though the effort to get through the day had stripped her of something only spirits could replenish. I didn't invite friends over anymore, for I was ashamed of my mother and the things that went on in our house. When my girlfriends called me at night I no longer wanted to talk to them, for I had become vigilant, was always listening for the sounds of my mother coming undone or my sister needing me. I felt that I could no longer be a child. There were more important things to do than talk on the phone about boys.

She stopped eating, and I watched her sometimes grow queasy, absolutely sick at the sight of food I had prepared and set before her, on the nights she made it plain to Kenya and me that if we wanted to eat, we would have to call for a pizza or make something ourselves. Once I heard her throwing up in the hallway bathroom. The sound was so wrenching, I rushed to her and tried vainly to open the locked door. She opened the door, clutching the doorknob, doubled over in pain, but shook her head and waved me brusquely away. Still, I stood outside the door, listening to the awful sounds of her retching until I heard it stop.

I felt like an orphan, and of all the things I missed most I missed my mother's touch. In her anger and bitterness and despair she had retrenched, pulled in on herself, had withdrawn from Kenya and me so completely that I barely remembered the feel of her hands on mine, the touch of her lips on my cheek. One night when I knew she was asleep, I crept into her room to lie beside her and feel her warmth and presence. But she lay in a stupor, in the grip of a tomblike sleep induced either by pills or alcohol. I saw both on her night table. I crawled beneath the spread and the sheets and huddled close to her but felt nothing. I clung to the nylon straps of her gown, breathed in the musky, stale odor of her skin, let my hands touch her lightly but decisively. My mother lay like a hulking inert mass, alive but devoid of anything that could reach or preserve me. I lay there a long time, waiting to feel something, for her love to invade me the way it used to, just by our bodies being close. Nothing happened. I grew cold, frigid, beneath the spread beside her. She didn't touch us anymore, and so in a way I guess we were no longer real.

When her girlfriends came to visit, they brought casseroles so she wouldn't have to cook, and my mother donned another persona for them. They knew my father had left, but my mother had told them they were in the midst of a trial separation. They'd congregate in the family room, kicking off their shoes, comforting my mother with gossip and complaints about their own lives. When they worried that she was losing weight or that she looked like she wasn't getting enough sleep, she'd say, "Sure I look like hell. I'm losing my marriage, how else am I supposed to look?"

Her bravado would quell the questions, inspire more expressions of concern, pledges to do anything she needed. And even when my godmother, Constance, sometimes managed to ask me about my mother, I was torn by loyalty to my mother and fear of her, fear that had not yet fully bloomed but that had been planted.

During one of those visits, "Aunt" Constance came upstairs to use the bathroom, leaving my mother and her other friends downstairs. When she had finished, she knocked on the door of my room and asked if she could come in. She found me lying on my bed on my back, staring at the ceiling, a position I had adopted with growing frequency. Sometimes I'd lie like that for hours.

She pulled up a chair beside the bed and asked me how I was doing in school, if I wanted to go to Potomac Mills with her and her nieces on the weekend, and if I had talked to my father lately. She asked all this in a soft, mellow voice that was nothing like the raucous, feisty sound of her judgments and laughter in our living room. Then she asked me about my mother.

"How's her health, Teresa? She doesn't look good to me."

"She's okay, I guess. She's not eating as much as she used to."

"Is she drinking, I mean more than before?"

"Why are you asking me these questions, Aunt Constance? She hasn't done anything wrong," I said, turning away from the ceiling for the first time to look at her.

"I didn't say she had, Teresa, but she's under a lot of stress now and she tries to hide things, but I don't like what I see."

"All I see is my father isn't here anymore."

"She really needs to be seeing someone she can talk to about this. But she won't hear of it when I suggest it. I want you to watch her carefully."

"You want me to spy on my own mother?"

"I want you to call me if you feel you need to."

I sat up and stared at a woman to whom I had told secrets I had never even told my mother and said, "She misses my father. She wants him to come home. That's all."

A week before Christmas, Ma Adele took us to get a tree. The night we bought it from a lot on Georgia Avenue it began to snow, and the sight of the snow set Kenya jumping up and down with glee. At home we filled the tree with decorations, many of which my father had helped us make over the years, Black angels with papier-mâché wings and Afros and kente-cloth scarves around their necks. In the middle of the decorating my mother stopped and retreated to her room. While Nat King Cole sang "The Christmas Song," Kenya and I finished the tree as slowly and begrudgingly as if it were a form of punishment. Ma Adele brought cups of hot chocolate into the room on a tray. My father called us on Christmas Eve and asked if we had gotten the boxes he had sent us. We had. In the boxes were a small portable stereo for me and a computer for Kenya. He didn't send anything for my mother.

Kenya descended into some region of anger and despair from which neither my mother nor I could reclaim her. She started sleeping with me, burrowing into my side in her sleep, tunneling for some refuge that she never found. One night I felt the trickle of her pee, warm, surprising, soaking through my gown, turning the mattress sodden and damp. When I gently woke her, told her what she had done, her tears of shame were unceasing. I turned on the light and helped her out of her gown and into a fresh one and changed into a new one myself. Kenya sat in the middle of the bed, pleading, "Don't tell, Teresa, please don't tell."

I sneaked into the hall closet, hoping my mother wouldn't hear me, got new sheets and towels to put on the bed, then stuffed my urine-soaked sheets into the hamper. In the morning when my mother went out I rushed to the laundry room and washed and dried the sheets before she got back. Some force had entered the house when my father left, and we began, without ever talking about it, to sense the imposition of new, more fragile borders between us all.

Still Kenya's campaign to bring my father back home was unyielding. One evening when my mother was cooking dinner at the stove, Kenya, who had been morose, sullen, doodling instead of doing her math, threw down her pencil and walked to the stove and stood behind my mother and screamed, "I want Daddy back." My mother turned from the stove and whispered through clenched teeth, "Don't say another word to me about him." Looking at her face, I imagined I could hear her heartbeat thudding angrily, plotting some dangerous act. "Don't say another word, do you hear?" she said again, her voice quiet, precise, and so deadly as she stared at Kenya that I could not predict what she would do in the next moment.

What she did, what I would never have expected her to do, was to grab Kenya's shoulders so hard, Kenya screamed as my mother dragged her back to the table, where she lifted her like a rag doll and literally stuffed her in the chair, pushed the chair against the table so close that it was impossible for Kenya to move. Kenya sat stunned, her cheeks tear-stained, silent, trapped.

Standing beside Kenya, my mother poised her agitated, twitching hands like an arc over Kenya's head. Hands I had never seen before turned into fists that struck Kenya three times on the side of her face, hard sharp blows I could hear and feel in my heart. Then in an instant my mother crumbled onto her knees, lifted Kenya from the chair, and held her in her arms. Snot bubbles bloomed in Kenya's nose, her suppressed tears erupted as a symphony of hiccups. A wail thundered up from the pit of her stomach. A sliver of blood broke through the skin of my sister's temple where my mother had landed the first blow.

My mother motioned for me to come to her. Timidly, unwillingly, I found a place at my mother's side. I held Kenya too. My mother tried to quiet Kenya's tears and stop the flow of her own. They were both holding me close, so tight I wanted to break free. But I held on. What else could I do?

One Sunday morning I woke up and heard noises in the attic. I had not dared to go there since my father left us. Kenya was not beside me. The covers on her side of the bed were thrown back. Barefoot, I crept up the narrow, enclosed winding staircase that led to the attic and pushed open the door to see Kenya sitting on the floor in her nightgown. She was drawing on a large, poster-sized sheet of paper, seeming to be happy and possibly content. My father had not taken his paintings. Maybe he would come back. Standing in the doorway, I saw, too, how much Kenya looked like my father. She had his high, wide forehead, and when she drew she held her pencil or crayon with a steely grip just like he did. I could see the scar on her temple and it reminded me of the dreams that had descended after that night in the kitchen. I had wanted to tell Ma Adele or my father. But I loved my mother too much. And maybe, I thought, if I didn't speak of it, one day amnesia would replace this fear, this guilt, Kenya's scar would disappear, and time would move us backward to where we used to be. Kenya finally looked up, saw me in the door, and smiled.

"I'm drawing a picture to send to Daddy," she said. I slowly entered the space and sat on the floor beside my sister. I could smell my father's paints, his oils, everything about him in the room. How would I ever walk back out the door?

Kenya was the brave one. Watching her leaning over the large square of paper, her butt in the air, her face bunched in concentration as she drew, I realized that she came up here often. Now I knew that on other nights when I woke up and thought she had returned to her room, she had come here instead.

I had watched my sister grow younger, more waiflike and innocent, with the passage of each day that my father was away. It was as though she were shedding months and years, traveling, in self-defense, back before all this had happened, to where she thought she might be safe.

A small stack of colorful crayon drawings lay on the floor beside her, one of my father blowing out candles on a birthday cake, one of Kenya sitting in his lap as he read her a story, one of the three of us at the kitchen table playing Uno. She hadn't used crayons in years, had used watercolors or oils as soon as my father discovered her proficiency with the brush. The brash, waxy colors, the nearly primitive style of the drawings, didn't look anything like what I'd grown used to seeing Kenya draw.

"Maybe he just forgot the things we used to do. Maybe he doesn't remember," she said, coloring with hard, brazen strokes, a bright yellow sun poised over my father's head as he lay in a hammock in our backyard, the rays' cheerful hands reaching out for him.

"He wouldn't forget, he couldn't," I assured her.

"Then how could he stay away?"

"I don't know."

"I think he just forgot," Kenya insisted, the explanation less damning than anything else she could have easily concluded.

"Will you take me to the post office to mail these to him?" she asked, tossing the crayon aside and sitting up, resting on her knees, surveying the drawings with eyes that told me nothing.

"Sure."

She looked at me, however, to ask, "Can we send them special delivery so they can get to him fast? So he can come home soon?"

I promised we could.

Now I had something to hide, as well as something to fear, and while I masked my anguish poorly, I defeated the feeble attempts of teachers and the counselors at school to question me about my home life as my grades plummeted and I dropped my friends.

While my sister haunted my father's attic work space in the middle of the night when she could not sleep, or just when she needed to feel him near, I began to steal, stupidly, daringly, from the drugstore in the shopping center several blocks from where we lived. I stole small combs, or a wrist brace when I injured my arm in gym, toothbrushes, notebook paper and pens, functional things I could justify. When I walked out of the store calmly, easily, with some object that belonged to me for free, things made sense. Theft made the nagging pain at the base of my neck go away. Fondling a tube of lipstick, or a jar of Noxzema I'd stuffed into my pocket, made me think my father would come home.

By the new year my mother did not pressure me to do my homework; sometimes she spoke no more than a few words to me and Kenya all day. I'd find her asleep on the sofa when I got up in the morning. She gained weight.

It was a Saturday morning when it happened. I woke up to find Kenya dressed. She had combed her hair and was packing her clothes in a small suitcase Ma Adele had given her for her birthday. "What are you doing?" I asked groggily, wondering if I was dreaming.

"I'm going to find Daddy." She thrust a small drawstring leather pouch at me, saying, "I've got ninety-three dollars and fifty-five cents saved up from my allowance and birthday and Christmas gifts. I can take the train to Michigan."

"Are you crazy? Mom won't let you do that."

"Well then, I'll run away again. This time I'll stay."

Kenya headed out of my room, holding the suitcase with both hands. I followed her and then for a few breathless moments we stood at the entrance to my mother's room.

My mother was curled beneath the covers watching the Road Runner zip across the TV screen. She had a cold; Kleenex littered the bedspread. The room smelled medicinal and her throat was wrapped in a scarf. My mother turned to look at Kenya and me through bloodshot, puffy eyes, and for a moment it appeared she did not know who we were.

"I'm going to find Daddy," Kenya announced, moving into the room, standing at the side of the bed, poised, ramrod straight, as if to heighten the dramatic effect of her words.

Kenya's pronouncement brought my mother back to us in a way she had not been in months.

My mother turned off the television with the remote she had been clutching, and the light, sound, the atmosphere of familiarity the television had created evaporated. Staring at Kenya, squinting as though trying to bring her into focus, with a harsh movement that sliced the air like the wind, my mother threw off the blankets. Whom did my mother see in the moments after Kenya uttered those words, my father, out of reach, or did she really see my sister?

"So you want to go find your daddy?" she asked, untangling the sheets that swathed her. Kenya stepped back a little, automatically, reflexively, and brushed up against me, stumbling, dropping the suitcase.

A throaty, unfamiliar cruelty throbbed in my mother's voice as she said, "Well, I'll help you get ready." Barefoot, wearing a flannel nightgown, she brushed purposely past us into the hall where we kept our coats and got Kenya's jacket out of the closet. She strode back to us where we stood in the bedroom doorway, our fear so potent, I wondered how my heart still beat, and how Kenya managed the jagged, nervous breaths I heard wailing, muffled and awful at my side.

Dangling in my mother's hands, the navy blue pea jacket was tantalizing, hanging there in the air between us, nearly alive, the arms twitching and dancing. My mother bloomed mammoth, intractable as she stepped toward us, displaying the coat as temptation and trap. There was nothing in her eyes at all. No anger. No recognition. No fear. Kenya clung to me, her small, thin nails digging into my side through my pajamas. In a quick, fierce move my mother stuffed Kenya's arms into the jacket even as Kenya resisted and began to cry.

"Mom, she didn't mean it."

"No, she wants to find her father. I think that's what she should do," she insisted, her voice filled with conviction, pledging never to back down from this belief.

"Come on," she ordered Kenya, holding out her hand. Kenya turned and looked back mournfully at me. I convinced myself that this was a game my mother was playing, a ruse to teach Kenya a lesson. This was not real, and it would be over soon. Despite my sister's tears, my mother pulled Kenya down the hallway. At the top of the stairs they stopped. Kenya gazed down the steps in wary, panicked confusion.

"Go find your precious daddy," my mother taunted her. "Go find him. See if he cares," and turned away. In that moment Kenya panicked and turned around, grasping the sleeve of my mother's robe. But my mother, her face gnarled, twisted and angry, her voice throbbing with such tumult, it was unrecognizable, turned and pried Kenya's grip finger by finger from her arm, grabbed Kenya's wrist and pushed my sister away. Kenya tried to lean forward, flailing to hold on to the banister.

When my sister stopped falling, her left foot was caught in the wooden spokes of the banister and her body was sprawled over the last three steps. Her neck was twisted as though she were looking for something behind her, trying to see just where and how she would fall. When I finally looked at my mother, no more than twenty feet from me, it seemed as though she stood on the other side of the world.

He was going to be late and he wasn't even going to try to figure if he was stalling for time, or interpret the meaning of his bed filled with jackets, slacks, and shirts. He'd dressed completely from shirt to shoes three times, and still didn't know what to wear. Ryland stood in his boxer shorts, trying not to look at the clock, which would inform him that even if he was dressed right then, and ready to walk out the door, by the time he drove through Friday-night traffic to Georgetown, he'd still be late.

The thought of how late he was going to be drove him into the bathroom. Again. He'd used the toilet three times since he got out of the shower. When he finished, as he washed his hands he looked in the mirror. What would Lena see? Would she gaze at his face selectively, choosing to take in only the trimmed beard and the glasses he'd have to wear to read the menu and ignore the dazed quality that still haunted his face? It had taken a long time to construct this face. To reconstruct it and salvage it. For longer than he could stand to recall, he'd felt like a form of walking talking living breathing wreckage, mangled and deformed. And that's how he'd looked. Sometimes he'd go for days not even looking at himself in the mirror. But time passed and he got his face back. Not the old one, but a face that at least didn't scare away people who wanted to buy his paintings, or students he was teaching or women that he tried to love, in a fog of fumbling, hesitant actions he couldn't control or remember after the fact.

Wiping his hands on a towel, Ryland thought he didn't look too bad. And the other face, the awful one that had slowly decomposed, most days he couldn't even remember it. So he'd be late. But they'd waited for four years. But had they waited really? Certainly he was sure she had. In prison, how did time move? What else was there to do but wait? Didn't your life stand still? Whenever he'd thought of Lena at Farmingham, he'd thought of her frozen in time. Like one day she'd come back from the dead the way Kenya never would. Teresa told him about Lena singing in the choir of the small church on the prison grounds, teaching illiterate women to read. He heard that Lena had lost some of the edginess, the tension that he knew had fueled her ambition and everything that had happened.

Even if she hadn't willed it, even if she'd fought it, she'd come back changed. Life had happened to Lena, had found and altered her. The gates of Farmingham hadn't kept it out.

But surely he hadn't waited. Not for the woman who'd killed his child. What would he have waited for? He'd sent her the separation papers because he refused to wait. And yet when it was done, when they'd signed the papers, sold the house on Sycamore Street, split the profits, set up a fund for Teresa, all of it accomplished through lawyers, without even having to speak to each other, he'd still felt her as a burden. He'd washed his hands of her. But they still weren't finished.

And sometimes he woke up in the middle of the night, after he thought that he was free, and go look into the bathroom mirror at that face and know that because of the daughter who still lived and the one who died, liberation was a dream. They'd said till death do us part. Well, death had. But they were still bound. All the lawyers in the world, a ton of legal forms, wouldn't change that. He'd waited.

The only difference was she'd known she was waiting. He, foolishly, had no idea that he was.

Standing at the foot of his bed, Ryland looked around the room at the paintings of his daughter and wondered if Lena, when she saw them, would think him a genius or a madman. Kenya had become an integral force, taken for granted like his ability to move or think. He knew his daughter was dead. He knew she lived in these rooms with him too.

There had been between him and Kenya a bond stronger than what he had given her through DNA and love. With each year that passed, she became more a reflection of him. Teresa was an amalgam, blessed with Ryland's height and his ability to stand back from things, to be present and distant simultaneously. She had Lena's drive and her willingness to plow unstoppable through obstacles and the world.

But Kenya was a miniature expression of him. She too went for long periods without talking, but in her silence Kenya seemed to offer up her muteness as her expression. He took her to museums and galleries like the Phillips Gallery housed in a Victorian brownstone on P Street, or the Museum of African Art and the National Gallery, where they'd been dozens of times. Her favorite was the Portrait Gallery, home of the wonderful drawing of Langston Hughes by Winold Reiss, that made the poet look like a dusky, thoughtful angel. They saw the faces of their people there more than any other gallery in town. Kenya sensed this too and called it the gallery where they could see "us."

She had known instinctively how to fill a canvas. Was it art? She was not a prodigy. But she was clearly gifted. And it did not bother him when he realized that Kenya would one day be an even stronger, more original artist than he. Ryland saw the signs of this in a charcoal sketch she once did of Teresa. Kenya was eight then and she'd been drawing Teresa as Teresa sat unaware, deep in reading, as they all sat in the family room one Saturday evening. He was watching CNN, Lena was sewing. It was the kind of mundane, priceless moment of peace that kept him in his marriage. Rising to go into the kitchen for a glass of juice, Ryland walked past Kenya on the floor, stepped over her, and saw the image of Teresa she was drawing. He didn't stop, even when stunned by recognition of how daunting was her skill. In just a quick glance he could see the pathos and tenderness Kenya had engraved in the profile of her sister.

That night after the girls were in bed and Lena was in the shower, Ryland returned to the now-deserted family room and gazed at the drawing that Kenya had tossed on the coffee table before heading upstairs to bed. How could he warn her that the world resisted the addition of beauty, fought it tooth and nail. Should he tell her that her talent would spark envy and cruelty and that it could heal and answer prayers. Could he tell her of the sadness that would swallow her as soon as a canvas was finished, because created by human hands it was complete and still imperfect. Hearing Lena pad down the stairs, Ryland let the drawing fall from his hands back onto the table. No one had told him anything. But he swore he would draw Kenya a map.

But the paintings of his daughter had not quelled his guilt or his conviction that he should have gone to prison too. His crime was abandonment, dereliction of duty. He had never gone to see Lena at Farmingham because he'd have to witness what he surely thought he deserved. His departure had been cold-blooded. It had rescued him and doomed his child.

He had known for months that he had the job at the college in Michigan, but he didn't tell Lena because if he thought about leaving, he never would. He'd simply have to get up one morning and go, not thinking about his daughters and what felt like too many years and reasons why and why not. So he had signed the contract with the school in May and all summer hoarded and honored the knowledge that he would leave. Even when they drove to the Outer Banks in North Carolina and spent two weeks and he and Lena spent so much time with the girls, shopping, sight-seeing, swimming, boating that at night they were so tired, there was no need to talk, he had not said a word. At Adele's annual Fourth of July picnic he had grilled the chicken, and to Kenya's delight set off the fireworks when it grew dark. He held her in his lap, sitting on the back porch when she fell asleep after a day of volleyball and horseshoes and hide-and-seek. The sound of her light snoring was a kind of music to him that night as he held her heavy in his arms, his arms aching but not ever wanting to let her go. Sitting on the porch with Kenya in his lap, Ryland had watched Teresa beneath the oak tree in the backyard, laughing and flirting with the grandson of one of Adele's neighbors. He wondered at the love he felt for her even as he lost her more and more each day. How, he wondered, would he live without his daughters always near? Through all the nights like that he had said nothing. He would have to leave without their knowledge; there was no other way.

The night of his return to Washington, a cold, brutal rain
stunned and chilled him as he got out of the taxi, lugging
his suitcase. Standing on the sidewalk, he was rumpled,
tired, afraid to enter his house, and even in the darkness he could tell
the street was the same. The houses had not crumbled, the sidewalk
was not cracked. The cataclysm that had visited his house had skirted
everything around it. Ryland stood shivering, his ears able to hear the
sound of raindrops magnified, pounding the street, wondering why
his house was chosen, looking at the houses on either side of his,
mouthing the question "Why my house, why me?"

When he opened the door he found and met Lena standing in the
foyer. Wearing knee socks and one of his old robes, clutching a glass
of water, so startled by his arrival, she instinctively drew back and
stumbled onto the stairs.

He placed his suitcase beside the door, stripping off his coat and
throwing it on top of his bag. "After Adele called me, I caught the
first plane out."

Lena muttered breathlessly, "Ryland, my baby's gone."

"What happened?" he asked, standing before his wife, looking
down upon her, wondering how he would ever touch her again.

"I don't know," she whispered, slowly looking up at him. Everything on her face told him that she had just told him all she could.

But still he shouted, "What do you mean, you don't know? How'd she fall down the stairs?"

"We were arguing."

"And you threw her down the stairs?"

"It wasn't like that," Lena moaned.

"What was it like? Tell me why my daughter is dead," Ryland demanded, halting his manic movements and standing, arms outstretched at his sides in supplication.

"It all happened so fast."

Wide-eyed, astonished, Lena looked away from him and examined her hands. Her silence angered Ryland so that he grabbed her by the collar of her robe and lifted her from the stairs. "Tell me what happened. Tell me now."

Their faces were inches apart, and the sight of her eyes, red-veined, swollen from crying, forced him to release her, and Lena slumped onto the floor at the base of the stairs.

"Tell me something, please."

"She wanted to leave, to run away to find you. I told her if she wanted to leave, she could." Lena ran her hands through her hair, over her face.

The words had induced again the guilt that had washed over him in waves ever since Adele's call. If he had not left. If he had stayed, Kenya would be alive. He knew it. How could he expect Lena to speak the words he so brutally demanded of her, words that inflicted a punishment he was sure he deserved too. Rising from the floor, Lena sat again on the stairs. She buried her face in her hands, concealing yet magnifying the sound of her sobs. Then she looked at Ryland and told him, "We were standing at the top of the stairs. I told her to go if she wanted to."

"Did you touch her?" he asked, hoping she'd say no, that the answer would miraculously be true.

"I touched her. Yes. But not like that. Not like that," she protested wildly.

"You touched her and she ended up dead."

"If I pushed her, I didn't mean to. I was angry. I was hurt." Lena struggled up from the stairs, facing him now. "You'd left. And she wanted to."

"So you wanted to stop her from leaving for good. My God. Where is she?"

"There's going to be an autopsy."

"An autopsy?"

"To find out exactly what caused her death."

The thought of Kenya's body in a refrigerated morgue somewhere downtown unsettled Ryland so, he stumbled into the family room and slumped onto the sofa.

"And Teresa?"

"With Mama."

"Why's she there?"

"The authorities, the police, they said she couldn't stay here."

"Why not?"

"Ryland, please," she begged, backing away from him.

"Why not?"

"Because of what happened. They're investigating for possible abuse."

"Abuse? I don't believe this, any of it. When can she come home?"

"I don't know," Lena whispered abjectly, wearily. She stood before him like a magnificent edifice that had been razed. Their daughter was dead and Ryland sat trying to convince himself that he could indeed walk over to Lena, touch her, comfort her, even find in her arms solace for himself. When she began a hesitant, shifting walk toward him, Ryland halted her, saying, "Why don't you go on to bed, I can't sleep now, I'll be up in a while."

"Do you think I can sleep?"

"Lena, please." He was afraid he would break down and wondered why it was so important even in this moment to deny her that sight.

Alone in the family room, Ryland refused to believe Kenya was dead, knew he wouldn't until he saw her body. But he sat knowing, despite disbelief, that it was true. Although he did not believe her dead yet knew that she was, his daughter was already a fulsome, sensual presence, the smell of her skin, the tinkling bright sound of her laughter, his dreams for her, the sight of her moments after her birth, the sound of her wheezing when she had an asthma attack, the sight of her boyish, reed-thin body, nude and slick after a bath, the impatience glittering in her eyes when she wanted their attention, it all rose up inside him, a raging fist of reminiscence on which he feared he would choke. His daughter had died and her life passed miragelike before his eyes. He craved her, heard her, remembered her, and saw her. And crying, unable to feel his own tears, in one luminous, lucid moment, Ryland wondered how one could survive if memory did not exist.

He walked to the window and saw harsh, cold rain still pounding the streets and the wind littering the night with a wild hail of branches, leaves, and debris. The night, chilly and rainswept, the flooded streets were more welcoming than the room in which he stood. He grabbed his coat and walked outside to Lena's car. Before opening the car door, he turned his face skyward and opened his eyes but could not see the stars, saw only heavens closed against him, a grim sky of unparalleled darkness.

It was after midnight, but he was sure Adele would still be awake.

And surely he'd see Teresa. The streets were slick and dangerous and deserted, the residential areas he drove through, slumbering and unaware. Still, as he passed the sleeping houses, peering at them through the rain-soaked windshield, he wondered who inside them would open the door once the sun rose that day to find policemen or some stranger or friend standing on the porch, waiting to tell them their husband, mother, or child was dead. As he drove slowly through the streets, Ryland looked at the houses but saw in his mind the people inside vulnerable and asleep.

Block after block, the streets were flooded and trees struck by lightning, their trunks split in two, lay massive yet helpless across lawns blocking parts of the street. He'd heard and seen and felt the rain. Why hadn't he heard the thunder?

Adele opened the door wordlessly, her hair in rollers, wearing her gown and robe. Ryland slumped onto the sofa in the living room.

"What time did you get in?" she asked.

"About two hours ago."

"Have you been home?"

He flinched at the sound of the word but nodded his head and said yes.

"I spent all day with her there, cooked dinner. I wanted to stay until you arrived, but around four o'clock she told me to leave. But I talked to one of the neighbors, who stayed with her awhile."

"Where's Teresa?"

"Upstairs, asleep. I think. I hope anyway."

Adele sat before him in her favorite wing chair, her face bunched into a mask of befuddlement and puzzled pain that made her appear to be gazing past Ryland, to not be seeing him even as she looked straight at him. He didn't know it that night, couldn't know it, but that gaze would haunt her for nearly a year.

"Adele, what happened?"

"I don't know, Ryland. And does it matter?"

"You better believe it matters. My daughter's dead," he whispered through clenched teeth, although he wanted to shout the words.

"And you have another one who's alive."

"I shouldn't have left."

He stood up, for he found that it was impossible for him to sit down. Moving, pacing, made him feel in control.

"Was it so hard to love her?" Adele asked.

"You know, at this moment I don't know. I can't even remember." But he remembered everything. The sinking, damned feeling of being almost fifty and nobody knowing his name, the fear that he'd always be a modestly successful illustrator, graphics designer, and painter. The sight of Lena being promoted to manager and hearing her complain about the office intrigues while she earned five or six times what he pulled in. And he remembered the slow curdling of his admiration for her become fear that everything she did under the guise of helping him was a reminder that he didn't measure up. He remembered the canvases he'd destroyed—only he knew about that—three months before he left, so sure was he that he was a fraud. Sitting in his mother-in-law's house, Ryland remembered that it had been hard to love anybody for a very long time.

The time in Michigan helped him see all that. He'd even thought while he was away that maybe when he came home in the summer they could try again.

"Why don't you look in on Teresa?"

"I should," Ryland said, grateful that someone was telling him what to do, that he could stop pacing the floor and do something else with his body that was so jittery and on edge.

In the guest room on the second floor Ryland fell on his knees beside the bed where Teresa slept. The sodden, damp odor of his coat was overpowering, filled the room with a heavy stench. On his knees, beside his daughter, in the dark, without thinking, he joined his palms. Although he had not prayed consciously in years, he closed his eyes and mouthed the word "God." But the word brought forth nothing he could use or hold on to, not even relief. Opening his eyes, he saw that his movements had awakened Teresa.

"Daddy," she whispered, the word pulling him toward her, inspiring him to hold her tight. Ryland released her and turned on the light beside the bed. She blinked and shielded her eyes. His daughter in his arms had given him what the one-word prayer had not.

Teresa had wanted them all to know that she was no longer a child. But lying in the small bed, her face, which he had not seen in six months, was a child's face, unscathed, trusting even as it bore the evidence of shock.

"I'm sorry it took this to bring me back. To bring me home." He said the word for her. "How are you? Were you there when it happened?"

Teresa nodded. Watching the closemouthed assent, given up haltingly, persuaded Ryland not to ask what she saw. There would be no forgiveness for either of them if he asked or if she answered.

"Where's Mom?"

"She's at the house."

"Will you stay a little while?"

"I'll stay all night."

"No, Daddy. Mom needs you."

Ryland sat on the bed and watched Teresa fall again into sleep, and then he did as his daughter asked, he went home.

When he returned home, Ryland stripped off his coat and clothes and fell onto the sofa and slept there. Going upstairs the next morning, Ryland's hands reflexively shook the banister, appraised it with his touch. But it was sturdy. There was no weakness, no buckling of the wood. He had heard about families who lost children and kept the child's room as it was, who didn't change a thing, families who continued to set a place at the table each night for the dead child.

Now Ryland knew why. Inside her room Kenya's Rollerblades stood against the wall that was filled with her drawings. When Ryland opened the closet and fell to his knees, he succumbed to the fantasy of finding Kenya huddled among her shoes on the floor and looking up at him in mischievous surprise. In her closet there were dresses, jeans, shirts, and blouses, and her hamper. Ryland touched them all, each one. And as much as all these things had belonged to Kenya, as much as her fingerprints and her breath were embedded in them, not one item brought her back. Each object merely confirmed that she was dead. Ryland had entered his daughter's room seeking a moment of brilliant total recall. Not even holding the large ivory-colored seashell that they brought back from Dewey Beach, hidden in a corner on the floor of the closet, and that Kenya had painted a rainbow of colors inside and out, resurrected her. He had dreamed while asleep on the sofa that he'd heard a knock on the front door and opened it to find Kenya on the stoop, dirty, tired, but safe. He picked her up and held her in arms that had been useless until that moment.

When he rose from the floor, Ryland wanted to stand in the middle of his daughter's room forever. No other place in the world held air that he could breathe. Ryland remained there as long as he could, sobbing as he stood behind Kenya's closed door. And when the first spasm subsided he wept again, sure now that his tears would bring her back. She must hear him, how could she not? But after he'd sat on Kenya's bed for three hours, vowing to wait patiently for her, to never admit to her death, even knowing that such a lie dishonored his daughter and damaged him, he reached for the doorknob, wondering how he would find his way into the room where Lena lay. The carpeted hallway was now a route he had never traveled, a journey of more punishment than promise. Stepping out of Kenya's room into the hallway, Ryland silently asked his daughter one final thing, "Tell me something to say."

Ryland arrived at Hibiscus, a trendy Jamaican restaurant in Georgetown, twenty minutes late. Lena stood up when she saw him approaching, and it was she who reached for him. Hugging her stiffly, Ryland's hands fumbled at her back, and before they fell to his sides, Lena held his hands and looked at him with a trace of apprehension that belied the display of affection.

The first moments were awkward, yet he remembered her so well, he nearly felt as though they'd slept in bed together the night before.

"You look good," he said, because that's what he thought and could think of nothing else.

"That always surprises people."

"I guess it surprises me too."

"Thank you for coming."

"Why wouldn't I?"

"I didn't assume you would. Did you?"

Before he could answer, their waiter, tall, broadly built, and olive-complexioned, introduced himself as Raoul and handed them their menus. He told them the specials and asked if they wanted a drink.

"I'll have a scotch," Ryland told him.

"White wine for me."

"So Teresa told me you're working in a bookstore."

"Until I figure out what to do next. And you?"

"I'm teaching at the Corcoran part-time, and still juggling everything else."

The waiter brought their drinks and asked if they were ready to order.

"Give us a few minutes," Lena said.

As they looked through their menus, Ryland put on his reading glasses. Lena laughed gently at the sight.

"The body turns on you," he said sheepishly, then added, "So why did you want to see me?" Raoul had taken their orders and he'd sipped his drink, and felt it bitter, fortifying, travel down his throat.

"We're still married," she said as though reminding him of something he might have forgotten.

"On paper," he said quickly, the sound of the words steeling him in some way as much as the drink. The scotch relaxed and sharpened him.

"Will you go back to accounting?" he asked, to change the subject.

"I don't want to live my life that way anymore." In the muted light of the restaurant, even sitting across from him in a sheer pale pink dress that accented the dark brown color of her skin, a thin shawl over her shoulders, she seemed insubstantial, more like a vision.

"What do you want most now?" he asked.

Ryland had decided, in the car on the way there, that he would play the role she had mastered so well in all their years together, the one who got the first and the last word.

"I don't know," she said. "But I do know that I always envied you when I was at Farmingham. You were out here with Teresa. You could see her when you wanted to. You didn't miss anything."

"You know why I couldn't see you. Why I never came."

"Some days I did," she said, staring at him, nothing neutral about her now. She was there with him, substantial, no doubt.

"I'd make up excuses for you. Try to understand. Tell myself your absence was no more than I deserved. But I didn't believe it."

"I came there once. But I couldn't get out of the car. I sat in the parking lot for two hours, then went to a motel and spent the night."

"What were you afraid of?"

"I don't know. Maybe having seen my daughter in a casket made it difficult for me to see my wife behind bars."

He had said the words gently, he thought, but he suddenly heard them as she must have when he saw Lena flinch and look down into her wineglass.

"I don't know if I really wanted you to come. Part of me did, of course," she said. "But then if you had, I'd have had to go through with you what I went through with Mama and Teresa, watching them leave. I never got used to that. I'd go back to my room or a work assignment or hang out with the other women and all the time I was struggling to hold on to something, anything, from the time spent with them. Even when Teresa became impossible in the last year, I'd find myself holding on to even our arguments, because then her voice filled my head and she was with me. She was mine."

"Did it work?"

"Sometimes. If I was in a place, a clear, clean place in my head where nothing else interfered with the process."

"What do you mean?"

"If I didn't start thinking about Kenya."

"I never stopped."

Over dinner and dessert they turned away from themselves, discussing instead President Clinton's chances for reelection and the Million Man

March. And it was in this zone that they found satisfaction, the return of ease. Even when they talked about Bosnia, the stakes didn't seem as high. Wars might rage around them, but they had laid down their arms, hadn't they? They could even imagine possible surrender.

As they left the restaurant, walking to Ryland's car Lena asked, "Could we drive to Sycamore Street? If you don't mind. I haven't been there since I came back. I didn't want to go alone."

"All right," he said, deciding not to tell her about the evenings he'd spent in front of the house, long after it was sold, in summer and spring, just watching over it, not believing they didn't live there anymore.

The street was sheltered by darkness, and they approached the house with a reverence they had felt unnecessary when they lived in it. A tricycle and a basketball sat on the front lawn. Ryland had loved the wide porch, the two-level lawn that sloped to the street, and the slender columns that rose from a brick base on the porch. The bamboo shades Lena had kept at the front windows had been replaced by curtains. A young girl walked around the room that had been Kenya's.

"They seemed like nice people," he told Lena. "I never met the kids. He's a dentist. She teaches elementary school."

"Did they know?"

"They said they didn't care."

From Sycamore Street they went to Ryland's apartment. When he turned on the light as they stood near the door, Lena shielded her eyes at first not, Ryland knew, against the light, but against Kenya remembered, remade. And as she entered the space, she looked around the room slowly, reluctantly, then she could not have found a way to stop looking if she had tried.

"All I could do was remember her," he said. "In the beginning it was just punishment. Then I let her take over. She wanted to come back."

Lena sat down slowly on the futon sofa and gazed at Kenya's images around her. He retreated to the kitchen and poured them both a glass of wine.

"I was afraid to come here. I didn't know what I'd feel," she said, reaching for the wine Ryland offered.

"What do you feel?"

"Proud that she was mine, and the sadness that never goes away. I thought seeing this would make it worse. Maybe it will make it bearable."

Turning to look directly at him, Lena asked, "When did you know you could go on?"

"It was gradual. When you went to Farmingham I felt like I fell off a cliff. Then there came a point, somehow, where I could see things again."

They watched the eleven o'clock news and when *Nightline* came on, Lena removed her shoes and placed her head on his shoulder. At midnight she asked if she could spend the night. He told her she could.

In his bed they made love in the unmasked presence of their daughter. He was not surprised. He could not be. Although he had willed himself to forget, he remembered everything. And so did she. The language they had created before, an antidote to everything else, sprang up before their eyes with each touch. In the aftermath, the feel of her weight against him, their odors fierce and mingling, filling the room, she asked him, "Was there anyone else while I was gone?"

"A friend leaving a bad marriage. She needed me. It happened."

"Did you need her?"

"I felt that I did. And you?"

"It happened once."

"Only once?"

"The day you sent me the separation papers."

"Why did you want to stay tonight?"

"I couldn't leave. I saw the paintings and I wanted to be here."

"We shouldn't do this again."

"All right," she said softly, then asked, "Do you want me to leave?"

"I just want to be honest. I don't know what you expect."

"I don't expect anything."

In the morning they drove to a pancake house for breakfast. Over coffee Ryland said, "I need to tell you something. In the end, it will affect us all one way or the other."

"What is it?"

"There's a gallery that wants to exhibit some of the pieces I did for Kenya," he said slowly, stirring his coffee, although he had not put anything in it.

"The gallery wants to mount a show in early September. It's been on the schedule for a while."

"Why are you telling me now? If telling me was so important, you'd have asked my permission months ago."

"Wait a minute, I did this as a courtesy."

"A courtesy," she nearly screamed, and then whispered in amazement. "That's my daughter too. That's our life, not just yours. She's not your private property. Not to sell to the highest bidder. And of course you'll reveal how she died."

"No. That was part of the arrangement. The canvases and sculptures will have to say everything. It matters to me how she died. The world doesn't need to know."

"I think it's an awful idea, and if there was anything I could do to stop it, I would. I won't come to see it."

"I respect your decision."

"How could you do this?"

"How could I not do it?"

When their orders came they ate in silence. When Ryland's eyes unavoidably swept over Lena's face, he curtained his glance, turning her into a wall or some other part of the restaurant decor. Still, days passed and he knew that he wanted to be with her. Ryland had looked at his wife and seen his daughter too. She'd come back with Lena and he had the chance to rediscover Kenya through the admixture of who he and Lena had become. And so a week after their breakfast in the pancake house, Ryland called her.

"I want to see you again," he'd told her. "I don't know why. Some of it's tied up with Kenya. Some of it's about you. I know it's going to hurt, but I don't care."

They'd meet mostly at night, after he'd spent the day painting and she'd been at the bookstore. Starved for each other, still angry, not sure what they were doing, certain it possessed a meaning they could not yet name, they quenched desire and sought shelter and scraped old bruises, inflicted new ones, and grieved for their daughter and themselves. One morning in his bed Lena asked, hungering as she so often did for definition, "What are we, lovers, friends?"

Ryland could think of nothing for a while, then he told her, "We're parents."

And now that she was back, he wanted to know everything, to hear the story he had chosen so carefully not to witness and by that refusal he sought to deny. But of course he *was* the story too, was its beginning, its middle, its end, and postscript. He asked Lena everything and she seemed willing, even eager, to tell. On Friday and Saturday nights he took her to the small, nondescript jazz clubs that lined Georgia Avenue. There they nursed drinks at small tables covered with checkered wax cloths, in rooms fragrant with the scent of barbecue, fried chicken, and potato salad, cigarette smoke and reefer, rooms so small they felt like someone's living room or kitchen. The music on the makeshift stages glowed and warmed and amazed them. Ryland knew the bartenders by name in many of the clubs. For after Lena went to prison he had haunted the clubs, sitting silent, save the tense request for another scotch and soda, before the bartenders for countless weekends, the laughter and the brittle transparent need etched in the voices, combining with the drinks to dull memory, temporarily stealing away the pain. And even after he broke through the hard glaze sorrow had drawn over his emotions and got tired of waking up sick and hung over and could once again paint and work, he returned to the clubs to hear the music and to lose himself among the faces and bodies and voices of people who would always be strangers.

In the clubs, before a set began or during the break, Lena would tell him about Farmingham, about the earnest young Episcopalian priest who served as chaplain. He brought Baptist preachers in to conduct services some Sundays, stocked the library with works by Thoreau, Emerson, and Lao Tzu. Gentle and softspoken, he'd served in Vietnam, then entered divinity school on his return.

"We talked a lot," she said.

"About what?"

"Faith. What else was there to talk about in a place like that with a man like him?"

"Teresa told me you sang in the choir."

"Does that surprise you?"

"I always thought you had a good voice."

"I joined, at first, just to have something to do. After a while I felt like I was singing myself sane. But you know, some women actually cried when their sentence was over and they were released."

"For God's sake, why?"

"Maybe the women at Farmingham were the only friends they had. Maybe they were leaving a girlfriend behind or they were afraid when they left, once they were on the streets they'd screw up again."

"Did you cry?"

For a few moments she said nothing, then told him, "Yes."

They both sat waiting for his response. When it did not come, Lena told him, "When I thought of coming back home, facing Teresa, you, and Mama, you better believe I cried."

"They'd visited you. You'd faced them before."

"Not really. It wasn't the same. When they came to Farmingham, they were facing me."

"You deserved better from me."

"I killed our child." Before Ryland could answer, the first strains of "Misty" anointed the small room and began to hush the conversations. They both turned to face the musicians. As the song neared to a close, Ryland reached across the table for Lena's hand.

In his apartment that night, after he opened the door, Lena whispered, "Don't turn on the lights." They were both tipsy yet knew the topography of the apartment so well that they found their way easily to the bed. They lay in the dark, holding on to each other as though they were either afraid or terribly in love. Beneath their clothes their bodies were humid and damp, for outside the night air was cloying even after midnight. Lena held Ryland tight around the neck. Soon she heard his gentle snores. Was he resting or asleep? She lay for a while against him, the sound of the music still humming in her ears. Then she lifted his Panama shirt, massaged his stomach, loosened his belt. She removed her own clothes methodically, and naked, she removed Ryland's clothes, his socks and shoes, lay down beside him, and pulled the sheet over them both.

They had made love often since the first time. And she knew they were simply saying good-bye. Their sex was inevitably tragic, even as there was contained in it more knowledge of each other and so more pleasure than had ever been possible before. He was awake and she could smell his tears, longed to feel them but did not touch his face.

"You deserved better," he said.

"We all did."

They never said anything to me at all about what they were doing. Sometimes I'd sit in my window late at night, watching my mother step off the porch into my father's car. I never asked her if she still loved him. I was afraid she'd say no. I never asked him if he wanted her back. I preferred to believe that he did.

My parents existed during all this in some realm of their own. I was unsure what I was seeing but invested it with the substance of my deepest needs. One evening I came downstairs and heard them in the kitchen. I knew Ma Adele had gone to visit a friend. But I hadn't heard my father come in. The sound of my parents' voices that evening in the house was startling, original, a sound at once unexpected and perfectly right.

They were in the kitchen, not the living room, and so I imagined them at a point where they were entirely comfortable with one another. I envisioned them breaking bread and with a thousand tiny actions and the inflection in their voices, building something that could renew us. I walked quietly into the living room, a few feet away from the entrance to the kitchen, and sat on my grandmother's navy velveteen sofa, the material pasty and warm against my legs.

I sat hushed as I listened to my parents. Despite the closeness of the two rooms, I could not hear what they said. I heard a spoon sliding across the rim of a cup, so I knew my father was drinking coffee, and I heard, too, the scraping of one of the chairs against the tile of the kitchen floor. My father, I suspected, was shifting in his seat, restless, attempting to get comfortable in the straight-backed chairs that he complained to Ma Adele had not been designed for a Black man's body. After a while I no longer strained to hear the words they exchanged. It was too difficult, for their voices were muffled, as though they were engaged in a moment of dangerous intrigue. Then at odd moments I'd hear a question, an answer, or a declaration, clear and articulate. But because I'd missed the words that had preceded it, the statement, clear as it was, had no meaning.

I listened not for what they were saying, but just for the sound of their voices. And in the moments when I heard silence I refused to believe it was an obstacle or an ending. In my grandmother's living room, hearing the voices of my parents, I was patient, full of belief.

I couldn't remember times before when they'd sat courageous, face-to-face, talking like this. Of course, I knew in my head there had been. But because I couldn't recall them with the intuitiveness that really told me what I knew, even if I couldn't prove it, those times weren't real. Momentarily, bitterness cut through my calm. I felt flushed. I trembled and wondered why this conversation had cost us everything.

I suddenly heard my mother laugh. It was a gentle sound, drenched in a reflective recollection of something dear, perhaps even precious. It was a laugh in which I heard who she had been long before I was born or even yearned for.

My father's voice erupted too, his more resonant, possibly hesitant, seeming to catch him by surprise. And then he gave in to it and I could hear his relief.

I sat so long, my eyes closed, imagining my parents' conversation, filtering it through my senses, that I didn't know they were in the room with me until I felt my father's hand on my shoulder.

"You okay?" he asked.

"Nothing's wrong," I assured him, standing up quickly, suddenly aware of my body, the room, everything.

"You sure?" My father stood close to me, his bulk blocking out everything else. I turned to look at my mother standing a few feet away from us, near and yet farther, it seemed, than she had been in the kitchen.

"We didn't know you were out here," she said demurely yet almost as if she could tell I had been straining to hear them. "Why didn't you let us know?"

"I was just sitting here, what's to tell?"

"So you aren't with your young man, what's his name, Solomon?" my father asked as he sat down on the sofa, pulling me down gently to sit next to him.

"We don't spend every moment together. And, Dad, you know his name is Simon."

"Solomon's not a bad name." He shrugged jovially.

"Neither is Simon. We're driving down to Myrtle Beach next weekend for a few days."

"You didn't tell me," my mother objected.

"I'm telling you now."

My parents exchanged a glance full of love and fear for me and the urge to protect rather than let me go. I had not seen that gaze in years. For too long there was no place in my life where it could exist.

"Is he a good driver? That's what, six or eight hours, and where are you staying, at a hotel or with friends?" my mother asked.

"He's never had a parking ticket."

"You'll leave a number and the address where you'll be staying, right?"

"Dad, will you please tell her I'm not a child?"

"But you are, Teresa. The only one we have left."

They sat, a scene of highway carnage unraveling in their minds as they thought of my trip. But Kenya had met her death on the steps we'd walked up countless times. They still thought the unknown was the thing to fear.

"All right," I conceded. "We'll be careful."

"And the job at the law firm, how's it going?" my father asked.

"Some days interesting, some days pretty boring. It depends on what I'm doing."

"You still thinking about law school?"

"Maybe."

"Which side would you represent?" my mother asked.

"I don't know. The prosecution usually wins. But it would be a good feeling to prove someone was innocent."

I'd never really thought about which side of the courtroom I'd want to be on. I knew only that I felt that my mother's sentence was irrelevant. The years she had spent at Farmingham had induced no absolution, no penance that she had not imposed upon herself. There was no way the punishment could ever fit the crime. Real restitution was impossible. In the end the search for justice, the need for punishment, was futile. But I didn't want to live in a world without the quest, as unsatisfying as it was.

When my father rose to leave, my mother followed him to the door and out onto the porch. I stood behind the screen door, watching them. Once again they exchanged words I could not hear.

I never thought of a future for my mother that summer. But she did. One Saturday morning I went with her to look at apartments. As we cleaned up the kitchen after breakfast, before leaving, she told me, "I can't live in that room much longer. It reminds me of prison. In it I keep remembering how at Farmingham I'd dream sometimes that I'd never get out and that even if I did, there'd be no one waiting for me."

"Where did we go? What happened to us?" I asked, closing the refrigerator, astonished at the rendering of my mother's dreams.

"I don't know. The dream would usually end with me knocking on Mama's door. It opened by itself. But the house was empty." She rinsed our plates and stacked them in the drainer and then wiped her hands on a towel.

"And you don't have much privacy either," I ventured, thinking about my father, wondering if I could trick her into telling me the meaning of what was happening between them. But she ignored my implication, saying only, "It's less about privacy than the need for a place of my own."

"Are you going to live alone?"

"I hope not. I'd like you to come with me."

When I said nothing, she rushed on clumsily, apologetically. "I can only ask if you'll consider the offer, Teresa. I can't force you. I wouldn't want to. But it would make me so—"

"Mom, stop, okay?"

"You don't have to tell me now."

"Why don't we just go? Please," I insisted.

She relented and reached for her purse on the counter.

She was planning a future, but in that place who would she be? I saw her swallow vitamins in the kitchen, B6 and calcium tablets, two or three times a day, inoculating herself against hot flashes and mood swings. She was going through the change and yet had already left one cataclysm behind. What more, she must have wondered, lay ahead?

If she was changing, what was she becoming? Were the alterations only physical, or was she evolving in her mind as well? How much of what was happening to her was renewal, how much mere adjustment? She didn't look different. So whatever was happening to her was camouflaged. Would the next few years be ripening or ruin? She would bleed no more, could have no more children. But there must be more to it than that, I suspected. If she lost such miraculous potency, what would replace it?

I'm sure she would've wondered what was left, what was possible now. My mother stopped eating meat and smoking cigarettes sometime before Labor Day. And she began to walk religiously, every single morning. She bounded down the stairs in T-shirts and shorts and athletic shoes and walked for forty-five minutes around our neighborhood. Some mornings, as I waited at the bus stop to go to work, I'd see her a block away, sun visor perched on her head, walking fast, rhythmically, with a wide stride. If she continued at that pace, I figured she'd live another seventy-five years. Was that what she wanted? Was she bargaining with her genetic code for more time?

I'd been at home some mornings when she came back into the house from her walks, glistening with sweat, slowly entering the house, slightly surprised, it seemed to me, at what she had done. She made me think of some middle-aged Amazon not living her life, but charging through it. Haywire hormones and fluctuating estrogen levels pumped something into my mother. Even as she was being depleted, she was blossoming too.

How did my father enter her body when they were together? A body that he would remember but that was shifting and ever new beneath his touch. Romantically, foolishly, I fantasized that my parents experienced only sexual nirvana. How did my mother receive my father? Confidently, or like a beggar filled both with gratitude and wretchedness?

But I know her. I am pretending here that I do not, and I do. My mother would have determined after the first hot flash to never submit to another one. In the room across from mine that threatened to become the circumference of her life, she'd have dreamed of the rest of her life, hungering for it, tasting it in daydream, harnessing its potential and existing so full of it that she could not have answered my questions about menopause even if I had asked. Menopause would have given her back the searing, greedy appetites tapped down flat and made inconspicuous by prison.

In the next half of her existence, both less and more would be at stake. There would be no getting over my sister, but one day Kenya would let her go because she loved her.

A week before Simon left for Atlanta, Ma Adele invited him over for dinner. Afterward we sat out in the backyard, under my grandmother's oak tree.

"Have you thought about us?"

"Don't you know that's all I think about," I teased him.

"Come on, I mean it. I'm assuming we have a future. I want to know that we do."

"I thought you did."

"Look, when I leave—"

"Simon, you're going to college, not off to war."

"But I'm leaving you here."

"I'll be faithful."

"I know that. I just don't want to lose you."

"You won't."

"I want to be sure."

He handed me a small box retrieved from his shirt pocket. I knew what was inside.

"I love you."

When I said nothing, he said, "I don't know what else to say, Teresa. We can wait. When you graduate, you can come to Atlanta. They've got law schools down there. Good ones."

I opened the box. The gold band was unadorned yet beautiful. I kissed him gently but felt consumed with hunger for him, wondering if I could ever be satisfied.

"Aren't you afraid?" I whispered.

"Of what?" he asked, genuinely surprised.

"Marriage."

"Why should I be?" he asked, clearly puzzled.

"Maybe you didn't see things growing up in your house that made you afraid to fall in love. I did."

"My parents didn't have a perfect marriage," he said defensively. "They managed. I know there were times it was hard for them. I didn't always know why. But I knew it was."

"How'd you know?" He shifted beside me, nervous, squirming, looked toward the house where my grandmother was probably settled before the television. I did not feel resistance in his silence but rather a struggle through some region I would not let him circumvent.

"There was this period of a couple of years," he said. "It started when I was twelve or thirteen. My mother looked dazed a lot. My father worked all the time or was never home. But the year before the accident they were closer than I ever remember them."

"That didn't frighten you?"

"Why should it?"

"Did they argue?"

"That was the funny thing. Sometimes I wished they would. Just so I'd know they cared."

"You never thought you'd grow up and be like them?"

"What's wrong with that? They stayed together."

"They weren't happy."

"Sometimes they were."

"But your mother?"

"I don't know that my father caused everything she felt or didn't feel."

"Did you ever ask her?"

"I wouldn't have known how."

"I'm sure your father didn't either."

"What're you saying?"

"I just wonder if anyone was listening to her."

"I'll always listen to you. Don't try to analyze my love, Teresa, just accept it."

"They couldn't let go when they should've," I whispered, gazing once again at the ring.

"If you want to marry me, tell me. Tell me now."

His earnestness convinced me we could make a miracle. I loved Simon with all that was left of my heart, for like my father, he was a man who could speak his own name.

After Simon left, I showed my mother the ring. I went into her room, where she lay on her bed, reading. I still wasn't wearing the ring. It felt too weighty and momentous. It frightened me.

"It's lovely," she told me, gently lifting the ring from the box, examining it and then placing it back in the case and handing it to me.

"You'll wait until you graduate, won't you?"

"Yes."

"I'm a little surprised. But I don't think you could do better than Simon," she said, tossing her book aside, carving out with that action a space for me to enter.

"There's no way you and Daddy will ever be together, is there?" I asked, looking at the closed box in my lap.

"I don't think so."

"Why not?"

"There's too much to overcome."

"Did you try?"

"We did all that we could."

The dispassionate tone of her voice maddened me. She sat talking about my father, about herself, about me as though we were an experiment that had failed, not a family that she had destroyed.

"Why couldn't you do it for me? I'll bet you never once talked about me when you were together. You ruined it all. No wonder he didn't want you back. How could anybody trust you?" I screamed, heading for the door. But she followed me. In the hallway she caught up with me and grabbed my arm and whirled me around. I refused to look at her. If I did, she might win. I tried to break free.

"You killed Kenya and took away everything we had. You killed my sister." I had hoped the words would eradicate whatever was left that made her real, that made her unalterably my mother. But she barely flinched. There was nothing I could say to her. There were no words, no curse I could foment that she did not already know intimately and that she had not somehow survived.

"We've all been dead a long time, Teresa. Let me live. Let me come home."

I began struggling against her and not knowing why. Her strength surprised and subdued me. But when she finally released me, we stood facing one another, and I felt my arms reach out for her. For the first time since she'd come back I knew there was nothing else to do.

I went alone to the opening of my father's show. Ma Adele and my mother had sworn not to come, and they kept their promise. That night my father stood in the gallery, as he often did amid his work, somewhat awkwardly, as though he would really be more comfortable disavowing than claiming it. There were several dozen people there, a couple of them I knew had bought some of my father's other work.

The soft glow of a strip of track lights cast a generous, befitting luminance on my sister's face in the paintings. Love and remorse and desire for her presence drenched me as I looked at the canvases I had seen so many times before.

My father came up behind me and whispered, "So they really didn't come."

"Are you surprised?" I asked, turning around to face him.

"I thought they might change their minds."

My father spoke of my grandmother and mother as though they were one. I knew their pained refusals had been no conspiracy but an act they thought of as a gesture of singular, solitary survival.

In a burnt-orange silk shirt and black pants, his beard flecked with silver and gray, my father stood before me like some sculpted objet d'art. But standing there, he was also quietly grim. My mother could still hurt him. Maybe he still loved her after all.

"I wonder what I can paint now," he said. "There's hardly anything I've done since I finished these canvases that's satisfied me."

"How could it?"

"I'll give you a ride home when this is over."

"That's okay. I'll be leaving soon."

"You know how I hate all this. It's like I'm on display too. Besides, I want to show you off, introduce you to some people."

"Daddy, please."

"Indulge me," he gently commanded.

I gave in and let my father shepherd me around the gallery. We broke into several small groups of people, and he introduced me, spoke my name with reverence and relief, embarrassed me by talking about G.W. and my summer job at Hollingsworth, Jacobs, and Lee, and confided jovially his fear that I might indeed go into law, because of what I had seen of his life.

I stood next to my father dutifully and veiled myself against the curiosity in the eyes of these strangers. We shuttled between the small groups of men and women, a tapestry of attitudes and affectations, business suits, suede vests, jeans, shaved heads, and dreadlocks. There were, among the crowd, some of my father's students from Howard and the Corcoran. They stood longest before the paintings, arguing aesthetics, and I wondered if they could see more than they had been taught. Could they see what of necessity you had to feel?

After the last introduction, I told my father I had to go and promised to call him the next day. As I headed for the door, straining for a discreet exit, yet feeling as though I walked nude among them all, one of my father's students hurried toward me.

Her frizzy blond hair framed her face haphazardly. The deep purple shift she wore was so short, it appeared to be an afterthought or a mockery, I couldn't tell which. Her hand on my arm was insistent.

When I didn't slow down, she stepped in front of me to halt my flight. I looked into her blue eyes as they rested upon me expectantly. We were probably the same age. Could we have been friends?

"We were just wondering, you know," she began, nodding with her head toward the group she had left, standing before an image of my sister, clutching beer and wine in plastic glasses, staring at us uneasily, hopefully.

She stepped back a bit, willing to give me room to breathe but not to escape. "About your sister. It doesn't say anywhere, you know . . ."

The question hurled itself up through her throat, past kindness and wisdom. I felt it coming, and wanted to hide my face or push her aside. I did neither.

"What happened?"

I did not know. None of us did. Not even my mother. We never would.

My silence was leaden, stubborn. I refused to look at her. The girl stepped aside, confused, giving up on me, and I walked out onto Seventh Street, hoping to find Kenya in the dark night, waiting for me. I walked several blocks up to Chinatown, the humid night a temptation. I felt her as I had not in a long time as I stood on the corner, waiting for a taxi. No one gazing at me could have seen or heard my tears. They were virgin, freshly shed for the sister I would always have.

When I went home I called Simon. But he wasn't in. I went upstairs to my room and it was there that the loneliness set in. I had felt uplifted in the gallery, replenished by the sight of my father's artistry. But I now felt suddenly empty, depleted. Ma Adele had gone to Baltimore with some friends to see the Orioles play. Across the hall my mother's room was empty. She had moved out two weeks before. I came home from work one day and she was gone.

I visited her once in the apartment that was now her home. That

Saturday, the rooms were crowded with boxes and trunks filled with artifacts from our previous life. There was even furniture from the house on Sycamore Street, the circular glass coffee table and its green wrought iron base, even the black marble dinner table. My mother was doing part-time bookkeeping as well as working at the bookstore.

There were boxes filled with dishes and cutlery, cookware and linens. It was then that I remembered how Ma Adele had lovingly, patiently, helped my father and me dismantle our house, pack away all the objects that gave it its meaning and put the items in storage. The apartment that day was messy, expectant, and my mother stood amid all the items in cutoff jeans and a denim shirt, her hair tied in a scarf, happily surveying the task ahead.

I had come to visit and stayed to help her create a habitat. I washed dishes and stacked them in the cupboard, washed the linen and the spreads musty from years in boxes. The material residue of our life was amazing to me. I had taken it for granted before. We had accumulated so much—clocks, tape recorders, cameras, silver trays, a dozen blankets, two portable televisions, two VCRs, flower vases, books, Kenya's computer, pasta makers, wine stands, two Oriental carpets, three leather hassocks, a hammock, half a dozen photo albums.

Many of the items my mother would have to discard, but that day she pored over everything, carefully peeled back the layers of newspaper that surrounded a crystal bowl or a sequined black clutch bag, holding her breath all the while, and when the remnant from the past was revealed, I could see in her gaze the reassuring unfolding of memory.

After several hours of unpacking and storing, my mother stopped and made lunch. I sat in the kitchen on a stool, looking through one of the photo albums. My parents had captured everything. Our child-hoods had been recorded in minute detail, moving from baby pictures to vacations to just because. Thumbing through the photo album, my past seemed like something that I no longer needed to judge or explain. The pictures of Kenya reminded me not of what I had lost but of what I still had.

I felt all this so powerfully, so totally, but how could I tell my mother? I savored the pictures and kept them to myself. My mother, in her own apartment, stood preparing grilled cheese sandwiches in a cast iron frying pan that was nearly as old as I was. That was more than enough. I didn't know if just then she could bear more.

But in my grandmother's house that night I wanted to tell someone what I had seen, to talk about the amazing thing my father had done. Ma Adele's house could not contain me as I roamed aimlessly through the rooms of the first floor, turning on all the lights, fearing darkness, the lights drenching me in a transitory sense of comfort.

I called my father, but of course he was not at home. I hung up at the first words of the greeting on his answering machine. When Ma Adele came home later, she found me sitting on the porch. She walked up the stairs, saying nothing about the lights blazing in every room of the house, lighting it up like a sign of hope. She said nothing about my suitcase beside my chair.

Seating herself heavily beside me on the swinging two-seater, she asked me, "Well, how was it?"

"It was a beautiful show," I whispered, wishing I could say more, that my grandmother would understand.

Instead, I asked, "Who won the game?"

"The Orioles, twelve to three."

We didn't say anything else for a while. And then she asked, "Do you want me to drive you to her house?"

"No, it's too late. I'll call a cab."

"Suit yourself."

"Will you be all right?" I asked.

"Don't worry about me."

"I just need to talk to somebody about what Daddy did."

"You don't have to make excuses. You two have got more than that to talk about."

"Do you think we can?" I turned to see her face cast in the muted porch light.

"One way or the other."

She stood up and headed for the front door. "I'll call you a cab."

Inside the taxi, I realized I had not called my mother. But was it possible to infringe on her love? I slumped back in the seat, weary of rehearsal, the intricate weaving and plotting of affection, suddenly shamed by the way I had parceled out loyalty, measured out my regard.

But when the taxi pulled up before my mother's building, I could see she was still up. Maybe I would not have to know what to say. She knew I was coming. The lights were on for me.

The Edge
of Heaven

Marita Golden

A Reader's Guide

A Conversation with Marita Golden

Q: Your novel, *The Edge of Heaven,* realistically confronts the issue of incarceration in a way that few African American novels have—without excessive melodrama or polemics. In so many ways, imprisonment, whether it's a man or woman behind bars, causes untold damage to the psyche and the self. Why did you choose these issues as one of the central themes of your book?

MG: The novel was inspired by a rash of child killings in Washington, D.C., in which mothers or caregivers were responsible for the death of young children. While this was happening I began to wonder how such a tragedy would affect a family and I was especially interested in the effects on those family members not usually spotlighted in the media coverage or the conversation surrounding these tragedies—that is, the surviving children and the spouse of the "guilty" parent. The more research I conducted, the more I realized that when the parent responsible for the death of a child is punished, the punishment is inflicted on the entire family. Just as does the actual death, that punishment kills something in all the survivors.

Q: What message were you trying to get across by focusing on each of the character's reactions to this crime individually and collectively?

MG: I wanted to show how organic or interrelated the notion of crime and punishment and guilt and innocence is in an entity like the family. In a way the book is a kind of chorus of voices, a chorus of grieving and rebirth in which the sensibility and emotions of parents and child and even the grandparents are necessary to render the entire story.

Q: It has frequently been said that it takes an act of will to keep a marriage and family together. Your novel chronicles the slow unraveling of the marriage of Lena and Ryland. Is their marriage doomed from the start? What has taken such a toll on the union of two intelligent, caring people?

MG: It would be fairer to say that the marriage is fragile from the start. Lena brings to the marriage much of the emotional baggage related to the death of her father and his absence in her life. For her, creating a kind of idealized family that she did not have as a child is paramount. Oddly enough, it is this dedication to the conventional that at first seduces Ryland as he finds it an intriguing antidote to his more nontraditional lifestyle as an artist. But as in many marriages, the same qualities that draw individuals to one another can repel them. Lena loves the fact that Ryland seems to be his own person as an artist but cannot accept the financial insecurity that goes along with his career. Her attempts to make him over in her own image, so to speak, alienate him.

Q: Many reviewers took notice that the perpetrator of this serious crime was a member of a middle-class family and not a person from a dysfunctional unit in the so-called underclass. This was obviously a very deliberate choice. Can you share the thought process behind this choice?

MG: I wanted to have the tragedy unfold in a family that would mirror the lives of most of my readers and a family wherein the dynamic of poverty and "social dysfunction" could not be blamed for the tragedy. No one in the story and even I as the creator of the story knows exactly why Lena kills her child. There are many objective explanations and clues in the book, but as in all tragedies, the truth is elusive. For me as a reader and as the writer of the story, the most compelling relationship is between Lena and Teresa as they struggle to find a way back into a zone of love and acceptance. Kenya's death ruptures their union, and most of the story is about their halting, unsure steps toward one another.

Q: While the language and images here are rich and powerful, your narrative maintains an emotional distance in many sections of the novel, almost as if you were letting the story tell itself without obvious editorializing. Was it your intention to let us, the readers, experience the novel as if we were eavesdropping on the action? What are some of the gains and losses of such a choice?

MG: The tone of the book echoes the mannered, somewhat intellectual, and even analytical way in which Teresa has attempted to make peace with her difficult legacy. It is almost as if Teresa is telling a story that does not belong to her, that belongs to and happened to someone else. For her to claim the story as her own is to acknowledge how much the story has cost her, how much she has lost because of it. In a sense Teresa in the first-person section is telling a story, one that she has had to embrace and distance herself from in order to survive psychologically. One of the advantages of this tone is that the story can become one that the reader can embrace because it becomes a kind of construction and a revelation on the part of the characters.

Q: **How difficult is it to adopt these three points of view? Do you identify more strongly with one character?**

MG: I think I identify most with Teresa because she acts as a bridge to her mother and her father with her hopes that they might reconcile. She was the only witness to what happened that tragic morning and before she can move into a coherent sense of herself as a woman and as someone who might be a mother someday, she has to make a kind of peace with her mother. Teresa probably bears more emotional weight in the story than any other character. I found it a challenge to adopt the three different points of view, one that was exciting and kept informing me of the different meanings of the story.

Q: **The acclaimed novelist Gail Godwin once asked, "What person in the world goes through life in a straight line?" Describe your approach to the structuring of** *The Edge of Heaven.* **What does the abandoning of the conventional approach of linear time say thematically about the characters and their lives?**

MG: This is a narrative that unfolds in the country of memory for all these characters. They are haunted by an event lodged in the past but which is vivid and fresh and painful for them each new day. And so memory is what they want to escape from and yet memory is all they have in terms of the love for their deceased daughter and sister. We know that memory is very unreliable as a reference for truth. But is quite accurate as a repository of emotions. And so because so much of the story unfolds in the past yet throws its shadow over the present, I felt that I was not bound by any conventional sense of time, how it had to exist or work in the novel.

Q: You purposely downplay the sensationalism of the crime, the death of a child at the hands of her mother, with a subdued, straightforward writing style. Why did you take this approach?

MG: I felt that the death of the child and the manner in which it happened was inherently dramatic and tragic, weighed with so much potential emotion that I did not want to overwrite or exploit the emotions involved.

Q: The husband, Ryland, is a complex, measured man, a black man not usually seen in African American novels. How are you able to so convincingly portray a man's sensibility?

MG: I have always found the opportunity to create a complex male character challenging and an endeavor that could be very satisfying. My father was very important in my life, I have had important platonic friendships with men, I have a son and am happily married, and quite frankly I have felt a sense of mission in my work to portray black men in a myriad of ways, the idea being not to depict them as "positive" but realistically. And for me, a realistic portrayal is subtle and ambiguous. Even when I presented a character who sexually molested his daughter in one of my books it was important, I felt, to dramatize how he had been abused as a child so that his monstrous act did not seem to be just another act of savagery, the kind that is too often equated with black males.

Q: How long did this novel take to write? Describe your method of researching it, especially the prison scenes, which are entirely believable and authentic. Did you seek out women like Lena and Kelly, the woman Lena meets in prison?

MG: This novel took about five years to write. At one point I put it aside and worked on and completed a nonfiction book. It took me quite a while to access within myself and my imagination the depth of emotion that I had to infuse the story with, despite its seemingly cool tone. I interviewed several women who had served time in prison and talked with lawyers and public defenders who had handled child abuse cases. One of these women told me that the real punishment begins when a woman in prison goes home, and that comment stayed with me and became the thematic core on which I built the story.

Q: In the novel, you emphasize the themes of forgiveness, redemption, and renewal. Are these things possible in a situation such as this? Are they elements that can enable a family, in the most trying of circumstances, to persist and survive?

MG: The families that endure, survive, and serve the people that are a part of it seek redemption, forgiveness, and renewal because they are driven or forced to or because they choose to. The family in this novel is fractured by the tragedy, but the novel ends with the possibility of renewal between Lena and Teresa. The novel actually ends with a beginning, with Teresa deciding to move in and live with her mother. This decision in itself is just the start of a long journey whose outcome neither mother nor daughter can predict. But for me as reader and writer of the story, I was more concerned that these two women at least take the first steps toward healing rather than with showing the conclusion of that process.

Q: What psychological elements in Lena's personality, which also inform her treatment of her husband and with her interaction with her children, contribute to the pressures that cause the tragedy involving Kenya?

MG: Lena's need to control people and situations around her and her masked but very real vulnerability made it impossible for her to adapt or adjust to the crumbling of the world she had created with Ryland, and that inability to accept the impending dissolution of her marriage pressurized her and made her lose the emotional grounding she had spent so much of her life erecting.

Q: What are your writing habits? Do you have writing rituals, as many authors do?

MG: When I am working on a book I set up a schedule that I adhere to pretty strictly. Generally I write at least three to four days a week for three to four hours.

Q: You have written in many genres, nonfiction as well as fiction. Why do you choose not to specialize?

MG: I find that writing in more than one genre allows me to experience and create the world in a multitude of ways. In a sense I write fiction to create alternate spaces and places in which I can meditate on and dramatize enduring themes; I write nonfiction to try to tunnel toward an understanding of actual experience.

Q: Many writers say their goal in writing novels is to offer their readers a well-crafted tale. What did you want to accomplish with *The Edge of Heaven?*

MG: I wanted to create a world which my readers could inhabit for a finite period of time, a world in which they would find reflections of themselves, their journeys, their crises, their yearnings, and their lives, even though the exact situation might be completely foreign to them. I have been gratified by readers who have told me that they identified with Ryland and Lena and Teresa as a family, saw shadows of their own domestic struggles even though they had not lost a child in the way that Kenya is lost.

Topics for Discussion

1. How important is the author's choice to use the three generations of women—Ma Adele, Lena, Teresa, and Kenya—as the focal point in *The Edge of Heaven*? In what ways are these individuals similar yet different? And how does that impact on the outcome of the story?

2. Usually an author explains all of the details of a crime at the very start of a novel, but that is not done here. Instead, the reader is given the details of the incident in fragments, in flashbacks that interrupt the ongoing action of the book. Does this approach weaken or strengthen the power of the novel? Does it allow the author to flesh out the characters and their actions at the expense of the overall plot?

3. The older daughter, Teresa, who is often the conscience of the novel, sets the tone for the entire book by addressing its key themes in the opening lines of *The Edge of Heaven*: "My mother returned that summer from an exile both imposed and earned. Nothing had prepared me for her departure. I was unsure how to claim her homecoming. But I share her talent for perseverance, for we are joined by more than I can bear. My mother came back to recognition and reckoning. I thought she came home to me." Discuss the importance of these words and how they set the stage for all that occurs afterward in the novel.

4. Kenya, the younger daughter, is the pivotal character in this domestic tragedy, offering a metaphorical mirror in which the actions of those around her are viewed. How might her strong personality factor into her death?

5. The author makes several insightful comments about the awesome responsibility of parenthood. What is she saying with Lena's statement to her husband: "Are we good enough? As people, as a couple?" Is this doubt and insecurity concerning mastering the task of parenthood common? Do Lena and Ryland have reason to fear their parenting skills?

6. The fate of Lena in her marriage is one shared by many women in our society, especially when passion and communication are no longer present. The author aptly describes their situation: "But living

within the borders of her marriage, Lena knew three things, that she loved Ryland, that he had failed her, and that she would not leave him." Is their union worth preserving? Are the measures they take to save their marriage effective or is it beyond repair?

7. Some critics have questioned the author's depiction of the incident which takes Kenya's life. Is there a reason for how the child's death is presented in an almost ambiguous manner? Are we sure that Lena intended to kill her child? Was it murder or an unfortunate accident?

8. Ryland, the father and husband, is portrayed with fairness and realism, unlike many African American men in recent black novels. What role does he play in the untimely death of his child? Should he blame himself for what happened to Kenya?

9. In the key scenes following Kenya's death, Teresa cares for her emotionally numb mother in a reversal of familial roles. How do these scenes reflect the healing power of love within the family? Is the lack of anger and bitterness in the scenes accurate?

10. What effect does the imprisonment of Lena have on her daughter Teresa? Does the nature of the crime that led to her mother's incarceration change her affection for her mother? What emotional adjustments does Teresa make to cope with her mother's return?

11. How does Ma Adele attempt to relate to her daughter after her crime? Upon review, discuss how her reaction to Lena's behavior and failed marriage show the contrast between these two women from two different generations.

12. What is the author emphasizing when she recounts Lena's words about her fellow female inmates: "They weren't so different from me. And in many ways, I was like them. They were individuals, not numbers. That's how I became their friend." What is the author saying about women in prison and the families they leave behind in the outside world?

13. The memory of Kenya's death disrupts the lives of all who survive her. What psychological damage occurs within each family member? How is Lena's response to the loss different from the others'?

14. Ryland's passion for his art is significant and has cost him a great deal. How does he use it to heal himself after Kenya's death, rather than reaching out to others for comfort and solace? Why is his art so important in his honoring of his daughter's memory? What role did his art play in the erosion of love in his marriage?

15. In *The Edge of Heaven*, Metropolitan Baptist Church becomes a haven for Lena when she seeks to find a way toward personal redemption after her release. Is the author's depiction of the woman's acceptance by the congregation an honest one, considering the conservative nature of the black church? What is symbolic about Lena seeking forgiveness at the church where her daughter's funeral was held?

16. Kenya, in many ways, seems to be a reflection of her father, especially in her love of art. Is this likeness a major reason for her mother's animosity toward her? Does this resemblance in Kenya's temperament contribute to her death?

17. Teresa's love and loyalty for her mother begins the family's quest for healing and forgiveness. The author's gift for language shines in Teresa's words about her mother: "I slept beside my mother at night on Sycamore Street, trying my father's place, loyal, loving, needing her despite everything. I lay next to my mother and listen to her sleep, partial, nightmarish, my sister's name breaking through her sobs. And as terrible as it was, there was no other place for me. She was my mother. I knew they would take her away from me. We would all pay for what she had done." What do these words suggest about the daughter's love for her mother? And what do they say about the emotional cost of the crime on the family as a whole?

18. Upon her release from prison, Lena confronts the tremendous struggle to re-integrate herself into her family and community. Which scenes reveal how difficult this goal will be? In reality, would an African American family be so forgiving of a mother convicted of such an unspeakable crime?

19. Reviewers have cited the author's exceptional ability to examine family relationships and the psychological depths that move her stories

"beyond race and the confines of the black community." What scenes in this novel best exhibit her skill in this area? What elements of *The Edge of Heaven* make it of universal interest?

20. Redemption, forgiveness, and renewal are never easily achieved. At what point in *The Edge of Heaven* can readers begin to hope that Lena's family will survive this terrible ordeal? What images and metaphors does the author use to indicate this possibility?

Excerpts from reviews of Marita Golden's
The Edge of Heaven

"Marita Golden begins *The Edge of Heaven* after the tragedy, giving us hints of how it occurred through the unfolding of the story. And though we realize what happened before she lets us know the details, we remain enthralled in the telling. Perhaps that's because even those of us in the most imperfect of families worry we could lose what holds us together through a single event. But *The Edge of Heaven* offers redemption, showing that tragedy doesn't have to ruin us forever. After the worst thing in your life happens, there is always time left to find peace."

—*Detroit Free Press*

"In the sensitive hands of Golden, this is more than just a story about disappointment and loss. *The Edge of Heaven* chronicles the passion of a young couple, the powerful relationship of two sisters, and the bliss of simple moments shared by a loving family. Yet such moments of calm and perfection are fleeting in any family's existence, and it is the love that remains that is the true redemptive force of this breathtakingly beautiful novel. An emotional tour de force . . . an awe-inspiring tribute to the power of the American family."

—*Dallas Texas Weekly*

"*The Edge of Heaven* is a fresh, original book. Golden depicts relationships and emotions with a keen eye. Her characters speak and act realistically—a welcome change in this genre. . . . When readers finally arrive at the inevitable depiction of the tragedy at the heart of Lena's story, they can be assured that they are in the hands of a writer who understands the intense feelings on display here. Golden goes for the emotional jugular with such skill and intelligence that it's likely even the most jaded reader will be won over."

—*Time Out New York*

"In novels like *And Do Remember Me* . . . Golden has vividly captured aspects of the experience of race in the U.S. in the late twentieth century. Three generations of women occupy the center of *The Edge of Heaven*, which opens as Lena, Ma Edele's daughter and Teresa's mother, comes home from prison. . . . Golden skillfully displays the contradictory emotions they experience as they are reunited and slowly grant the reader glimpses of the past that explains those emotions."

—*Booklist*

"Readers will be thoroughly thrilled with Golden's new novel, which compassionately peels away the layers of a family's grief to reveal one woman's passage from repentance to renewal. Three generations of women struggle with the devastation of loss and the journey back to love as they head for a precarious reunion in contemporary Washington, D.C. . . . These vividly rendered characters come to life, leaving the reader to cheer their strength and humanity. Highly recommended."

—*Library Journal*

"An acclaimed chronicler of black women's lives (*And Do Remember Me*, 1992, etc.) shows what happens when a good marriage goes bad. Set in the sophisticated milieu of black professionals living in Washington, the story is told by Teresa and her parents, Lena and Ryland. . . . Before everything went wrong, her mother had been someone to admire: a successful accountant in a top firm and a loving mother and wife. . . . [As] Golden persuades us, these women can be strong on their own terms. Emotions run high—the plights of black (and white) women let down by men and the world are sharply etched—but telling insights often soften the rage and give it balance. For Lena and Teresa alike, life will go on. Golden, in her fourth novel, is writing in top form."

—*Kirkus Reviews*

"Golden has a rare gift for the poetry of language. As in her previous novels, in particular *And Do Remember Me*, the unexpected metaphors and marvelous images of *The Edge of Heaven* powerfully evoke the pull her characters fell between commitment to family and self. . . . Golden's touching story of three fierce, passionate people stumbling toward understanding, forgiveness and resolution is a triumphant journey from grief to renewed hope."

—*San Francisco Tribune*

"Fiercely intelligent, brimming with ethical questions, never overtly political, the novels of Marita Golden have an old-fashioned earnestness about them. . . . This is a powerful story, which Golden tells with great sensitivity and respect for her characters. . . . In a departure from her previous novels, Lena's troubles can be traced not to oppression by the white world but to her eager participation in that world. In enjoying the fruits of inclusion in white corporate America, she also paid a grievous price in the destruction of her marriage and her daughter's death. . . . Golden seems to be suggesting that the Singletarys' tragedy is colorblind and could just as easily have befallen other families, black and white."

—*Washington Post Book World*

ABOUT THE AUTHOR

MARITA GOLDEN has distinguished herself as a writer, teacher, and literary institution builder. Born and raised in Washington, D.C., she grew up in a household where at the age of fourteen her mother told her she was going to write a book one day and her father, a raconteur and history buff, supplemented her formal education with his own in-depth knowledge of African and African American history.

In her first book, a memoir, *Migrations of the Heart*, she transformed her own experience of marrying a Nigerian and living in Nigeria for several years into a story that has resonated with a wide audience and has become a book used on college campuses around the country in women's studies programs. Her novels, *Long Distance Life, A Woman's Place, And Do Remember Me,* and *The Edge of Heaven,* have dramatized the intersection of the personal and the policitcal, as well as the everyday tragedies and triumphs of contemporary African American life. In her nonfiction book *Saving Our Sons,* she explored the continuing contradictions and challenges faced by black parents raising male childen in America today. She is also the editor of *Wild Women Don't Wear No Blues: Black Women Writers on Men, Love, and Sex* and the co-editor of *Skin Deep: Black Women and White Women Write about Race.* Her latest book is *A Miracle Every Day: Triumph and Transformation in the Lives of Single Mothers.*

In 1983, with Clyde McElevene, she formed the African American Writers Guild, a Washington, D.C.–based organization that offers workshops and support programs for black writers in the metropolitan D.C. area. An active member of the national literary community, Marita Golden has served as a member of the PEN Faulkner board and is currently on the advisory board of the Mobil Pegasus Prize. She is president of the Zora Neale Hurston/Richard Wright Foundation, which presents a summer workshop for black writers and awards the nation's only national award for college fiction writers of African descent.

AND DO REMEMBER ME